AT THE END OF THE MAGIC

JEFFREY HEWITT

*Even after all this time
the sun never says to the earth
"You owe me."
Look what happens
with a love like that —
it lights the whole world.*

-- Hafiz

Dedication

To my wife, Megan, for being stronger than me. To my parents, who introduced me to the world of books. And to the authors who wrote those books, who taught me magic.

Acknowledgments

A special thanks to everyone who helped make the writing of this book possible. Megan, my first and best reader, Rachel, Tonya, and countless others of my coworkers who chipped in a word or two (or an ending). Once again, the talented Tim Denee for his evocative cover art and willingness to work with someone who doesn't possess a single punctual bone. Please visit Tim's website at www.timdenee.com Lastly, my editor Jennifer Schoonover who made the book tons better both by her apt suggestions and excellent powers of editing. You may visit her blog at http://firewaterpro.com/blog

Disclaimer

None of this is real and is totally all in my head, man. Any resemblance to places, persons, or events real or fictional is strictly coincidental, and all in your head, man.

At the End of All Magic
Jeff Hewitt
Hand-wrought Edition
Copyright 2013 Jeff Hewitt

Visit my webpage at www.jeffhewitt.net for news, updates, and sneak peeks at other of my works. This work also available in print and e-formats at many online retailers.

This novel is in no way protected by Digital Rights Management (DRM.) It is yours to copy and share as you wish. However, it would not have been possible without the love and dedication of the artists involved. Please continue to support us and others who create art so we can keep on creating adventures.

Cover art by Tim Denee
Edited by Jennifer Schoonover

ISBN-13:978-1495963230
ISBN-10: 1495963233

Prologue

YELLOW LEAVES FELL FROM silver oak trees straight as lines in an orchard where no man ever stood. A king, imposing and impossibly tall, waited at the foot of a dais. Sitting empty at the top was a throne of twisted vines and unfurled leaves. The dais stood at the center of the orchard, which itself imposed order on the otherwise wild glade that surrounded it. Just outside the organized central garden stood the machine. Black coal smoke billowed in the distance, huge and dark as a thunderhead.

"We'll never again see a sky so pure," muttered one of Oberon's guards. The three stood at the foot of the empty dais together, Oberon between his unwavering but terrified guards. Oberon towered over them at nine feet, but the machine god that glared at them with mechanical malevolence matched him easily.

"This age passes, another comes. It is the way of things," said Oberon.

"I hope they choke on it," hissed the guard. Oberon said nothing, just watched the brass man. Two red eyes glowed from a cylindrical head, and steam and smoke flowed freely from mesh vents on the sides. Long, articulated arms held together with bolts and wires gave it a spindly appearance. One arm ended in a huge circular saw. A furnace grate on its belly gave off heat like the fires of Hell itself. The air shimmered around the mechanical man, and the grass beneath its feet burned. There was a crackle as the brass man opened his mouth, and black smoke poured out as it moved up and down.

"The time of fairy things and magic is done," the machine told them. It advanced, stuttering and jerky like an old man with arthritis. The saw on the end of its arm spun to life, whining like a hungry dog. As it passed the oak trees it savaged their trunks, causing them to fall amongst their brothers. The trees wept golden autumn foliage, and the saw spun.

"We'll see," said Oberon. He nodded to his guards, who screamed a futile defiance as they charged the brass man. They raised spears handed down to them by their fathers, inherited from their own fathers back before man knew song and nightmares of saber teeth. The brass man let the saw spin, and two more of the dying fairy race lay at the feet of industry. Mechanical laughter came from inside the machine, wherever its steam-powered heart hid.

"Do it, and have done," Oberon stated in disgust. He turned and walked up his dais, to sit on the throne of vines one last time. How many sunsets had his court witnessed over thousands of years? How many magics performed, illusions delighted, justices wrought? And here at the end of things, to face a metal saw.

"A machine god. The world of magic is no more," said Oberon. The brass man walked his steady, jerking walk to the dais. The saw whined. Oberon looked up at the sun, and smiled. The blade came down, slicing through the fairy king. When it struck the dais, thick smoke burst out in a sudden blast. The whining stopped and the brass man, the new machine god of Earth, waited patiently for the smoke to clear. When it did, it saw no body like the others. Instead, Oberon's empty armor and robes lay on the throne, and a thousand times a thousand birds of paradise flew out in a storm of wings and calls. The world was, for one moment, a writhing, fluttering whirlwind of colors and song. Then, just as suddenly, they were all gone, and all that was left to do was to burn the grove. If the machine god had been able, it would have smiled.

Chapter 1
Andrew the Wizard

ANDREW DALE WAS PISSED. He fumed in the only quiet corner in the garish ballroom, and sipped a drink that made him grimace. Only an hour or two more and he could slip out, perhaps unnoticed, perhaps unmolested by the court that tormented him. Perhaps.

"Shit." He noticed the king and his entourage approaching him. He tossed his drink back and suppressed a violent cough. It wouldn't be so bad if they'd let him alone even for a little bit. Living on the run hadn't been this bad; at least in the woods you were left alone. Being at court was like dancing with a poisonous and irritable snake's daughter: no missteps allowed. *Well...*he reflected...*at least you can see a snake's fangs.* The Sun King was a huge, imposing man, towering over everyone in the room. His face was large and friendly, his skin black and shiny, and his teeth white and perfect. His entourage was full of equally beautiful people of all variety and colors, from a woman with scaly, indigo skin and gold-rimmed eyes to a little walrus in a tuxedo.

"Andrew!" roared the king with a jovial laugh.

"Your majesty." he said, bowing.

"How are you enjoying the party?" said the king. Andrew spared a glance for the drunken revelers.

"Most entertaining," he said.

"Wonderful! Listen, this young man here," he began, indicating the formally dressed walrus "…is interested in seeing a bit of magic. "Oblige him." Andrew looked down at the walrus. Its face was unlined with the deep scars so common on elder walruses, and his tusks white and smooth. The little walrus puffed up his slight moustache, quite proud. Andrew sighed inwardly.

"I'd be delighted," said Andrew. He looked around

for inspiration. He stepped over to one of the courtiers accompanying the king and pointed at her drink.

"Is this water, ma'am?" he said.

"Yes, good wizard."

"Do you mind if I borrow it?" he said. "I promise to give it back." There was a slight chuckle. The woman, dressed in rippling gold cloth and wearing a dazzling sunny tiara, only laughed and nodded. Andrew took the glass and held it up to his face, looking into it. He walked back over to the walrus. The walrus shuffled eagerly, trying to get a better view. Andrew knelt next to him.

"What is your name, sir?" said Andrew.

"Nyark, son of Nyargh, of the Northern Circle," said the Nyark.

"Very good, Nyark. You're quite far from home. Was your journey pleasant?" said Andrew.

"It was long, and these parts are quite warm, but I am happy to attend the Sun King at his leisure, of course," said Nyark.

"I'm glad you deigned to join us," said the King. He gave a great laugh, his entourage along with him. Nyark looked down. Andrew smiled and said:

"I see your boutonnière is white with green fronds. Are you a newlywed, sir?" Nyark's face, such as it could, lit up.

"Indeed! I was married the day before our ship left for Aethero," said Nyark.

"Is there a point in all this, wizard, or are you conducting interviews today?" said the king.

"At your majesty's pleasure, I will be coming to the point in just a moment," said Andrew. The king waved his hand.

"Do get on with it, before the party dies of boredom," said the king. The fops and dandies tittered and whispered amongst themselves.

"I'll try to provide some measure of entertainment,"

said Andrew. He directed a sour look at the crowd of hangers-on; had they tasted it their faces would have sucked inwards. He turned back to Nyark.

"Is your wife beautiful?" said Andrew.

"She is the first star that rises over the ice, so rare and beautiful she is." Andrew smiled.

"Would you cast a quick breath on my glass, here, whilst keeping your bride in mind?" said Andrew. He held the glass down for Nyark, who shuffled forward and huffed on it. His whiskers tickled Andrew's hand, and the glass fogged.

"Watch it closely," said Andrew. He focused on the glass and spoke under his breath. A few of the powdered idiots scooted closer, no doubt trying to spy on his magic for their masters, but they wouldn't be able to understand it anyway. The glass became cold, quite cold, and the condensed air on it slowly turned to frost as waves of mist dropped from it. The water turned a dark, deep blue. The biting cold slowly crept up Andrew's veins, but he held the class calm and steady. The water swirled, and then appeared as the ocean does from beneath the surface. Light shone through the top and gave everything a soft glow. Two shapes took form in the deep ocean water, and grew larger, until they resolved into a pair of walruses.

Nyark's eyes grew with wonder as he witnessed himself and his wife on the first night they met, swimming and dancing underneath the ocean and the ice. Every detail was perfect, the dance steps, the playful banter, and the reveling in the deep cold and ice of their home. The freezing cold crept up Andrew's arm until it bit into his shoulder, and despite the cold pain, he was sweating. After giving the young walrus a good look, Andrew held the glass up for all to see. Amazed gasps and the susurrus of quiet whispering filled the room. When he could stand the cold no more, he pried the glass from his frozen hand and looked into it, muttering again.

The frost dissipated, and the light from inside winked out. Andrew took out his handkerchief, wiped it down, and handed it with a bow back to its owner.

Everyone broke into applause, Nyark most of all. Andrew gritted his teeth and bowed to his audience, hoping for dismissal so he could go warm his arm. The king's eyes were on him, and he knew that it would not be over yet.

"Is there anything else I can do to please his majesty?" said Andrew.

"Yes. Iona here is curious about you, as she is new to court. Please indulge us by answering her questions," said the king. Andrew directed his attention to the young woman the king pushed forward. She wore a formal yellow gown with a huge skirt, and her hair was piled high. Flowers blossomed in her hair. She was pretty, with delicate features. Andrew knew this song and dance quite well. He knew what questions she would ask. He could see her rehearsing them, her eyes worried. *Another humiliation for the tittering morons.*

"Sir wizard, where did you learn magic?" she asked.

"From my uncle," said Andrew.

"Would you be able to teach others your art?"

"I'm afraid that's quite impossible. The ability to perform my style of magic—real, practical magic—was lost when my world gave up magic for machines."

"There is no way for someone here to learn it?"

"No. It's a trait of my race, though some are able to learn to sense magic."

"How is that done?"

"I do not know the particulars, but I understand that people sensitive to magic feel it in their guts, a kind of nausea or cramping. I gather it is not pleasant."

"Are there any others like you?"

"No. Not that I'm aware of," said Andrew. His voice tensed momentarily. Iona dropped her eyes. Andrew tried to find the strength to forgive her. *She doesn't know better.*

"What does it feel like to perform magic?" she asked next, looking at the floor.

"Like falling in love. Like the first time you look into someone's eyes and you know, in your heart, in your mind, that person is meant to be with you...always. The wrench in your stomach when they walk away, the flight of heart when they come back. When you look into that person's eyes and realize...you would die for them," said Andrew. He looked at the king. "Or kill for them." Tears were falling down Iona's face. He stepped close to her and gently put his hand under her chin, lifting her head so he could see her eyes. The court was quiet, whispering. He was saying and doing things he didn't normally. Andrew knew the king was watching him closely, burning him with a deep glare.

"It is not your fault, Iona," he whispered to her. Her eyes streamed freely, tears dripping off the bottom of her jaw. "Ask your last question, so that this will be over."

"Sir...Sir Wizard, then, you are alone?"

"Yes. I am the last."

"That must be painful," she murmured. The court muttered around them. *She's off the script.* "I've grown used to it. There are many peoples who are alone and come to the end of things by themselves. I don't feel it, for I am basked in the love and admiration of our good king's court. I hardly feel alone at all," Andrew deftly moved back to the words the king desired to hear. The young woman looked back up at him with gratitude, and fear. Andrew's heart was heavy, and his arm ached terribly.

"If I may propose a toast to our king!" said Andrew. "He took me in when I was alone, and has provided for me. Without him, I'd likely be another street urchin with nothing to show for myself but dirty cheeks," said

Andrew. The king looked pleased. *How nice for you.*

"Cheers!" said the crowd, and those with drinks tipped them up. Andrew turned on his heel and was striding away when he heard a shriek of disgust and the sound of the entire royal court spitting and coughing.

"Saltwater!" someone yelled. Andrew wondered who it was, but he was around the corner and he didn't want to risk the king's wrath by coming around for a peek. Deciding he'd had enough of the king's entertaining for one evening, Andrew walked towards his small room in the servant's quarters. He didn't even warrant an apartment with the rest of the court, even though the king insisted on dressing him in the finest clothes. *Just another pet.* He was about halfway there when he heard someone fall into step behind him. He ignored the newcomer and continued to walk towards his room. He strolled, as though on a pleasurable promenade. He stopped at a freestanding brazier of coals to warm his arm. The castle was drafty and cold in the best of times, and since the long winter the stones deep in the castle were chilled. The person cleared her throat. Andrew ignored her.

"Andrew, you can't ignore me forever."

"It would be easier if you didn't talk to me."

"Andrew, I have to talk to you."

"Do you ever get tired of being the king's lap dog?"

"Stop it!" commanded the voice. He sighed and turned to face his interlocutor. It was a woman, a sliver shorter than him, with cropped black hair and a lovely face, with a figure to match. She was wearing her formal uniform as captain of the king's guards, and it fit her well. She was a sight to behold.

Andrew couldn't stand to look at her, so he settled for a musty tapestry behind her.

"What can I do for you, Guard Captain?" said

Andrew. She gave him a sorrowful look.

"You can say my name, Andrew, it won't bite you."

"If it's all the same to you, Guard Captain," he said.

"Despite our mutually unsatisfactory past, I would like it if we could be civil with each other one day. Or, that you could say my name, at least." she said, trying to catch his eye.

"What did you want to speak to me about?"

"You know damn well what I want to speak to you about."

"I'll return the stockings. It just a lark."

"I...what? You know...never mind. I'm talking about your performance in the ballroom, just now."

"Did the king find my display of magic unsatisfactory?"

"No, it's..."

"Or my etiquette—did I address a duke incorrectly?"

"No, you were well...."

"Or perhaps I stepped on someone's foot while they were dancing?"

"Andrew! You turned everyone's drinks into saltwater! You've managed to piss off the entire royal court. Again! Even twice in one day!"

"To be fair, the royal roofers need to make sure everything is secure before they ask me to conjure a storm."

"That's as may be, still..."

"I will apologize tomorrow and everything will be all right. I perform and kowtow and scrape and beg and am humiliated every day. Is that not enough, that I must also be spineless?"

"You know what the king wants."

"I do."

"Some deference might go a long way, is all I'm trying to say to you."

"I'll try it sometime."

"You might be killed before then."

"If I am, I'll try to do so in an amusing fashion."

"I should have phrased that differently. You might be dead, by your own hand as likely as any other."

"Tragic, I'm sure, for the king."

"Tragic for me, for you...Andrew, I know you feel alone, but you're not. We grew up together."

"Yes, and now you're arm and arm with a...a man, I suppose, who strives on a daily basis to make me less and less! Humiliates me, belittles me, reminds me of my less-than fashionable past! I call you a lap dog, but at least a lap dog may get a pat on the head or a treat. I am less than that, less than a kept animal. Every day I feel the whip of his scorn against my back."

"If you could try to act with a bit more humility when he calls on you..."

"Oh! I beg many pardons!" yelled Andrew. He threw himself on the floor. "Let me make it up to you! Shall I use my magical talents, born at the beginning of time and created by a god, to clean your boots? Am I low enough yet? Am I low enough yet!"

The guard captain reached down, seized Andrew by the shoulders of his jacket, and hauled him to his feet.

"On your feet! Quit acting like this!"

"I'm sorry, Ashna! I can't be the foulest thing in the palace and be quiet about it anymore! I am more than that!" said Andrew. He pushed Ashna away from him, catching her by surprise and knocking her against the wall. A gale of wind blasted against her, shoving her back against the stone and ripping down the tapestries. She gasped as the wall knocked the breath out of her, but she kept her feet. Andrew, chest heaving, his face a deep red, looked mournful. Ashna took a step away from the wall and ran her hands along her body.

"Are you finished? Are you going to use your magic to hurt me? Maybe kill me?" she said, after a long moment. Andrew swallowed and looked down. He shook his head.

"You know I would never hurt you with my magic. Or kill someone."

"Except my father."

"I never killed your father. I wouldn't do that! Why do I have to keep saying it?"

"Because that's what happened."

"You mean that's what you were told," Andrew countered. Ashna gave him a look and he shook his head. "This is why I can't do what you ask. He's lied to you, turned you against me for so long, and…you believe him. I'm sorry, Ashna. I know…I know it's not you. I just can't…live the way he wants me to anymore. To be a plaything. I am a person. I am a man. If I can't even hold my head up, then what do I have?"

"You have your magic, Andrew. You have a place to live and food to eat, clothes to keep you warm. You have…" said Ashna, before trailing off.

"What, Ashna? What else do I have?"

"Nothing. Never mind. It was…all a long time ago, wasn't it?"

"A long time ago, for some. Not so much, for others. It's all in one's perspective."

"I wish things were different."

"They won't be. Not while he's in the picture."

"Why do you give him this power over you? I know you're stronger, Andrew."

"If I was stronger, I'd be on my own. As it is, I would be back to telling fortunes and creating fairy-lanterns in a week. He doesn't give me any money, you know that. To keep me as his faithful pet."

"I have enough that I could…" began Ashna, but the darkness that fell over Andrew's face forced her to stop.

"I don't need your money. I never did."

"It's not just about the money."

"That's what it always comes down to."

"It doesn't have to."

"It does. Because I cannot be independent, can't be my own man, without it. He's not going to give me any, and no one is going to pay me when he's made sure everyone knows what would happen if his faithful servant was able to procure means of escape."

"There must be a way, Andrew," said Ashna, looking into his eyes. Andrew looked back, and the hardness in his face gave her chills. It was hard to look at someone so cold.

"There are prices even I won't pay. Even if I wanted to," said Andrew.

"That's not something I'm asking you to do. You know that."

"I know. You'd be rather a bad guard captain if you did."

"Just....Andrew, for your sake and mine, can you cool it down? You're making both our lives harder. It doesn't have to be this way," said Ashna. Andrew looked at the floor.

"I can't make it easy for anyone. If it becomes easy, it will become natural," said Andrew. He looked at her once more, and Ashna thought he might be about to say something, but then the peculiar look in his face disappeared. The mocking countenance returned.

"I want something better for you, Andrew. Something better for us," said Ashna.

"If it involves some magic, I can help you. Otherwise, Guard Captain, I would like to return to my room. Good evening," he said. Andrew turned and walked away. Ashna watched him walk out of sight, and sighed.

"But it does involve magic." she whispered.

Andrew turned the corner and kept his steady pace. His heart was aching. He stopped and leaned on the wall, one hand supporting him. Something in his throat hitched, and all he could do was wheeze. Andrew closed his eyes and started taking deep, slow, breaths. He stood back up, and with a more even stride, walked back to his mean apartment. The halls echoed with his footsteps. Even amidst the revelry of the constant balls and galas, he was alone. The walls were bare except for occasional torches or candles, and wall hangings became less frequent and more threadbare the closer he got to the servants' quarter. He arrived at the small wooden door that led into the wing, swung it open, and stepped through. Inside the servants' quarters, the walls were unadorned and cold. Smokey torches hung at corners and ends of hallways, but the middles of the halls were left obscured in semi-darkness. No light came from outside, not that the small windows let much in. He began walking again, turning corners here and there, until he finally came to his room. He had to crouch to fit through the doorway.

  It was more of a cell than a proper room. A single narrow bed lined one wall, and a small desk with a three-legged stool completed the furniture. He was not allowed to keep the clothes they dressed him in. Instead, another servant handed them to him in exchange for the old clothes. He was allowed to wear his undergarments at that time, but was given fresh linens to change into. The servant, often the laundress, didn't go away until he or she had collected everything. Andrew did his best to keep clean. The servants, though they had to cater to him somewhat, were the closest things he had to friends other than Ashna. At the very least, they didn't berate and degrade him when he tried to be himself. He even helped some of the children (when he had a spare moment) with their studies (if they were allowed to study, precious few were) and on occasion, worked a bit of magic for them. He felt glad to do it, but had to be careful because the King would grow jealous if he knew the children of scullions and butchers were enjoying the same magic as he. Better magic, at times, because a glad heart worked all the harder.

He stripped off his formal coat and hung it on the back of the door. Andrew paced his room for a little while by the light of the single small stub of a candle. The room was chilly, and he tried to warm himself a bit before laying down on his bed. Finally, when he felt warm enough, he took off his pants and boots and slipped under the thin covers. The only thing soft enough to offer comfort was his pillow. The sheets were coarse spun, but clean. He lay in bed facing the narrow window that overlooked part of the castle's courtyard. Despite the darkness, he could see the light of the stars. The constellations, familiar to him now, reminded him of the time when they fascinated him, back when he was still young and new to this magic land of Aethero. His heart started aching again, so he pushed those memories out of his head and rolled over, facing the cold stone wall. His last thought, the final thing that crossed his mind as he fell asleep, was one of regret for being so cold to Ashna. Then sleep took him, and he dreamed.

Ashna watched Andrew walk away from her and sighed. *When will it all kill him?* Why won't he reach out? She smoothed her dress uniform out and turned to walk back to the party, when a small shadow detached itself from a nook in the wall. She recognized it instantly.

"Salim, what are you doing here?" The shadow coalesced into her son. He was a small, lanky boy, with dark skin and hair to match. He had his mother's fine, beautiful eyes. It was easy to tell when he grew up he would be as handsome as his father.

"I wanted to talk to Andrew," he said.

"You know Andrew isn't allowed to do magic without the King's command," she said with a small smile. Salim looked ashamed.

"I was just going to ask for a little magic," he said. "It's my birthday soon."

"And I'm sure he'll do a great bit of magic for your birthday party,"

"I hope so! He made my cake dance last year. Do you remember?"

"I do! But Salim, you know it's your bed time."

"Yeah, I guess so. Will you walk me to my room?"

"Of course, sweety." Ashna took Salim's hand and started walking towards the young prince's quarters. For a long moment, their echoing footsteps were the only sounds. Then, Salim whispered:

"Were you and Andrew fighting?"

"I suppose, young Prince."

"What about?"

"Well, that's hard to explain to someone your age." They turned a corner, and Ashna was silent for a long moment.

"Did you know Andrew and I grew up together?"

"No I didn't! Are you related?"

"No, we were friends."

"How did you meet?"

"He was being raised by his uncle, but his uncle couldn't take care of him anymore after a while. So, he came to live with me and my father. We lived in a theater and put on shows."

"What kind of shows?"

"Magic, juggling, acrobatics, sword fights,and plays. All kind of things! We had a wonderful time."

"Do you miss living in a theater?" They turned another corner, and were approaching the prince's room.

"No, I'm happy here. With you. With the King."

"Sometimes I wish Andrew was my father." Salim blurted the sentence and stopped dead in his tracks. His eyes were huge. Ashna took the prince and stepped quickly into his room. She looked about, but they were alone.

"Salim! Never say that again!'

"I'm sorry, it just slipped out."

"It's okay."

"Will you tell my dad...the King? What I said?"

"No, of course not. Sometimes....sometimes we say things we don't mean, and we regret them." Salim looked at his hands.

"I don't know why I said it." Salim walked over to his bed, a large, opulent, and soft affair that dominated the little boy's room. He sat down, his shoulders hunched.

"I don't know why I said it..." Ashna sat down next to the boy, and put her arm around him. She hugged him close.

"I know the King isn't always very nice to you Salim. Shhh, it's okay to talk about it here. Between you and me. Don't ever let anyone else hear this, of course, but between us, it's okay. The King isn't very nice at times. He's not even very nice to me, sometimes."

"Does he hurt you?" Ashna hesitated. She never had to deal with this line of questioning before. Salim was getting older. Old enough to ask questions, now. To see and understand things that never bothered him before.

"Salim...it's hard to talk about. I know you feel the same way. Some of us have to live in fear of the King. You and I are some of them. Many others do, too."

"Not Andrew." Ashna was forced to laugh.

"No, not Andrew. He's a special case."

"He knows magic!"

"That he does."

"I wish I knew magic. I wouldn't be afraid of anyone."

"Me too, Salim. But for people like you and me, our smarts are our magic. When I was performing in the theater with my father, we could do things that Andrew couldn't."

"I don't believe it!"

"I'll show you sometime. Now, it's late, and you need to be getting ready for bed."

"Okay. Thanks for talking to me, Ashna. And…thanks for not telling."

"Of course not, sweety." Salim slipped off the bed and ran into his wardrobe. He reappeared in his dressing gown. His eyes were red with sleep. Ashna turned down the covers and tucked him in.

"Good night, Salim."

"Good night." He yawned and rolled over, asleep almost in the same instant in the manner of small children and excitable dogs. Ashna watched the little boy sleep. How could she explain to him that even she was scared of the King? A little boy couldn't understand it, but he was getting there. And he was right about another thing: Andrew was the only person who wasn't afraid of the king. She leaned down and kissed the boy's cheek, and then crept out of his room.

She walked the corridors, checking in with guards at their posts and seeing inebriated guests to their carriages or rooms. She thought about Salim's face when he asked if the King hurt her. She thought of his face when Salim said he wished that Andrew was his father. She thought about the man she had talked to the year before. Ashna lingered outside the King's chambers for a long time. She did a lot of thinking. Before she went in, she hurried to her quarters and penned a letter. She fetched one of her guards and sent him out with it. And then she attended the King in his chambers.

A dozen servants struggled to get the singing, tipsy deity to bed while changing him into his nightgown.

"Ashna! Guard Captain! I trust you dealt with the problem?" he roared.

"Yes, Your Majesty. As far as anyone can correct

Andrew's behavior," she said. The servants tugged one last time at a few errant laces on the robe and then left the room. Ashna tried to remain calm, but being alone with the King made her uneasy. Especially in his bedchamber. The King smiled at her, winning, charismatic, and evil.

"Well, perhaps I should apply some iron to him," he said, leaning on one of the huge bedposts.

"I think he would object strongly to such treatment, Majesty," she said.

"I don't care what he objects to! He is walking a very fine line indeed, sassing me in front of my court. I will not have this type of insolence be a daily occurrence anymore. I'm quite tired of it," said the King. He lurched forward and Ashna reached out to catch him. He wrapped huge arms and hands around her shoulders and drew her closer to him. Ashna's heart raced.

"Come to the bed, Ashna. There are matters of security I must discuss with you," he said, leaning down to try and press his lips to hers.

"I think not, Majesty. You're drunk, it's late, and I'm not feeling up for this. It's very late."

"Nonsense!" he said. He crushed her to him harder, and Ashna felt panic rising in her throat.

"Into this bed!" he said in her ear. His breath was rank and hot on her skin. Ashna leaned with him until he fell back on the covers.

"That's better, now..." he trailed off. "What is that? What is poking me? Take off your belt, stupid woman!" he said. He got up on his elbows to look at her. The King felt a chill go through him when he saw Ashna holding an eight-inch dagger with a wicked point and gleaming edges poised above his crotch. The tip was just poked through the fabric.

"If I were you, Majesty, I would seriously consider going to bed and sleeping it off," said Ashna.

"I...you can't do this. I'll have your head for this!" he

gasped when Ashna put pressure on the blade.

"You'll do no such thing. I've written out a very nice letter detailing some very...interesting...events that perhaps you would not like shared with the world, yes? It's with the Turtle Enclave, with directions to spread my letter to every foreign outpost in the world should my death ever be discovered," she said. She twisted the blade a little, watching the light from the candles on the walls play on the King's stunned face.

"I've put up with your shit for eight years. I'm not going to forget what happened when we first came here. Nothing will ever change it. But I swear to all the gods if I have to, I'll cut your throat. You will not invite me to your bed again, and I don't care if you're drunk or sober. I am your guard captain. I will protect you from enemies close and far. But if you ever, ever try this again, I will gut you like a pig and leave you in the street for the dogs. The only person in the world from which you have no protections, not one...is me," she said. She forced herself not to smile when she saw how soaked his robe was with sweat. She sheathed her dagger and removed herself from his now limp arms. She walked to the door and opened it, then turned.

"Oh, and if I should fail to check in with the Enclave at some time during the week, those letters will be sent out regardless if a body is found or known. Just a...point...to keep in mind, Your Highness. I hope your sleep is restful." she nodded and strode out of the room. The King found he did not sleep well that night at all.

Chapter 2
Unfamiliar Stars
20 Years Ago

THE NIGHT WAS GETTING ON, close to ten or eleven. Andrew sat in the front with his uncle, too excited about the day's events to be tired. His uncle, Maeryl, sat beside him, occasionally flicking the reins and talking to the single horse pulling their cart piled with their modest belongings. A lantern hung high and forward, like an angler fish's lure, to light the path. A glitter of twinkling lights hung on the horizon: the city of Aethero. A band of glowing light dotted with stars, huge in the sky, crossed the darkness like a luminescent river.

"Uncle, do you know the constellations here?" said Andrew.

"I know a fair number of them, Andrew," said Maeryl. He was older, perhaps in his fifties, and dressed as you might expect of a wizard: robes, floppy hat with a point, the works. He leaned down to his nephew's level and pointed up into the sky. His finger designated a large, bright star.

"That, first off, is the Nameless Turtle. You remember the story I told about Alexander and his friend?" said Maeryl.

"Yessir!"

"Well, that's his friend. She's a North Star, like our own on Earth. Follow that star and you'll find your way home, it will always guide you the right way," said Maeryl.

"Even if I need to get South?" said Andrew.

"Yes. The world here is governed by magic, Andrew. Though the world around us appears to be like at home, at least at first glance, it is all magical. We're riding on the back of a giant turtle."

"Uncle! Everyone knows Earth is like a baseball!"

"Earth, yes, Andrew. Aethero, Alexander? That's a whole other story. When people tell you something here that sounds like a fairytale, I tell you, son, take them serious. They're deadly serious here. Take everything literally until you know otherwise, you understand?"

"Yessir."

"Good. Now, to her left you see that little cluster of stars, kind of like a wobbly circle?"

"Yessir."

"The Five Brothers, that is. It's a good story, but I can't do it justice right now. They're guarding an island in the ocean of the stars, where their mother lives. But you're too old for such stories."

"I like your stories, Uncle. I'll never be too old!" said Andrew. Maeryl smiled and ruffled his hair.

"That's because you're still a boy. One day you won't want to hear stories anymore."

"Nuh, uh! I'll always like them. They take you places you could never go."

"Well, I hope you keep that sense of wonder, Andrew. I really do," said Maeryl. He looked sad in the dim light, but Andrew was too busy scanning the stars to notice. Maeryl pointed at another group of stars, this one more spread out.

"See how those stars connect? Similar to our Big Dipper?" he said.

"I think so."

"That's Mustafa the Whale. He was one of the first beings in the universe."

"Whales were first?"

"Yes. Before the stars, before the planets and the turtles, the sky was totally black, like the deepest of oceans. In that darkness, Mustafa sang the first song, the song of creation and light. Stars began to dot the sky, slowly, in a flowing river of light and music. He created other Whales, and they sang along with him, until a chorus of voices created all that we see today. From the smallest blade of grass, the meanest insect, to the gods that walk amongst the people of Aethero."

"It was all created by songs?"

"Yes."

"Can things still be created by songs?"

"Only if you have knowledge of the Whale songs. They're very, very old. I'd say only the first gods know them. The Sun and the Moon might, I suppose."

"What about planets?"

"They came from that beach you see in the sky. You, of course, remember the Milky Way in our own sky?"

"Yessir!"

"It looks much the same, except here where there are no lights at night it's much easier to see," said Maeryl, using his hand to indicate the huge band of light that swirled across Aethero's sky.

"While the Whales sang, they created that beach there in the ocean of stars. They sang turtle eggs into being, and in the fullness of time the eggs hatched. The turtles swarmed the beach, a billion, billion baby turtles, and they crawled into the ocean to become the planets themselves."

"All the planets are on the shells of turtles?"

"They are here."

"That's silly!"

"I suppose. Just don't tell any turtles that, you might offend them."

"Turtles can't talk!"

"They can here, Andrew."

"Wow! I hope we meet one!"

"I'll take you to meet some. They've got a...an embassy, I suppose. Are you familiar with that term?"

"Sure! Diplomats live there, and they go to conferences to work out treaties and argue and things!"

said Andrew.

"I can tell you've been paying attention in school. That's good, young man."

"I like learning."

"Good. I have a lot to teach you," said Maeryl. He looked up ahead at the light bobbing in the darkness, and added, almost to himself, "And not much time."

"Why not?" said Andrew. Maeryl looked down at his nephew and smiled.

"Oh. I'm just an old man, Andrew. Ignore me!" he said. They continued riding in the darkness for a good while, but now in silence. Andrew tried his best to stay up so he could see where they were going, but his next memory was of his uncle touching his shoulder.

"Wake up, Andrew. I need your help setting up for the night. We've gone far enough." Andrew yawned and rubbed his eyes. The sky was still dark.

"I...thought we were going to ride all night?"

"We were. We didn't get as far as I wanted, and it's almost time for the trolls to be out. We want to be hidden when they get active."

"Trolls!" said Andrew. He looked around in the darkness, but Maeryl laughed.

"It'll be okay. Are you ready to learn some magic?" he said. Andrew nodded eagerly, wide awake, but then he hesitated.

"Mom and Dad said I can't learn magic until I'm older. They said it's dangerous," he said. Maeryl's face fell.

"That's in the past. Our circumstances call for something different now."

"They won't like it," Andrew insisted. Maeryl sighed and drew the horse up on the side of the road. He got down from the cart and began going through their bags. Maeryl muttered quietly to himself until he located a jar full of white powder. He opened it and took it back to

Andrew, who was still sitting on the cart seat. Maeryl held the open jar up to his nephew.

"What is in this jar?"

"I dunno."

"Taste of it," said Maeryl. Andrew dipped a finger in the powder, hesitated, then touched his tongue to his finger.

"It's just salt, Uncle."

"Right. Salt has powerful properties. It's not just for making dinner taste better. Tonight it will help us sleep safely."

. "Mom and dad said..."

"I know what your parents said, Andrew!" Maeryl interrupted. Andrew wrapped his arms around himself and looked down.

"Andrew, your mother is my sister. I love her very much, and I wouldn't go against her word in regards to her child. I love you, too, and things have changed. You have to listen to me, without question, from now on. When I tell you about something magical, you will listen. When I tell you the words of a spell, you'll memorize them. When I ask you to help me, you'll do your best. This isn't Earth, this isn't your home, and I am not your father or your mother. I am your teacher, and if you want to survive to adulthood you will listen to me."

"I want to go *home*!" said Andrew, his voice shaking.

"We can never go home," said Maeryl. He turned and began shaking out a small measure of salt in a wide circle around their cart, muttering words. Andrew began crying in earnest, sobbing into his hands. When Maeryl completed the circle, he screwed the lid back on the jar and placed it back in the cart. He climbed up beside his nephew, and after a moment, hugged him close.

"Why can't we go home?"

"You know these last few months have been hard. You're old enough, and smart enough, to know something was going on, right?"

"Y...yes."

"There was a war. An invisible war to the regular person, and more or less invisible to you because of your age."

"Who was fighting?"

"Oberon, the king of fairies and god of magic, against a machine god. No one knows its name," said Maeryl. He wiped his nephew's face with the sleeve of his robe. "The machines are what people began to look to. The new factories, with their black smoke, dominated the landscape. No one leaves out milk for the sprites or fairies at crossroads anymore. They shovel coal and put petrol in tanks. The machines belch smoke and fire, and people worship at them."

"They worship machines?"

"In a sense. All this, all the changes, all the people moving to the cities, has changed the face of Earth. Magic could not be sustained because no one believed in it anymore. Somehow, out of this, the machine god was born. It, along with its clockwork armies, attacked Oberon and his fairies. They had existed for many thousands of years, teaching gifted humans magic. They were not prepared for an assault by soulless metal men. They fell, and wizard kind fell with them. We exist through sustaining magic itself. Without it, we wither and die. Like a candle in a jar. We just...go out."

"What about...mom and...d-dad?"

"They gave you to me, because you have yet to be touched by magic, you should be able to survive longer. I...made a deal. I had to make a great sacrifice to bring you here. Your mom and dad, they loved you very much. They wanted you to grow up, even if it meant without them."

"Why didn't you bring them?"

"I couldn't, Andrew, that's not how it worked."

"It's not fair!"

"Life often isn't. That's the first thing you must learn here, because we are on our own. No one in Aethero can do the things we do. When we are found out, unless we are well protected, we will be hunted."

"I don't care! I want to go home!"

"I told you already, we can't..."

"I hate you! I hate this place! I want my parents!" cried Andrew. Maeryl tried to hug him close again but Andrew just threw his uncle's arm from his shoulder and stumbled off of the cart. He started to run for the barely visible barrier of the salt.

"Andrew, stop! You're going to get hurt!"

"I don't care!" he yelled back. He ran for the circle, and just short of it he felt something grab his ankle. He screamed as he fell to the ground and landed on his stomach, the scream cut short by the blow as it knocked the wind out of him. His eyes screwed shut and he tried to cry and gasp for air at the same time, choking. Maeryl stood on the horse cart, a root in one hand and the other stretched out. From out of the ground another dirty root broke through the soil, and wrapped around Andrew's ankle.

"Let me go," wheezed Andrew. Maeryl wrenched at the air, and the root drew Andrew back towards him. Andrew tried to sit up to fight the unrelenting force, but was unable to peel the tendrils back from his ankle. He cried out and Maeryl pulled at the air again, dragging Andrew along the ground.

"You're hurting me!" he cried. Maeryl leapt from the cart and knelt next to Andrew.

"Look behind you," he said.

"No! I hate you, I hate you!" said Andrew. Maeryl took Andrew's head in his free hand and forced it around. Andrew grudgingly looked to the darkness. A pair of burning eyes, seeming tall as a tree, stood just out of the circle of lantern light, just on the other side of the salt barrier, and looked in at them.

"What is it?" said Andrew, whispering without realizing it.

"Possibly a troll. Maybe something worse. Whatever it is, it didn't want to take you home," said Maeryl. He slipped the root into his pocket, and the one around Andrew's ankle relaxed and slid back into the torn ground. Andrew rubbed his ankle. Maeryl touched it gently and Andrew winced.

"I may have pulled a tendon. I'm sorry. You weren't listening to me and I had to do something. Do you understand?" he said. Andrew nodded.

"This is why you have to listen to me. We are in a strange place with new dangers. I have to teach you magic, too early, perhaps, and you have to learn. We are on our own out here."

"Will it be the same in the city?" said Andrew.

"It will be worse. People are a whole different sort of monster," said Maeryl. A low growl, more felt than heard, menaced them from the burning red eyes floating just outside their light.

"Why?"

"If they find out what you are, what you can do, they will try to take you. They will try to steal you from me, to sway you, to make you theirs. No one can do what you and I can, Andrew. Remember that always. We are strangers here, and no matter how well we ever seem to fit in, our magic sets us apart."

"Mom said our magic makes us special."

"It does, and that's the danger. What makes us special makes us valuable, and there are two of us but many, many monsters," said Maeryl. He helped Andrew to his feet.

"I want to go home," said Andrew, very quiet. He looked at the burning eyes outside their circle and shuddered.

"We *are* home, Andrew."

Chapter 3
Opportunity

ANDREW WOKE THE NEXT MORNING when a thin beam of sunlight snuck through his window and touched his cheek. He sat up in bed and rubbed his eyes. He felt like dammit; his dreams kept him busy. He stretched and blinked. The morning was chill, and the stone walls of the castle gripped the cold like a miser's coin. He got out of bed, put on his socks from the night before and began pacing to keep warm. He wanted to pace, to set his own routine before they came to drag him back to court. Sometime later, when the sun was no longer sneaking into the room but fully invading the space, a knock came at his door. He opened it to reveal Ulga, the elderly laundress who brought him his clothes every morning.

"Good morning, Andrew," she said with cheer. Andrew muttered something and handed her his old clothes.

"You're too young for so much grumpiness," she commented.

"I've earned my grumps," said Andrew.

"You've never told Ulga why you're so sad."

"You would be as I am if the King had you in my position," said Andrew.

"The King is hard on everyone."

"The King is hard on his son. Then he is spiteful to me. The rest of you he merely tolerates."

"Perhaps this will make you feel better." She handed him practical clothes: a thick wool tunic and pants, along with his tall leather boots.

"No court today!" said Andrew, brightening.

"No, indeed! Your time is your own," said Ulga. Andrew smiled even brighter than the light bursting through the window and hugged Ulga. She patted him on the back and pulled him off.

"Don't be making any moves now, young'in!" she laughed.

"On such a beautiful and innocent maiden? I would never dream of dishonoring you, miss," said Andrew. He turned and quickly changed into the plain workman's clothes. It felt good not to be wearing silk in garish colors, for once.

"Are the children in school today?" asked Andrew, sitting on the side of the cot to pull on his boots.

"Not at all, the professor was sick and they've been given the day as well," said Ulga. Andrew felt a tiny pang, feeling perhaps that the leave was a subtle way of calling him a child. When Ulga saw his face, she patted his shoulder.

"Andrew, the instructor has been ill for a while. It must have gone serious last night, that's all," she said. Andrew smiled at her.

"Oh...I'm just...I guess I don't know what to do. I'm usually attending the king. I haven't had a day of my own since...I don't know when," said Andrew. He looked at the wall, his eyes vacant. Ulga gave him a moment and then politely spoke up.

"They could always use a man in the courtyard to help with loading and unloading and such. You could do an honest day's work," she said with a wink. Andrew grinned and stood up from his bed.

"I may just do that," said Andrew. He looked at the stooped, elderly woman and a smile came to his face. He looked over her shoulder and quietly shut his door. He leaned down close to her ear.

"Is there anything I could do to help you out? For bringing me such good news?" said Andrew, whispering just above silence. Ulga looked thoughtful, but Andrew could see apprehension in her eyes.

"No, master wizard, I think...even if you were to help, it may perhaps be a hindrance. If...anyone realized," she said. Andrew's face fell.

"Not that I don't appreciate the offer, young man, it's just..."

"I know what it is. Thanks, all the same, and if there is something you can think of,"

"I will let you know, Andrew. Go outside. Enjoy your day," she said.

Andrew hugged her gently and then walked into the hallway. He walked slowly about the halls of the castle, watching the servants come and go, as invisible as thoughts while the courtiers and lickspittles whispered in corners and laughed in small groups. They didn't notice Andrew at all when he wasn't sussed up like a bad whore for the king's amusement. One dandy, a particularly greasy man called Dauer, even walked smack into Andrew at some point and upbraided him for being so clumsy. Andrew stepped aside and muttered an apology, smiling privately to himself. *He sings a different tune when I get creative.*

Andrew wandered by the kitchen to get something to eat, and earned a bit of warm dark bread and some cheese for his efforts. The staff was friendly and helpful, but he could tell they wanted to remain aloof of his company. *No bother. I wouldn't want to be mixed up in my problems either.* He walked with his little bundle of food to the courtyard of the castle proper, still wet and muddy from the storm he conjured the day before. He found a bench to sit on, and watched a crew of laborers unloading a cart of various supplies, their breath fogging the air, steam rising from their bare skin. They sang while they worked, and Andrew felt a small pit of envy form in his chest. *No one notices them. No one makes them perform. They're expected to bow when someone important addresses them, and not a worry in the world for what the*

King will think of next. He munched his bread and cheese and considered the tower located in one corner of the broad, square yard.

It always made him smile, even just a little bit. It had a noticeable lean. The King ordered it built many years ago, but skimped on the price of good foundation materials. Since then the weather slowly wreaked havoc on the tower. One side was sinking, bringing the whole thing to a sharp angle. The King yelled and berated, but no one could fix it, and no one could think of a good way to bring it down without damaging the castle itself, thus costing the crown even more gold. *That's a good lesson in fundamentals and miserliness.* Today the tower sported some wooden beams, thrust into the dark mud of the courtyard and up against the tower to help support it while the ground dried out. They had to do that every time it rained now, otherwise the tower would groan and the courtyard would empty of people as they watched it shift, even minutely. Andrew wished he had some money; there was a large (and secret) betting pool amongst the staff of the castle on when the tower would come down. He saw a group of school-age children laughing and wrestling in the mud. *There'll be some baths tonight!*

Finished with his meal, Andrew folded the cheesecloth from his meal and put it in one of the pockets on his trousers. *A marvelous thing, pockets.* He wondered. *When was the last time I wore something with pockets on it?* There was a commotion, and he looked up. One of the laborers had taken up too much in his arms, lost his balance, and fell from the cart. There was an audible *crack*! And the man began howling with pain. Andrew and some others rushed to his side. The man was clutching his shoulder and moaning. Andrew noted a distinct shape pressing up from the man's skin. The workers knelt around him.

"Fetch a surgeon!" someone said. Andrew got on his haunches next to the hurt man's head.

"Wait. Let me take a look," he said.

"Who are you?" demanded one man. He was tall and burly, with a thick handlebar moustache. Andrew recognized the air of authority, and figured him for a foreman.

"Andrew, the court wizard. This looks like something we can take care of right now, and it will be much to his relief, believe me," said Andrew.

"You'll not use no magics on him, hear me?" the foreman grabbed his arm. "We don't want trouble with the King."

"No magic needed. Here, you men help me lift him onto the cart. Careful, now!" said Andrew. With his careful guidance, they set the man on the cart, face down, with the arm of the damaged shoulder over the edge and pointing down. Andrew waved them away and firmly took the man's elbow and wrist.

"What's your name, good man?" said Andrew.

"Eustin," came the reply through gritted teeth.

"Eustin, I'm going to make you feel better, but I need you to help me, okay?" said Andrew. His voice was calm and even, and he subtly rubbed the man's arm. He could how tense Eustin was, his muscles knotted. The man's face was dark, angry red, and he was sweating profusely.

"What do I do?" he said. His voice was strained; his teeth clicked into a grimace between words.

"Think of a good, nice place to be. Some place you feel like you could always go to," said Andrew. "And be safe. Maybe be with the wife or a girl if you have one."

"Had a wife. Died last year of pox," said the man.

"Sorry to hear that, Eustin. What was her name?"

"Was my Reena."

"Was she pretty?"

"Lovely, she was. So delicate, not like me, all rough

and tumble."

"Gentle soul?" said Andrew, in that same, even tone. He began to gently pull the man's arm down towards the ground, careful to keep the elbow and wrist straight and even. He felt some give in the man's arm.

"As a kitten, she was. Loved her very much," said Eustin, sounding dreamy. Andrew continued the gentle downward pressure until there was a subtle boney pop! Eustin gave a huge sigh of relief, and tension visibly drained from his beet-red face.

"Oh, lord, oh lord...." whispered the man. "That's so much better. Thank you, thank you!" he said. Andrew helped him sit up, legs dangling over the side of the cart, and tied up the man's arm with the cheesecloth from his meal.

"Don't thank me yet. Go see the surgeon and make sure I didn't ruin your arm permanently," said Andrew. The man gave him a startled look, but he wasn't sweating or red any longer, so Andrew felt confident. Eustin thanked Andrew again and another man walked with him to go see the doctor. Andrew was about to leave when a hand clapped on his shoulder.

"No magic?" said the foreman.

"No magic. Just a bit of medicine I saw a long time ago," said Andrew.

"Good. Thank you," said the foreman. "I'm Davies," he added, sticking out his hand. Andrew took it and shook. Davies' grip was powerful but not crushing.

"I'm glad I could help someone," said Andrew.

"Me too. Seen that happen a few times meself, but never seen anyone treat it like that before," said Davies.

"I took a chance. I hope he's okay," said Andrew.

"'M sure he will be. Eustin's a good tough sort," said Davies. The big foreman turned and said to the other men gathered in a loose group:

"Back to work, men! Bags don't unload themselves,

and no more playin'!" The men wandered back to their work and began unloading the carts again.

"Well, thank you again," said Davies. As he turned to walk off, it was Andrew's turn to grab his shoulder.

"Wait," said Andrew. Davies turned to him with an inquisitive eyebrow raised.

"Yes?"

"I...could I offer my help?" said Andrew.

"You mean unloadin'?" said Davies.

"Yeah. You're a man short now, and..." Andrew cut off short. He could tell from the look on Davies' face that he made a mistake. Andrew sighed.

"Never mind. I know it would just bring you more trouble. Have a good day," said Andrew. Davies motioned for him to stay.

"No, no, not that. I mean...we could use ya. If you don't use magic, you know? Keep it low profile. No one recognized you at all until you announced yourself, and these men are with the merchant's crew so they don't know you from anyone anyway. If you can keep it to yourself, I'd be happy to have the help," said Davies. Andrew's heart warmed, and he beamed.

"That is, if you feel like getting your hands dirty," said Davies.

"I do. Thank you, for this," said Andrew.

"We'll see how thankful you are after hauling a dozen fifty pound bags of grain!" said Davies. Andrew took a cue from the other men and stripped off his tunic, baring his pale skin to the sun despite the chill in the air. He joined the line of men tossing grain down the line where another man waited with a handcart.

As they worked, they sang songs to break up the monotony. Andrew was thrilled! He felt glad at the labor, feeling the richness that comes from working as a team with others and with his own two hands. He sang too, though off key, and after some time they even became comfortable enough with the newcomer to gently poke fun at him. He took it all in good stride, joking with the others as they moved on to another cart, unloading more bundles and bales. As he handed off the items to the next man, he was even able to forget about his worries for a time.

They came back when he heard a familiar voice ring across the courtyard, and all the world held its breath.

"Salim! What are you doing?" boomed the voice of the King. Andrew looked and saw the giant man striding across the courtyard, heedless of the mud. Andrew followed the king's gaze and realized what he was screaming about: Salim, the prince, was playing in the mud with other children. Andrew hadn't even noticed that the little prince was among them at all, had barely noticed earlier that the children even existed. The other children melted into the shadows cast by the leaning tower as the king strode towards his son, now standing alone and holding his hands behind his back. The king knelt down and grabbed his son by his shirt. The boy was around nine years old.

"What have I told you about playing with the common children? These mongrels! You're filthy! This is disgusting. You're not acting like a prince but a pig! A filthy, low hog wallowing in its own filth," said the king, shaking the crying child for emphasis. Andrew felt a fire flare up in his chest, fierce and angry. He began walking towards where the king was shaking the helpless boy. Everyone in the courtyard was silent, unmoving; completely entranced by the display of rage and cruelty. They all jumped when the king swung his hand back and dealt the child a vicious slap across the face.

"That's for shaming me! In front of my own subjects! How dare you, child?" he slung his hand back for another cruel blow when Andrew caught the King's wrist and held it.

"He's acting like a child, not a pig, and you're a disgrace and a bully for acting this way!" said Andrew. He wrenched the king back off of Salim. The king slipped in the mud and fell against one of the beams holding up the tower. It shifted and cracked. The king sat in the mud, covered in it, and stared at Andrew with a terrifying mix of rage and shock. Salim ran behind Andrew's legs, and hid behind them. The bottom dropped out of Andrew's stomach when he saw the king's expression. *Oh shit, what have I done?* The king drew in a huge breath, no doubt to start another, even more rage-filled tirade as he struggled up out of the mud, when he put one of his huge hands on the beam. There was another *crack!* And the beam gave way. The tower shifted, visibly, and one of the other beams slid through the mud. With a monstrous groan like a dying whale, the tower began to fall. Deafening cracks and snaps filled the air as the tower fell. It was ponderous and slow, and the air pressurized under the moving bulk.

Andrew turned and grabbed up Salim, and looked over his shoulder at the king. The man was paralyzed, staring up with wide-eyed horror at the slowly collapsing tower.

"Run!" yelled Andrew. The king didn't seem to hear him at all, didn't seem to know what was going on.

"Run!" he yelled again. The tower fell past any point of stopping, carried by its momentum, and anyone underneath would be crushed. Andrew could see he had only a few seconds. He dropped Salim, dropped to the ground himself, and snatched up a huge handful of mud. He feverishly caked it over his right hand with his left, his eyes on the tower, his lips moving in a flurry as he said the words of a spell. The ground next to the king began to writhe and rumble of its own accord, and seconds before the tower crushed them all, a huge, muddy hand roared out of the ground and slammed into the tower. With a crash, the tower stopped falling, but began to come apart. Masonry fell as mortar crumbled, and the giant hand struggled to hold up the weight.

Rivulets of sweat poured down Andrew's body as all his muscles and tendons stood out. His right arm was held up, as though clutching the tower itself, the force of his magic and will alone keeping the building from killing them all. Struggling under the stupendous weight, he grabbed Salim in his other hand and began pushing the child to safety as cut stones and powdered mortar fell around them.

"Go," he managed to say through clenched jaw. Salim finally came to his senses and ran out of the courtyard. The king still looked up at the tower, unable to move. Andrew backed out of the shadow of the tower himself. His face began turning many shades of red, and his muscles bulged against his skin. *Just let it go,* said a voice in his mind. *End it all, here. No one could say you didn't try.* He was soaked with more sweat than he thought possible. *Just. Let. Go.* He knelt, and began molding an object out of the mud. Slowly, as it came to shape, a litter with tiny, muddy legs lifted the king as it came up out of the mud. It walked quickly across the courtyard, deftly dodging the falling stones. Just as it came to a safe place, Andrew fainted, and the tower, along with the litter, collapsed. The hand of mud melted all at once, and the tower finished its descent with a deafening roar and a wet *thud* as it crashed down. The ground quaked beneath the feet of the startled crowd, and the rush of wind knocked many down. The world shook, then calmed.

The crowd rushed to the king's side, and the workers with Andrew got him up and awake. As the people around him talked excitedly and clapped him on the back, Andrew saw the king looking at him from across the courtyard. Their eyes met, and Andrew saw death writ clearly on the king's face. Davies, the foreman, pulled

Andrew to his feet.

"You saved the king, Andrew! What power! You're a hero!" said the man, shaking Andrew's hand with fervor. Andrew couldn't break his gaze from the king's own, and he felt a deep and forbidding chill course through him. *I will not live long to regret this.* Andrew struggled through the crowd, fear looming over him like a crow over a cradle. As he ran from the courtyard the king's face filled his vision. Seething hatred spelled out clear as ten-foot letters on a face twisted with rage. *I should have just let the tower fall. Should have ended it. It's over now, all over. I don't have much time.* Andrew ran through the halls of the castle, trying to collect his thoughts. *I'll flee. I can disappear into the city.*

Andrew skidded to a halt in a juncture of hallways. One led to his quarters, but there was no point in that. He didn't have anything precious, or even any clothes. As he bent over, gasping for air, he felt a shudder run through him. He thought he could hear yelling from the courtyard. His thoughts raced, and making his decision, he turned right and sprinted for the kitchens. *Get a bag. Get supplies. Keep it together.* He ran and ran, his lungs burning with the effort. As he neared the big double doors that lead into the kitchens, a royal guard stepped in front of them.

"By order of the King—" the guard began to shout, a pike leveled, but Andrew was already committed. No more gloves. He thought. Andrew hardly broke stride as he waved his arms towards his face, as if gathering the air, and then blew at the guard. The air howled as it was whipped into hurricane fury and blasted the guard into the doors and the doors to the ground. The kitchen was flung into a frenzy of disorder as the winds gusted and knocked down cooks and utensils and foods off the walls. Andrew stopped as he came to the guard, who moaned and tried to roll over. Andrew put his foot on the man's chest and took his dagger. He hesitated, then ran farther into the kitchen. He grabbed a rough burlap bag from the floor and dumped out a few dozen onions, then began to fill the bag with various things from the shelves. Spices, root vegetables, a few cooking implements, and a few loaves of bread. Anything he thought he could use for spells or to survive on the streets. He'd made do with less in the past, he could do it again. *Gonna need a shirt, at least.* He made his way back to the guard, who was just sitting up, and clocked him with a pan. The metal of the pan rang against the guard's helmet, who slumped back to the floor. Andrew ripped the guard's cloak from his shoulders, heedless of the royal purple. He needed to keep warm; he could worry about being conspicuous later. As he fled the kitchen, he didn't notice the many castle workers huddled in a terrified silence about the room.

Gotta get out. Head for the gate. No, there'll be guards. Gate will be down. Servant's entrance! He turned down a hallway and nearly ran into a pair of guards.

"Stop! You're under arr—" began the guard on the left. Andrew cut him off by dropping the bag and the dagger and burying his hands in the man's beard.

"What!" Started the guard, but Andrew gave a colossal wrench and the guard's beard grew out in great lengths, flowing almost like water. Andrew spoke a word and the hair continued to grow. The guard's helmet fell off as his hair pushed it off in a great wave, and he fell to the floor under the weight. The hair spread slowly across the stones, making a sound like the gentle whisper of a snake through leaves. Andrew whirled to face the other guard. He was shaking so hard, Andrew could hear his breastplate rattling. Andrew kept his eye on him while he picked up his dagger and bag. Andrew walked carefully through the growing hair, heedless of the muffled screams, and turned his back on the paralyzed guard. He took off running to the end of the hall. He was only two turns away from the servant's entrance to the back of the castle. He turned the corner and heard someone yell behind him. Looking over his shoulder, he saw a two more guards struggling to get through the huge mound of moving hair, and the second of the first pair slumped against the wall in a dead faint.

He ran towards the last juncture with the sounds of pursuing guards on his heels and slid to a stop. Four guards were on the doorway. Four guards stood between him and freedom. He scraped the blade of the dagger he held against the wall before they could make a move, catching the sparks in his hand and blowing into them. They grew in number until he held a huge handful of them, the light flickering as they sparked and danced in the air. The men on the door lowered pikes.

"You have one chance to cease your magic and give up peacefully!" said their leader, a sergeant. Andrew could see fear in their eyes. Could almost hear the sound of dry mouths whispering prayers.

"You have one chance to stand aside. I will not be held. Not ever again," said Andrew. He held the sparks, fire and dazzling lights pouring from his palm.

"In the name of the king, I order you to perform no magics! You are under arrest!" said the guard sergeant. He even managed to sound like he meant it.

"No," said Andrew. He blew into his hand and the sparks shrieked down the hallway, filling the air with flashes of light and heat as they impacted into one of the guards in front. He went down and screamed as his breastplate turned from shining gray to dull red. The other guards leapt over the fallen man and charged down the hallway. Andrew reached into his bag and drew out a pinch of salt, which he rubbed on the dagger. It immediately turned to rust, and the heads of the pikes the guards carried crumbled into red-brown dust even as they converged on him. Andrew ducked under the swing of the first guard and kicked the legs out from under the second. The tripped man's pike haft hit the floor, and Andrew picked it up as he stood and slammed it into the chin of the first guard as he tried to recover from his missed swing. The sergeant tried to make a stab at Andrew with his sword but the tight corridor made it hard for him to get past his own two men.

 Andrew spoke to the wooden haft he held and thrust it at the standing sergeant. It grew with sudden force, sprouting leaves and branches, slamming the sergeant to the ground and back as a sapling suddenly filled the hallway. Andrew quickly let go of the growing tree and it fell on the guard he tripped, knocking him back to the floor and trapping all three under its weight. The sound of snapping and rustling as the tree grew was nearly drowned out from groans and screams of the guards trapped underneath. Andrew knelt and laid his hand on the trunk. The tree stopped growing. The guards struggled under the tree, their eyes wide with terror.

 Andrew gathered his items and began to navigate around the branches, pushing them aside and stepped carefully between limbs and leaves. He made his way to the end of the hall, where the first guard struggled to get his smoking breastplate off. Andrew hurried over, kicked the man's pike aside, and drew out a little jug of water from his bag. He poured some into his hands, rubbed them together, and then wiped them on the breastplate. Great gouts of steam *whooshed* into the air and the armor cracked open like a crab shell. The guard panted, his expression wrenching Andrew's stomach with its mix of gratitude and stark terror.

 "I'm sorry," whispered Andrew.

 "I am too," said a voice behind him. Andrew spun about to see Ashna standing over him, a cudgel in her hand.

"Ashna, wait—" said Andrew, but she brought the stick down on his head. His world exploded into brilliant flashes of light and a sharp blast of cold cut through him. *Iron!* Was the only thought in his mind before the freezing daggers of ice stabbed into him. Ashna looked down at Andrew, writhing on the floor, the hair where she hit him with the iron club already falling out in clumps. Her face was expressionless as she gave orders to her remaining guards. Two men hauled Andrew up from the floor and carried him off. Andrew's head lolled and tears streamed down his contorted face. His head was swollen and red where she had hit him. *You can't cry here, Ashna. Hold it together until you can get away. Just...hold it together.* She oversaw the operation to remove the tree from the guards on the floor, and the surgeon reassured her that the burned guard's injuries were minor. Not a single person died during Andrew's attempt to get away.

Chapter 4
A Magic Lesson
18 Years Ago

THE AIR SHIMMERED with heat above a small clearing in the woods that surround Aethero. Andrew and Maeryl stood in the center, focused and quiet. Maeryl still wore his robes and pointed wizard hat. Andrew tried to keep the heat from distracting him, but the sweat was getting into his eyes. *Isn't he hot under all those clothes?* He crushed his eyes closed. *No, don't think about that. 'A canny enemy will use anything to distract you, big or small.'* Andrew refocused his thoughts on peaceful things. A still pond they encountered last week, alive with fish that flashed neon colors and sang sorrowful melodies. The snug house of a badger they paid a visit. The clearing they were in, now. Sitting in the living room with Mom and Dad...Andrew collapsed on the soft grass as Maeryl's presence suddenly filled his mind and bade him *sleep.* Maeryl helped Andrew sit up and gently woke him.

"Ugh. You got me, huh?" said Andrew, his eyes foggy.

"Yep. What distracted you this time?"

"I...it was nothing. Just a thought," said Andrew. Maeryl helped him to his feet and brushed the loose grass and dirt from his nephew's clothes. Andrew was growing fast. He was already approaching five feet tall, and he was bulking out subtly. Maeryl sighed inwardly. *I must find us a safe place. I'm aging the poor lad. He needs someone his age to help him grow up right.*

"What was the thought? I find it helpful to think about what's on our minds, that way we can address them and control them in the future."

"I don't understand why we need to spar, Uncle. If

we're the last two wizards, then I won't ever need it," said Andrew. Maeryl appeared not to hear him.

"How about a quick break, a drink of water, and then we'll try again?" said Maeryl. He put his arm around Andrew's shoulder and led him to the wagon, where he drew a cool mug of water from a barrel. He took a deep drink, topped the mug off, and handed it to Andrew. Andrew wiped the sweat off his face and took a pull on the mug of water, relishing the coolness in contrast to the heat of the day. It was good that magic could provide them with a cool drink, even if Maeryl claimed it was an indulgence.

"Uncle, why is keeping the water cool an...indigence?"

"Indulgence. I guess your uncle is just old-fashioned, Andrew. Magic was hard won from the Fairy King many thousands of years ago. It made us equals in their power. As it was both a gift and a prize of war, we learned to never squander it. I'm also being cautious."

"Cautious how?"

"You remember how I told you that magic is kind of like borrowed energy?"

"Yes, uncle."

"Borrowing the energy causes...hmmm...a disturbance that some people can sense. Trained wizards can feel when others use magic. Some creatures in the wild can, too. That's why you see...saw a lot of wizards with owls. Owls like the way magic feels."

"They do?"

"Yep! Some creatures don't like the way magic touches them. It's an irritation, like a bad itch that you can't scratch. If you get them sufficiently riled, they'll look for the source of irritation and try to get rid of it."

"So some animals will attack wizards?"

"Sometimes. It was rare in my day, as most of the wild things were moved on to more remote corners of the world, or died out. It's sad. Your grandmother saw a unicorn, when she was very young. When I was your age, unicorns were unheard of. Before we left, no one living had seen one at all," said Maeryl. He looked sad. Andrew couldn't stop thinking about the last Christmas he spent at home. The warm fire, the little glass of sherry his dad let him sip. A tear slipped down his cheek and he wiped it away with his arm.

"I...was thinking about the last...Christmas with mom and dad. I couldn't...remember what they looked like," said Andrew. Macryl hugged Andrew to him as they sat next to the wagon. Their horse, tethered to a nearby tree, flicked its tail at buzzing flies.

"It's okay, Andrew. You need not feel guilty or anything. Sometimes I forget what your aunt looks like."

"Aunt Willow?"

"Yes. She died a long time ago, and time is the enemy of memory. When I try very hard, when I am scared I will forget her, my mind comes up blank and I feel like I have lost her forever. Then, when I am not thinking of her and I am in the middle of something, her face will come back to me. Her warm smile and long, red hair."

"Do you still miss her?"

"Terribly."

"Does the pain ever go away?"

"It hasn't for me. Some people I've known have acted like it, so maybe they were lucky. Or not, depending on how you look at things."

"I can't remember mom and dad at all."

"You're just trying too hard. Let it fall to the back of your mind."

"I can't when I'm trying NOT to think about it."

"Then list me all the magical uses of salt."

"Uncle!"

"We've had a good break, and I'm trying to help. All the uses of salt," repeated Maeryl. Andrew sighed.

"When sprinkled with a spell of protection in a circle it will bar the entrance of any enemy, magical or mundane, and block spells. When used on iron it can cause rust. It can be used as a gift for pixies, brownies, naiads, and...and...."

"Think Andrew. Tall, very thin...."

"Um."

"Pan-pipes."

"Elves!"

"Good. Continue."

"It can be used to bless a house to remove an evil spirit. A little in a vial can be carried for good luck, but luck magic is unreliable."

"Is that all?"

"I think so."

"What would be the opposite of a protective circle, perhaps?"

"Oh! It can also be used to bind an enemy or magical being in one place."

"Correct! Remember when you thought salt was just for sprinkling on dinner?"

"Uh, huh!" said Andrew. They laughed together as the wind picked up gently, ruffling Andrew's hair. It was getting long, almost to his shoulders. Maeryl noticed. *We need to get to a town. He needs new clothes and a haircut. My, but he's growing fast.*

"Oh!" said Andrew.

"What is it?"

"I just remembered my parents," said Andrew. He looked down into his mug of water.

"That's good, though, isn't it? You see what I meant, now?"

"I do, uncle," said Andrew. As the young boy looked into the water, Maeryl was suddenly reminded of a spell he learned around Andrew's age.

"Would you like to learn a new spell now, Andrew?"

"I guess so," said Andrew.

"You'll like it, trust me," said Maeryl. He stood and rummaged through the wagon until he came up with a clear glass, which he filled with water. He then walked Andrew through the steps of the spell, until the water turned dark and Andrew found himself looking into his living room, a few years past, during the last Christmas he spent with his parents. He watched them laugh together as he opened presents and his parents sipped hot drinks before the roaring fire.

"Oh...thank you, Uncle." whispered Andrew after a long look.

"You're welcome. That charm only works if the person looking remembers the scene very well. It can help you to remember, but if you keep them close in your heart, you will never have a problem repeating this spell. For yourself, or for others, if you need to," said Maeryl. Andrew nodded and continued staring into the glass. Maeryl let him look a while longer, then spoke the words that unbound the spell. The glass returned to clear water, though it had the smell of wood smoke. Andrew gave an anguished cry when his parents and home disappeared. Maeryl hugged him close, and then knelt in front of his nephew.

"You cannot spend too long looking into the past. You will lose your way," was all he said.

"I...I won't, Uncle," said Andrew.

"You'll never forget the face of your father or mother, Andrew. You've a good heart."

"I miss home," said Andrew.

"I do too."

"Can we ever go back, you think?"

"I don't think so. There's no magic there to sustain us."

"No magic, anywhere in the world?"

"Okay, you caught me. That is, perhaps, a bit of an

exaggeration. Let me say that there could be pockets of magic, places where one might live, but they would be so remote that we would be forced to live alone, and in secret."

"Why in secret?"

"Same reason as here, Andrew. The Machine God would seek us out and destroy us, as a matter of course. He would not tolerate the presence of magic. Here, there are people who would try to use us to use our magical talents for evil. This must never happen."

"Oh."

"I'm sorry. Truly, if I thought it was safe for us to return, we would. I miss Earth, too, you know."

"I miss having friends," said Andrew. Maeryl felt a pang of guilt sweep through him.

"I know how you mean, Andrew. Maybe when you're a bit older we can try to find a little town to call home. For now, though, we have to keep on the move."

"Do you miss anything from home?"

"Oh, yes. The familiar streets of Atlanta, even after the war. A soda straight from the fountain. Beer. Oh yes, I miss a good beer."

"Uncle! That can't be all!"

"No, there are many things. Other wizards, for instance. I think you would have enjoyed growing up with other wizard children. The magical games were a hoot to play, and even more fun to watch as an adult."

"What kinds of games?"

"Hide and seek like you wouldn't believe, for one. Races where participants could make themselves lighter, or fly, or others change the ground to mud or to ice. Magical dueling, non-lethally, was big amongst adults. For children, it was another sort of game. You would take on a form, and your opponent would take one that could defeat it. You might become a cat to chase a mouse, and the mouse into a dog to chase the cat, and the cat into wolf, and so on. But more intricate, of course, if the youngsters were especially clever. Sometimes that game was used as an exam by masters for apprentices."

"Did wizards go to school?"

"Not as such. It was more like the Socratic model. A master or instructor posing questions to students, challenging them. It was a loose network of learning, with different scholars or philosophers even taking different points of view and teaching them to those that followed. Apprenticeships were very big, and magical traditions were often passed down through families. Your father and I learned from our father, who was taught by his father, and so on until the time when we first learned magic."

"You said it was won from the King of Fairies?"

"Yes. In the very early times, the only magic, applied magic that is, with spells and the like, was that of the fairies. Their king Oberon, who was also a god, gave the fairies spells and taught them magic. Humans, over the centuries, picked up on some of these spells and the uses of magical substances, like salt and silver and iron." Maeryl took a sip of water, contemplating the forest before continuing.

"Then, a war broke out between fairy kind and human. Fairies used to steal human children and replace them with changelings, fairies in the guise of human children. Children taken by the fairies were never seen again. The war started after a number of children from a village in China were stolen. The villagers trapped a fairy with a bowl of milk and a cage of iron, and from it they learned the location of their children. They destroyed the fairy village they found, and that was the first battle in a long and grievous war. It was fiercely fought, and in secret, mostly. The casualties were blamed on the Black Plague, but it was really a last-ditch effort by Oberon to destroy humans. When it failed, and his armies were turned back, a treaty was signed. Fairies would co-exist with human kind, staying behind the vale, so to speak, and Oberon would gift mankind with magic. The men and women who fought him gained the ability to use and teach magic, and a number of magical texts were written to keep the knowledge alive. There was a stipulation: magic could only be inherited by blood. The peace lasted, and relations even grew to the point that they were no longer so cold, if not very warm, over the centuries. Then the machines came. And...well, you know the rest of that. Here we are."

"Oh. What happened to the Fairy King?"

"He...he was killed. Or so most people think. He went away, that's certain," said Maeryl, suddenly uncomfortable looking.

"What about...changelings? What was bad about them?"

"Kidnapping is wrong, no matter what, even if you leave something else behind. And the something else is a big part, too. Changelings were just...wrong. Off. They would have a fairy-like characteristic—you could always tell if you were looking. Some had cat's eyes, and others long, pointed ears. They were often mischievous and would cause their 'adopted' parents much heartache. After a few years, they too, would disappear. The horrified parents would lose the only other 'child' they had. Some people believed a changeling to be the shell of a human with a fairy soul in it."

"What do you believe, Uncle?" asked Andrew, looking up at Maeryl. Maeryl smiled again and tousled Andrew's hair.

"I think it's time to get back to teaching."

"Awww!"

"You must keep learning."

"I know, I know. Uncle Maeryl, I have one last question."

"Okay, go ahead."

"You said the Black Plague was caused by Oberon?"

"Yes."

"But people eventually stopped him. Did they have to kill?"

"Yes. That's the way of war."

"How could they stand up against magic?"

"We humans are devious creatures. Amulets and iron charms, and a variety of other things can protect someone from magic. If they are cautious, that is."

"You told me slaying with magic was wrong."

"It is. It's prohibited by human kind especially."

"Why? We might have to use magic to fight fairies again one day."

"We'll cross that bridge when we come there. Against other humans, it is a very, very bad thing to do."

"I thought all murder was wrong."

"It is! Murder by means of magic is especially heinous."

"Why?"

"Think of it...think of it like this. Could you capture a frog?"

"Of course! They're not so fast or so smart or anything."

"Would it be wrong to kill a frog?"

"Oh, yes. It would be cruel."

"Could the frog stop you, even if it fought as hard as it could?"

"I don't think so. I'm a lot bigger than a frog."

"Good, you're right. Now, think about this. Have I ever struck you?"

"No, uncle."

"Why do you think that is?"

"I dunno. You're bigger than me?"

"That's part of it. It's wrong to hit someone who is smaller and cannot defend themselves, and I also personally believe it's wrong to hit children."

"Okay."

"As wizards, we must treat other humans as children. Not in the way we talk to them or treat them, but in the way we do things with our magic. There will be times where you or I will have to fight with magic. That's the way of the world. But we must keep in mind that our magic makes us giants. Everyone, Andrew, everyone, is smaller than us. And a child. We have a responsibility to use our magic correctly, so as not to become monsters ourselves. Do you understand?"

"I think so."

"Good! Now, tell me how much you understand about delving," said Maeryl. Andrew groaned.

"Don't groan at me, young man. There's much to do!"

"What next?"

"We need to practice," said Maeryl. Andrew groaned once more.

"Again?"

"Yes. It's an important part of our magic."

"I don't see why. You don't delve to call the wind or start a fire."

"No, that's true. However, if you want to affect a living thing, like a plant or an animal, then you'll have to delve or have delved something like it before."

"I've delved all the bugs around! It's pointless! I feel like I'm putting my fingers in a dirty old sock."

"Insects can be like that."

"Everything is probably like that."

"The bigger animals aren't."

"You won't let me delve the bigger animals. You won't even let me delve a squirrel." Maeryl sighed. He looked around the clearing, could hear the animals and birds rustling and singing all around them.

"If I help you delve a squirrel, will you promise to study the theory extra hard this evening?"

"Yes, sir! Of course! I'll be an expert by tomorrow!" Andrew laughed, his eyes sparkling. His uncle could best him in magic, but at begging, Andrew was king.

"Okay, okay." Maeryl scanned the trees around the clearing and picked out a squirrel. He focused on it, and the squirrel bounded over to them. He leaned down and picked it up in his hands. It was docile as could be, as if it ran to and was held by humans on a daily basis.

"This," said Maeryl, "is a squirrel." Andrew rolled his eyes.

"Unlike delving something as simple as an insect, animals are a good deal more complex. Many have emotions and thoughts of their own."

"Thoughts! Animal's can't think!"

"You'd be surprised, Andrew, and will be I'm sure. To continue, this particular squirrel is hunting for food."

"Nuts!"

"Shush. Close your eyes and find your stillness. Remember..."

"When we delve, we extend ourselves, and we must be at peace to do so."

"Correct." Maeryl watched his nephew close his eyes. Andrew's forehead crinkled, then relaxed. Maeryl sensed his nephew's calm like still water.

"I'm ready."

"You'll recognize the streams of light extending from you and from all living things, but especially animals and people. Using your wizard's eye, look at this squirrel." Andrew opened his eyes. They were utterly calm, and piercing at the same time. He could look through ten feet of solid iron if he wanted. He could look through the Earth to the other side. He could look through blood and bones. He turned his masterful stare on the squirrel.

"I see a web of lights, Uncle."

"You see this squirrel's living relatives, blood relatives, where the threads disappear like spider's silk on the wind."

"I see a few...nubs?"

"Those are dead relatives."

"Ah...the blood is the connection. Is that what I touch?" Before Maeryl could stop him, Andrew reached out and grabbed the web in the clumsy manner of a child. The squirrel shrieked and writhed in Maeryl's hands.

"Andrew, stop! Stop!" The squirrel lay silent and unmoving. Andrew's concentration broke, and his face was taut.

"Uncle Maeryl! I think I hurt it!"

"You certainly did, wrenching on him like that! Quiet now." Maeryl placed his hand on the squirrel's little chest and closed his eyes. After no more than a second, he looked at Andrew.

"You wrenched his heart, Andrew. I can feel torn arteries." Andrew teared up.

"I didn't mean to hurt him."

"I know you didn't."

"Can we help him?" Andrew begged. Maeryl's face was serious, but he nodded.

"The magic I am about to show you is very, very dangerous. Don't ever try it on your own. It's too advanced for you. I am showing you this because of our moral obligation to help anything we harm. Watch closely, but don't ever do this." Andrew nodded quickly, tears spilling down his cheeks. Maeryl drew the knife at his belt and drew the blade across the inside of the squirrel's arm. Andrew cried out, but Maeryl shot him a look that silenced him. Maeryl dabbed a finger in the blood.

"Watch." Andrew assumed the wizard's eye, and the blood went from dark red to bright white. He could see the web of the squirrel, much dimmer, so much dimmer now. The light was fading from the center out, with the interior nearly dark. Andrew choked back a sob that rose in his throat. He watched Maeryl take the bright light of the blood and speak some powerful, terrible words. The kinds of words that make you scream inside, afraid like you've never been afraid before. The darkness in the woods, the pad of the panther's paw, the tread of night coming after the dawn. The language of death. The language of blood. But even amidst the primal fear that washed over Andrew, he watched his uncle. Maeryl spoke the terrible language, focusing on the dying web of light in his hands.

To Andrew's astonishment, the lights began to brighten. The web was slowly reknitting, again, working from the inside out. The strands stopped fading and became warm. Soon the hurt that Andrew had caused was gone. Andrew let go of his wizard's senses, and saw that the squirrel was no longer bleeding from the cut in its arm, and breathed well. Maeryl sat the critter down and watched it. It took a few tenuous hops, looked back at them, and then broke for the woods. Maeryl smiled. Andrew broke out laughing, the tension easing out of his body. Maeryl turned to his student.

"Did you see what I did?"

"Yes, Uncle."

"Do you think you could perform the same spell?" Andrew shuddered.

"I don't want to. The words you spoke...they were terrible, like the center of the Earth speaking through a tomb, or something." Maeryl nodded.

"The language of blood is a terrible one," said Maeryl.

"Where did you learn it?" Maeryl hesitated.

"A teacher whose lessons I should not have pursued. They came at terrible cost."

"But you were able to save that squirrel."

"I could have made it worse, too. Arteries, veins, the heart...these things are very sensitive. Blood magic is nothing like the other magics we know. It is an ancient magic, the very first magic was written in blood. It is always dangerous."

"But...but the squirrel is okay."

"Yes. I hesitated to do even what I did, but I thought you would benefit from the knowledge. Personal responsibility is an important lesson. Gentleness is, too. It is better that we show responsibility and gentleness than have to do what we did. Do I make myself clear?"

"Yes, Uncle."

"Good. Let's take a quick break, and then we'll go over the delving theory. I want your rapt attention, young man."

"Yes, sir!"

Chapter 5
The Northern Star

ANDREW WOKE UP IN A HAZE of pain and blurred vision. His scalp throbbed and burned. He tried to sit up but the motion immediately made him vomit.

"Okay. I'll just lay here a bit," he whispered after retching. *What happened?* His last memories were so vague. A crumbling tower, an adrenaline- and terror-filled escape...being struck. Ashna's face, looking sad. *Why...did she...?* He felt like throwing up again. He felt the lump on his scalp as he lay on his side, and grimaced. It was very tender to the touch, and from the feel of the angry, smooth skin under his fingers, he guessed it must have been iron. Nothing else would make his hair fall out like that. He sighed and let his hand fall to the floor in front of him. Through the blurriness he could barely see it. After what seemed like hours, he finally managed to sit up enough to look around him.

He was in one of the cells below the castle, that much was obvious. It was dark, damp, and cold. *Everything,* he reflected, *you would want in a castle dungeon. Perfect. Maybe a rat will come by and let me out. A talking rat, yes, that's the ticket. Maybe a princess who was transformed by an evil...well, wizard, but that doesn't make any more sense than a talking rat. Maybe she was a rat princess, cursed to find true love in the human world by a...rat witch. She roams the castle looking for the One, the only One that could set her free. With true love's kiss! Yes, this is a constructive escape plan. Any moment now the door will spring open.* Andrew tried to shake his head at the notion and paid dearly with a stab in the brain. *Let's not shake our head at our own foolishness. Also, let's stop talking to ourselves and see what we can do with this cell.*

Using one hand to cradle his head, he slowly groped around the stones with the other. *Ooh, more damp. Nice. Good, gritty feel to the stone. Unyielding and oppressive. Where did they find this stuff, a morgue?* He used his senses to probe a little deeper and was rewarded with a thunderous blast of pain in his head. He slumped where he was sitting, and dry-heaved through another spell of nausea and world-spinning. *Oh...Boy. Seems they've reinforced the walls with more iron.*

He crawled to another corner of his cell and found a pile of moldering hay. *Best bed in the house, by the smell. Premium mold, this.* He felt along the walls again, this time going more slowly, and only suffered a wave of vertigo when he discovered more iron bars sunk into the stonework. He was in a cage. The stone doesn't even matter. *They could put me in iron manacles and I'd be just as trapped. The cell is an affectation to show me how much time and money he has to waste. Asshole.* Andrew didn't bother going near the door. He could see it was banded with iron, and didn't feel like dry-heaving for another ten minutes just to confirm what he already knew. He dragged himself back to the hay. Despite the mold, it was the softest thing to rest against.

Andrew leaned back and closed his eyes. He was sweating hard, and the lump on his head throbbed such that it felt like someone was hitting him again. *Well. Locked up good and tight, here. No rat princess as of yet. How am I going to get out?* He mused on a variety of escapes, each more unlikely than the last, and the last one involved summoning a dragon and riding out while throwing lightning bolts at the king. *I don't even know any dragons.* Good luck getting one to save a stranger. He reflected on the implications of forming closer ties with the draconic community, and how they would respond to a gift of smoked lamb. *Poorly, I'd guess. They can have smoked lamb whenever they want. Lucky dragons*. Ashna's voice came to him, a whisper in his ear.

"Dragons like virgin maids, or so Maeryl claimed. Do you know any virgins?"

"Not if I can help it."

"You could also try gold. Dragons love gold."

"I don't have any gold."

"Got any lead? I know a neat trick to turn it into gold."

"Ha! I won't fall for that twice, sneaky wench," said Andrew. He opened his eyes, and found that he could see much more clearly than before. Ashna stood before him, wearing a red and gold juggling costume. It clung to her shape in a way that made him dizzy.

"At least you're not Ashna from ten years ago. That would make it even worse."

"Is there something wrong with my shape today?"

"Not at all. Just...different. Lovely, still, either way."

"Thanks, Andrew. Even in your dreams you're kind of an ass."

"I do my best."

"You try to act like an ass?"

"Listen, this self-examination is great and all, but I'm trapped in a cell banded with iron. I need to escape before the king comes up with a particularly interesting way of killing me. I can keep arguing with myself, or I can come up with an escape plan. Any ideas?" he said.

Ashna began juggling casually with iron-banded cudgels. "Nothing comes to mind."

"Oh, good. I'll just watch myself juggle. How productive."

Ashna made the clubs vanish and sauntered over to Andrew. "There's other ways to pass the time, you know," she whispered. He could smell the perfume she used to wear to drive him crazy, and it still had the same effect. He put his hands up and around her waist, drew her down to him. Her lips sought his and they kissed eagerly.

"Wait, if you're me, thinking out loud…" he started.

"In love with yourself, eh?"

"Andrew," said a voice.

"In love with *you*," he said.

"Andrew," said the voice again. Andrew stirred, watched the ghost of Ashna fade away in his arms.

"I love you, too," she said, the sound of wind slipping under a door. Then she was gone. Andrew opened his eyes again, this time through a haze of pain. *Oh yes, the real world. Much better.*

"Andrew!" said the voice, equal mix exasperation and tremulous fear.

"Ugh..w-what? Who is it? Why are you bothering me? I'm trying to formulate an escape plan. Unless you've brought some gruel or bread crusts or something, just go away."

"Andrew!" said Ashna. Now her voice was all exasperation.

"Oh. It's you. The same applies. Bread crusts or solitude, please. I have nothing to say to you, Guard Captain," said Andrew. He tried to turn over so he couldn't see the face at the bars in the door, but that was the side of his head where she had clubbed him, so he had to be satisfied with a slight turn of the head and body and shut eyes. *God, I feel like I'm ten again.*

"Andrew, I'm sorry. I want to talk to you about what's going on, please," said Ashna. Andrew remained silent.

"I didn't mean to hurt you so badly. I didn't know that would happen to you." Silence.

"Look, when I asked you all those years ago about ways to stop a wizard, I didn't realize you'd be honest with me. How was I supposed to know?" said Ashna. Andrew shifted and said not a word.

"I know I hurt you, Andrew. I know that. I'm sorry,

okay? I've said I'm sorry. You're acting like a child. You know I care about you and I always have, and I know we've had our differences, but—"

"*Differences*? We've had *differences*?" said Andrew. He sat up rapidly and gagged as the world spun, but he remained upright. "You call clubbing me in the head differences? Becoming the mistress of the most vile, evil, disgusting monster in all the world differences? A monster that treats me like a slave, demeans me in front of the world, keeps me as a plaything is a *difference*? You're right, we DO see things awfully different, Guard Captain Ashna Lillifran. Go run to your monster and sleep with him or whatever it is you two do to have fun when you're not telling me to be complacent and he's not making me more miserable. I've had enough of the both of you, and I swear to God I'll...I'll..."

"Kill me?" whispered Ashna.

"No. No. No, just go away, please. This is too much. I've nothing left, please just let me have my solitude."

"I can't leave you alone."

"So you're here to remind me that everyone I've ever loved has abandoned me? Perfect. You're doing a great job. Maybe his highness will gift you with extra treats today."

"You're not being fair."

"I'm glad you've got so much to say about differences and fairness outside my nice cozy cell. You should really sleep in one of these sometime. The haypile has exquisite aromas and the rats are the friendliest you'll ever meet."

"Fine. Don't listen to me, even for a second, because you'd have to stop pitying yourself long enough to hear what someone else had to say. God forbid! How awful that would be for you," said Ashna. She turned to walk away but stopped herself. Andrew found himself without anything to say. Ashna turned back and put her hands on the bars.

"I wish you would stop pushing me away. I know things happened in our past that neither of us are proud of. We both have regrets about things that we can never change. Things we said we can never take back. Things that we did or someone did to us that led us to this place. You're stuck in an iron cell in the dungeons of a monster that treats you like filth. I understand that. I know that you think everyone in your life that you've ever loved has left you. Maybe that's true, but not for me. I haven't left. We're on different sides of the door, but we're still here. Together. Me and you. I want to help you. I want to open the door, Andrew. I want more than what we have. I'm not happy either, but I don't let that define me. Don't open your mouth, I'm not done yet. I don't let it define me, and there are some things going on that even you don't know about. I haven't been able to tell you because you never let me talk to you. You hog all the pain and suffering in the world to yourself and leave no room for others to feel bad. I can't reach out to you, so I suffer alone, and inside. I need someone too, Andrew. Same as you. We're both dying inside, or maybe even dead. Do you know what it did to me to hit you with that club? To see your hair fall out and your skin turn red in seconds? To watch them haul you into a dungeon I helped build on the orders of a man I hate? I cut out my own heart, back there, Andrew. To survive. So both of us could survive."

"That's rich. You kept me from getting out when you hit me, and I'm supposed to feel sorry for you?"

"No, don't feel sorry for the way I felt when I hit you, Andrew. Feel sorry because I'm just as trapped as you."

"How? HOW? You've got money and the means of disappearing into the world like I never could. I know *magic*, Ashna, no one in the world can do what I can do! If I ever used my gifts outside the castle I would be known in an instant. I would be hunted for the rest of my life. I can never escape him, this place, you, my past. It's all here, all the time!" said Andrew, hitting his chest. "I can never escape what he's turned me into. A slave, a hunted man. A commodity. And now, now I've gone and done something he can never forgive. I made him look weak. And now, I get to be weak. Even weaker. An ant dared bite a giant, and now I'll be ground into a speck of nothing, even less than I was before."

"There are things that keep me here, too, Andrew."

"What could keep you here? What keeps you from flying free whenever the fancy might strike you?"

"You, for one," she said. Andrew snorted and turned his head so she could see the angry welt where she hit him.

"Right. What else, then?"

"Salim," she whispered. Andrew could only look at her.

"Salim?"

"Yes."

"The prince? Salim, the king's son?"

"Yes."

"Why?"

"He's mine."

"What?!"

"He's my son. I gave birth to him," said Ashna, her voice very small.

"But...he's the king's...you *slept* with him!"

"Andrew, I—"

"I can't believe it! I was right! You're here to torture me you evil bitch! Rub it in my face while I'm down, good old Ashna coming to the king's rescue!"

"Listen to me, dammit!"

"Right! Sure! Next you'll tell me you still love me and come up with an elaborate escape plan!" Andrew managed to stand and begin walking around the cell slowly, waving his arms in agitation. "We'll summon elephants to knock down the walls! Alligators to fight the guards! Magic fairy dust will blind them to our escape and we'll ride out on a unicorn made of love and rainbows!" He didn't hear Ashna open the cell door, so when he turned around and came face to face with her, he was a little off-guard.

"We'll name the unicorn Francis, and just as—!" Ashna hauled back and slapped him across the face as hard as she could. Andrew went down in another blaze of agony and began retching. The slap felt like it slammed his brain against his skull, dribbled it around, and dumped it in a pain basket. The world spun wildly and he felt so sick all he did was dry-heave and moan. Ashna pulled her hand back, tight in a fist, to hit him again. Her chest was heaving and her breaths were coming in high-pitched gasps...she tensed...and let her fist drop to her side. When Andrew was able to see again, he saw her sitting in the corner, her arms wrapped around her legs.

"Why did you do that?" he groaned.

"You don't get to be broken today."

"What do you mean?"

"The king raped me, you piece of self-centered shit."

"He...he...?"

"Yes. Raped me. You heard me. He forced himself on me. Held me down, and...well, you heard me. He raped me. Are you happy? You're such a selfish pig," said Ashna. Her voice was cold and distant. Andrew coughed and struggled to stand so he could walk to her, but wasn't able to get his legs working again. He crawled to her.

"Ashna, I'm sorry," he said. Ashna was crying, tears streaming freely down her face. She tried to push him away but he managed to crawl up and put his arms around her. He hadn't touched her since they arrived at the castle, years ago. And yet, holding her felt as natural as the first time he ever did, when they were teenagers and falling in love. Ashna settled against him, put her head on the nape of his neck and sobbed quietly for a while.

"When...when did he...."

"Salim's eight. You're a fucking wizard, you do the math," she said into his chest. Her tears were hot against his skin.

"I'm sorry. I'm sorry," he said to her, stroking her hair. Her bodied shuddered, wracked by her pain. Andrew felt like an ant again, or even less than an ant. A tiny dung beetle.

"I didn't know."

"How could you? The only pain and suffering in the world were yours, how could anyone else have any?"

"I didn't mean to be so blind."

"You did a good job of it."

"Why didn't you ever tell me?"

"Would you have listened?"

"I...I don't know. I'm sorry."

"It's in the past. I love Salim. I'm sorry I hit you."

"Mutual remorse forgives all sins," said Andrew. He held Ashna for a long time. Two broken puzzle pieces fitting together.

"What about the guards?"

"I told them you couldn't get past the iron no matter what, and honestly, you scared them to death. I'm amazed they were even near your door after you grew some teeth today."

"I didn't kill anyone, did I?"

"No, of course not."

"Good...just...good. I was afraid I would."

"You held back. Just enough."

"What now?" said Andrew, looking into Ashna's eyes. She sat up.

"I help you escape. As long as you help me with one thing."

"Of course, what is it?"

"We take Salim with us."

"But..." Andrew began to argue, but the look Ashna gave him killed his words in his mouth.

"Well, that's going to take some doing. Are you prepared for a fight?" said Andrew.

"I'm ready to kill. If that's what it takes," said Ashna. "I just don't know where we can go."

"I have an idea," said Andrew.

"What?"

"I planned on following the Northern Star."

"The Unnamed Turtle? Why?"

"My uncle told me a long time ago if I was lost I could follow it and it would lead me home."

"Why would you trust him? He left you more than ten years ago and you haven't seen him since."

"Despite that, the advice he gave me before he left has always been sound. Especially when it comes to magic."

"Will it take it some place safe?"

"Do you have something better?" asked Andrew. He looked into Ashna's eyes, looked at the crow's feet at the edges of her lashes, just coming to be. He saw for the first time some of deep lines that marred her otherwise flawless beauty. She felt gaunt in his arms. *She's suffered every bit as much as me. Probably worse*, he thought.

"I'll get us out of here," Andrew tried to assure her.

"No, we'll get us out of here. We're not doing this alone anymore," Ashna countered. She looked for a moment like she wanted to kiss him, but instead she stood and helped him to his feet. "No sense in waiting around."

Despite the situation, Andrew's heart was lightening. "Except I've been dearly injured by the only person in the world I can trust. Otherwise, I'm a hundred percent. Never felt better. May I lean on you?"

"You always did before."

"I love it. Off to fight everyone in the castle, are we?"

"Andrew! You're in no condition to be fighting," said Ashna, looking at him. He laughed, but he saw she was serious. He adjusted the arm around her shoulders so he wouldn't put so much weight on her.

"Then...ah, I seem to have misunderstood. Does all the other stuff still make sense right now to you, or am I hallucinating?" Andrew wondered. He looked at her sideways. "You're not going to start juggling, are you?"

"Um. Whatever that means. No, I didn't plan on doing much fighting. What you did today has put every guard in the castle back in diapers. They're terrified of you. I figure you could work some magic, maybe cause a stir, and we'll be out no problem. They know you fought off near a dozen guards without getting hurt yourself, or even slowing down, and the rumors about other stuff you didn't even think to do to them is circulating."

"Ooh! Like what?"

"Let's not inflate your swollen head any further. Here, come out into the hallway. I've got something for you," said Ashna. She helped Andrew into the hallway, and the bags leaning on the wall immediately piqued his interest.

"For me?"

"For all of us."

"Fine. What's in mine?"

"You'll see," she said. She helped him sit on the floor next to his bag, and he opened it. It was a wealth of helpful magical items! Roots, spices, chemical and alchemical compounds carefully labeled and in stoppered jars. Feathers, rocks, rusty and clean daggers, a vial of what looked like blood, wax, string, anything and everything he could ever think of for use in a spell. He fetched out a particularly gruesome root and grinned in a way a fox would find unsettling.

"A mandrake!" he said. He took out one of the daggers and began carving the root.

"What are you doing?" said Ashna as she strapped the other pack to her shoulders. Andrew just gave his little grin again.

"Oh, you'll see," said Andrew as he shaped and trimmed the root into the rough shape of a person. It looked eerie, and misshapen, but the form of it was there.

Ashna suppressed a shudder as she knelt next to Andrew. She took in a breath of his scent. She closed her eyes. Faintly of moss and earth, like always. Rich and heady...wonderful. Ashna reached out to him and put a hand on his back. Andrew flinched, and she withdrew her hand.

"Sorry."

"Don't be. It's just...I'm not used to being touched. It's been a long time," he said, looking at her for a moment before scraping at the root a few last times. "Hand me that candle," he said. Ashna gave it to him and watched as he lit it and began to dribble wax on the rough figure's feet. When he had enough, he stuck it to the floor and let the wax drop all over it.

"You're not going to steal someone's body, are you?" asked Ashna.

"Oh, no. Nothing like that. Though the results will be spectacular either way," Andrew added. He made motions as though drawing in the air to himself as the candle melted over the figure. The flowing wax made it resemble a melting person. As Andrew muttered and motioned, Ashna heard a sudden steady dripping sound.

"Is that—" she began but Andrew motioned her to silence and continued his spell. He reached into the pack she handed him and drew out the vial of blood, which he opened and poured over the creation. The dripping grew louder, and Ashna gasped when she saw movement from around the corner of the hall. Something moved along the ground, flowing as smoothly as a snake. At first it was a small thing, but it grew as it came closer. When it came into the light of the torches nearest to them, Ashna saw it was indeed a clear liquid. It flowed under the figure and climbed it, pooling around the crude feet and climbing up the legs. As it did so it lifted the figure off the ground, and Ashna could see rough-looking feet forming on the floor. More and more of the liquid flowed into the room, and she jumped back as she saw fluids coming from the ceiling to drop on the growing monster of wax and root. Andrew concluded the spell and stepped back to where Ashna was to watch the creature grow.

"What is it?" she said.

"Mostly wax. A little blood and magic," Andrew shrugged.

"Is it...dangerous?"

"Could be, if the wizard had ill intentions."

"But with you it won't be?"

The magician smiled. "No, I didn't give it any kind of intelligence of its own. It's a puppet, nothing more. There's nothing to lose control of," said Andrew. The figure was now half as tall as them, still growing as more and more fluid rushed into the room and dripped down.

"What's that stuff it's made of?" She pointed to the fluid dripping from the ceiling.

"Oh. More wax."

"Where did you get it?"

"Here, there. You know...the castle."

"Don't you think someone will notice all the wax candles melting and pouring down into the dungeon?"

"Yes."

"And that doesn't concern you?"

"You already said they're terrified of me after today. What about candles melting on their own and flowing across the floor to some unknown purpose?"

"Well...okay," said Ashna, eyeing the wax man as it grew. The head took shape, and the wax flowed down to fill out broad shoulders. It reached its maximum height, standing over Ashna and Andrew by a full foot. Andrew walked around it with an air of a proud parent. Ashna shut away the part of her mind gibbering in horror and tried to keep herself calm and focused. She walked around the front of the creature where Andrew was standing, and she looked up at the monster. Its face was a disgusting mockery of a human's, with melted, partially formed features that suggested mute horror at its own existence.

"Andrew."

"Yes?"

"We're trying to rescue my son, not give everyone in living memory nightmares for the rest of their lives."

"Why can't it be both?"

"If you were eight and you saw this walking towards you...."

"Point taken. We'll figure out where he's at and leave it outside. If we make it give him a horsey-ride maybe he'll be able to ignore the other bits."

"Like the melting face of Hell itself?"

"We'll put a bag over it when we find him."

"...Okay." The last of the wax fell on the monster that stood before them. Andrew put an arm around Ashna and led her behind the monster, where they bent and picked up their packs of supplies.

"You ready for this?" said Andrew.

"Yes," said Ashna. There was a faint hiss as she drew her sword.

"I'll need you to make sure no one interrupts me while I'm controlling the wax man. I'm going to bind it with my own actions, so if I have to run or anything...it'll be coming along, too. We'll just take it nice and slow, okay?" said Andrew. Ashna nodded.

Andrew took a torch from the wall and spoke, drawing some fire out of it. He made a gesture like throwing seed in a field and the fire leapt from his hand

and fell about the wax monster, catching here and there. Andrew spoke a few more words and the flames turned blood-red. It flickered slowly and oozily, like the fire itself was made of oil. Ashna's breath quickened at the sight of the burning monster.

"Fuck, Andrew," was all she could manage.

"I know!" he said with glee. He spoke a word with such authority that Ashna felt it as pressure in her chest and the monster animated. The nightmares Ashna had imagined before grew that much worse. It flexed with a ripple, as though it was impatient, and it made a sickening squeaky sound as it moved. The fire flickered and oozed around the monster. Andrew took a step, and the monster lifted a waxy leg and strode forward. Andrew concentrated hard, his brow knit, as the monster shambled from the dungeons and climbed the stairs. Andrew followed close behind, Ashna with sword drawn just behind him. Andrew heard the soft sounds she murmured.

"Why are you whispering?"

"I'm praying."

"Why are you praying?"

"For the safe return of my son. And that I might forget that monster ever existed."

"Ah. Say one for me, too. For freedom."

"Done."

They came to the door that led into the dungeons. Ashna dug into her pack for the key.

"No need," said Andrew. The monster reached forward and placed hands on the door. The wax of its arms flowed into and around the wood, and the monster ripped the door from the hinges. The squeal of the iron gave the door a voice of pain, and the sloppy wax sounds only added to the horror. The door clattered to the floor as the wax man threw it down, and bent to step through the now open doorway. The rooms of the castle were muted, as it was late at night and recently all the candles went missing. The sparse torches on the walls flickered and gave the castle an eldritch quality, something out of a dream. The waxman, rearing to full height and wreathed in crimson flames, made it a nightmare.

Andrew peeked around the burning wax man to see guards pressed up against walls or huddled on the floor, faces pale and frozen in total horror. Nothing had ever been seen like this in Aethero, and Aethero was a weird place. Andrew smiled, drew in a great breath, then let it out. The monster mirrored this, but instead of just breathing out, it gave a gurgling roar that shook the floor. Ashna put her hands over her ears. The roar shuddered through her and made her heart skip a beat.

When the sound of the roar finished echoing, the immediate room was totally empty save for Andrew, Ashna, and the wax man. Andrew turned to speak with Ashna, and the wax man looked over its shoulder. Ashna tried very hard not to look up at the creature's face.

"Where to?"

"I...God, Andrew....I think he'll be in his room," said Ashna. Andrew nodded and walked that way. The floor thumped with the blunt stride of the wax man. Andrew walked along behind it, with Ashna at an angle to watch their sides. She wondered if there was any point to her doing so. *No one is going to mount an assault on us with that thing around. I don't know if I could drive the guards to it myself.* She was proven wrong when they rounded the corner that led to the royal quarters. A group of a dozen royal guards, in breastplates and holding shields and pikes, stood before the doorway. They brought up their shields in response to the group coming into view, but Ashna could see start terror writ on the faces of the men. Yet, they held ground. Ashna felt pride at the sight, but cursed herself at the same time for the constant drills and training she put them through. *Well...you never did think you'd be facing pike formation behind a wax monster, either.* Andrew didn't break stride, so the monster continued plodding down the hall towards the raised metal. The red light of the flames cast about an eerie gloom, making the scene look as though it occurred at the bottom of a pool of blood.

"Halt!" cried one of the men in the front of the formation. Andrew raised his hands, and the monster mimicked his action, neither slowing down. The men in front tried to back up but were blocked by their comrades. When Andrew and the wax man were within a dozen paces, the front rank broke. The men dropped their shields and pikes and scrambled to get away from the monster, screaming in horror and trying to push against the other men. The next rank seemed ready to break as well when a voice, deep and commanding, stopped them all dead in their tracks.

"Stand, fight!" it commanded. Andrew himself stopped. The monster lurched but maintained its footing.

"Impossible," said Andrew. Ashna grabbed his arm.

"What is it? Why did you stop?" she asked. Andrew was trembling. The guardsmen reformed, and a figure stepped in front of them. It was a man, wearing dark robes. His hair was long and white, with a beard to match.

"That's…" said Ashna.

"No!" cried Andrew. Maeryl smiled.

"Andrew, my nephew. I've missed you."

Chapter 6
Monster
16 Years Ago

"WHAT'S THE NAME OF THE TOWN?" said Andrew as their cart rumbled along a rutted track.

"Blaine. Simple name, and they're simple people, so I'll thank you to keep your magic to yourself."

"You always say that when we go into a town."

"There's a good reason for it."

"I've never done anything!" said Andrew.

"I know you haven't, and I also thank you for your restraint. I find that I feel a bit better if I remind you. Please forgive your doddering and worried uncle," said Maeryl with a genuine smile. He tousled Andrew's hair. Andrew tried to twist his head out of the way.

"I wish you'd stop doing that!" he said.

"I will when we've got it cut, which is our first order of business in town here," said Maeryl. "We both need a trim," he added. Andrew's hair was down to his shoulders, and Maeryl's white beard and flowing hair were grand and ridiculous even for a wizard. *It will be good to have shorter hair for the summer. Lord, but it's hot!* thought Maeryl. He looked at his nephew, and how much he had grown in the last four years. Even living it rough in the wild Andrew didn't lack for food, and had begun the inevitable growth spurts and temperament changes. He was starting to be a handful for Maeryl to raise on his own, and he had thought a long time on the problem.

"So we're coming into Blaine for a haircut and then we're gone?" asked Andrew. As they approached the town, the sound of voices carried on the moist summer air. The smoke from cooking fires was visible over the tree tops, and as they came around a bend the first of the modest cottages came into view.

"Well, I've got some business to attend to here. I'm not sure how long it will take, honestly," said Maeryl.

"What kind of business?"

"Personal business."

"Hmph," said Andrew. As they approached the town, Andrew suddenly grew quiet. Maeryl was confused as they passed the first of the cottages—friendly looking wooden and brick homes— until he saw the crowd of children around the pole in the center of the town. The children, mostly boys, kicked a ball around having a great time of it. He could discern no rules or structure to the game, just one child kicking the ball away from the others and the rest of the mob trying to get the ball away. The new possessor would break from the crowd and the pile-up would begin again. At least, that's how it looked to Maeryl. Perhaps to young eyes it makes more sense. He looked over at Andrew, who was lost in gazing at the crowd. His feet twitched and his eyes were wide and curious. Maeryl felt a strong pang of guilt wash over him. *He needs so much to be around others. Maybe this trip will yield us a place amongst these people, if only for a little while.*

"Do you want to join them?" said Maeryl.

"Oh...no, Uncle, I suppose not. I don't know the game and you're always telling me how we can't trust anyone. I'm sure it'd be dangerous," said Andrew, who turned his head and pretended to be absorbed in the passing buildings. Women shucked corn and chatted amongst themselves, the younger children playing on the floors of open homes or around clusters of wives and daughters. A few of the girls gave Andrew appreciative looks, and Maeryl laughed to himself when Andrew quickly turn his head away, face bright and red.

"You could make some friends," Maeryl suggested.

"I'll wait for you. Maybe if we stay long enough to eat lunch I can try and talk to some...of the others," said Andrew. He shifted in his seat and looked around from under his long clothes.

I'd better be careful, getting him cleaned up and in a new, small town. The boys might resent the newcomer, and the girls will preen and play. Oh, to be young and new again! He won't miss out much longer on being a child, I pray. They rode through the dusty square of Blaine, and came to a stop at one of the houses a little ways down a street from the open center. Maeryl hitched the horse to a post outside and gave Andrew a hand down. Andrew felt the eyes of all the town children on him, and tried to be small against his uncle.

"Here we are," said Maeryl. Andrew was grateful when they walked into the shop. It smelled clean, and a friendly woman of about fifty greeted them. She was wearing an apron and had her brown and gray hair up in a loose bun. The space wasn't very large, taken up mainly by a chair in the center and a stove in the back with a large kettle of steaming water on it. A leather strap hung from a wall near the chair, and a large number of razors and shears hung from a pegboard as well.

"Welcome! Oh my, I see that I've got some real work ahead of me!" she said.

"Thank you, and yes, we're both in dire need of a trim, I'd say," said Maeryl. The woman smiled broadly and gestured to the chair. It had a number of gears and springs that would allow for many fine adjustments to fit the person sitting it. Maeryl looked at it with appreciation.

"Amazing! I haven't seen a chair quite like this since...." he trailed off. The barberess looked at him searchingly.

"I designed this chair. You shouldn't have seen anything like it before; I never have," she said.

"I apologize. My nephew and I are far traveled, and it's much like a chair enjoyed by the wealthy and powerful far away from here. Not nearly as clever, though. My name is Maeryl, and this is Andrew," he said. He took off his pointed wizard's hat and swept an appropriate bow, which Andrew mirrored with somewhat less flair.

"And I'm Anni, nice to meet you," said Anni. "Thank you for the kind compliment to my chair. Who'll be first?" she said. Andrew was looking up from under his bangs and being especially quiet.

"How about it, Andrew? If you go first you can go outside and enjoy some time away from your boring old uncle," said Maeryl. Andrew didn't say anything but climbed into the chair. He started a little when Anni made some adjustments.

"Is that better?" she asked.

"Yes'm," he said. Maeryl settled himself in a more conventional chair and watched as Anni took out a rough bar of soap and drew hot water from the kettle.

"I'm going to give your hair a quick wash and then brush it out, if that's okay with you Andrew," she said.

"Please," he said. Soap was one of the things they were going to get on this trip into town. They had run out a few days before, and only diligent scrubbing with hard brushes and hot water had kept them relatively clean. Both would be glad of a bath and a shampoo. Anni sliced some of the soap off of the block and worked it in the bowl, creating a rich and thick lather. Andrew felt luxurious as she worked it through his thick hair. Maeryl looked on with envy, and had to remind himself he would get a turn too. *Never thought I'd miss being able to walk down to a barber and get a shave and cut*, he thought to himself. *Used to dread it terribly. Now...what a treat!* Anni made small talk with Andrew as she washed and brushed out his hair, and then finally set about cutting it.

Thick mounds of black soon riddled the floor like oversized caterpillars, and after a final snip Anni stood back and admired her work. Andrew's hair was now short and well-cut, sensibly fashioned for a boy his age.

"Oh, he cleans up well, does your Andrew," said Anni. "Better watch out yourself, Mr. Maeryl, if you do as well. I might have to take you home for supper," she said with a wink. Andrew moved to climb out of the chair but Anni laid a hand on his shoulder.

"What is it?" said Andrew, nervous.

"You look like you're just about ready for a shave," said Anni, looking at his uncle. Maeryl nodded; he himself had noticed the fuzz on the boy's face.

"You mean it? I'm growing a wiz...a beard?" said Andrew. Maeryl held his face still. *He almost said wizard's beard. Close call.*

"You sure are. Let me get my finest razor. A moment like this calls for the best," said Anni. She stepped out of the room and came back a moment later with a fine wooden case. It looked old and well-oiled and cared for. She set it on the counter of her shop and opened it. Out of it she took a fine, old razor. It was a little longer than a standard straight razor, with a dark red handle made of a fine maple wood. It was polished to a high sheen, and inlaid with silver scrollwork. She began to sharpen it against the leather strap hanging from the wall, and Andrew's eyes grew wide.

"You're...going to put that against my neck? To shave me?" he said, his voice small. Anni laughed.

"I'm the best shaver around here, young man. Never drew a drop of blood in all my twenty years of work. I tell you, kings have stopped in and said they've never had better!" she said, the soft strop strop of the scraping blade punctuating her words. She held the blade up and gently drew the pad of her thumb across the blade.

"Yep. Fine and sharp. Let's get you lathered up," said

Anni. She adjusted the chair so Andrew was leaning a bit back, and then lathered his face. Maeryl smiled at the little show. *He's nervous now, but he'll be the toast of the town when he's all done. His first shave! I'll have to show him how to do it himself after today, but I doubt we'll have to worry about that for a while. It was good to come into town today.*

Maeryl watched with an appreciative eye as Anni talked to Andrew, keeping him distracted as she shaved his nephew with practiced grace and precision. Soon enough she wiped his face with a cool towel and helped him out of the chair.

"There you are, young sir! Cut and shaved and ready for a dance, I'd say!" said Anni. Andrew looked in the smoky mirror set above the counter and inspected his face. Not a single cut, and his head felt much lighter without his hair.

"Thanks, Anni! I really like it," he said. He turned to Maeryl with a grin.

"My first shave!"

"I saw. You're growing up fast, young man," said Maeryl. Andrew glanced out the window at the courtyard. Maeryl smiled.

"If you want to go and see about making some friends, I think our friend Anni here is going to need more time with me than you," he said. He ran his hands through his own thick mane of hair and beard.

"I'd say! You're a regular lion, sir," said Anni. Andrew made for the door, but as Maeryl was sitting down he called out to him:

"Remember your promise, and be careful!" said Maeryl.

"I will!" called Andrew over his shoulder as he barreled out of the door and into the street. Maeryl watched him with quiet anxiety. Anni began fixing another bowl of shampoo and hot water.

"Good young man you have there. Polite and respectful," said Anni. She began rubbing soap into Maeryl's hair, and he closed his eyes.

"It's been a trial, raising him by myself. We're on the road a lot, and that makes it more difficult," said Maeryl.

"What does he do for friends?" said Anni as she rinsed his hair out.

"Me. I feel so bad, but it's been necessary. We're traders, you see. Can't stay in one place too long, you run out of customers and so on," he said. He felt a gentle tug at his hair as Anni began snipping his white locks.

"I understand, I understand. Got a man who comes through once a year, and his hair usually looks like yours. I know I can't be the only haircutter on Aethero!" said Anni. Maeryl chuckled.

"No, of course not. Maybe everyone says you're the best," he said.

"Now you're just trying to flatter me into lowering the price," she said.

"I wouldn't dream of such a thing. In fact, I would be willing to pay a little more if you could help me with some information," said Maeryl.

"I'm no gossip, sir," said Anni, pausing in her snipping.

"Nothing like that. I just need to know if there's a home for sale or rent in the town. Andrew needs a stable place to stay. I just can't raise him on my own anymore, and it's no good for him to be alone with his uncle in the wide world without friends. He'll grow up to be a hermit or something," said Maeryl, watching out the window as Andrew stood on the side of the play area and looked on with interest.

"Where are his parents?" asked Anni, resuming the haircut.

"Both died. Around four years ago, now. A...a sickness," he said.

"I'm sorry to hear it, sir," said Anni.

"Not your fault, obviously, but I appreciate your sympathy. In a way, it's also a blessing. I never would have had the opportunity to raise a child of my own without losing them. Life can be bittersweet that way," said Maeryl. His head began to droop under the careful hands of Anni, and soon a gentle snore filled the little barbershop. Anni finished up her work with careful patience, and then threw a sheet over Maeryl so he could sleep in peace. She looked at his careworn face and white hair.

Poor dear, looking after such a young man by himself. Needs a woman, he does, she thought to herself. *Maybe if they find a nice place to settle down I could set him up with one of the gals in town looking for a husband. Let's see....Now, Roose has been a widow a fair few years now. I bet she'd like a gentleman to keep her company again!* Smiling to herself, Anni cleaned up quietly and walked into the back of the shop to plan her matchmaking. Meanwhile....

Andrew enjoyed watching the other children play their game almost as if he were playing himself. It looked exciting and complicated. He wondered how it was played. Sometimes one of the other children would notice him and take an interest, but the lure of the ongoing kicking, laughing, and shouting proved too great and they would rejoin the game. Whenever Andrew saw this, he was relieved and disappointed in equal measures. *Show me how to play!* He wanted to shout. His heart fluttered about his throat and there was a taste in his mouth only describable as excitement. Suddenly, the boy currently in possession of the ball kicked it in Andrew's direction and it rolled to his feet.

Andrew looked at it like a cow would at a complicated math problem. He had a chance to look up as the horde descended on him, and he gave the ball a furtive kick. The children immediately gave chase, and the magic of childhood games was worked. Andrew was swept up in the moment and found himself carried into the crowd. As they mobbed around the maypole Andrew slowly got a sense of the shifting alliances and esoteric rules of the game. The goal was to get the ball around the pole as many times as possible while keeping possession. When it was lost, the capturing player had to go in the opposite direction and tried to complete as many circuits as possible.

While Maeryl slept and Andrew was caught up deep in a new game, a suspicious man slinked into town. He was tall, with rough features and dark clothing. He fit in well enough with the villagers, and on any other day he might have warranted consideration. However, with the weather so fine and the children all about in the courtyard (and a cart with two strangers!), the usual long noses managed to find themselves immersed in the inconsequential gossip of a small village. No one really took notice of a lone man walking about the town.

The stranger had a travel sack over one shoulder that clanked faintly from time to time. He made his way towards the center of the village, looking on with great interest as the children kicked the ball about. A brief wind kicked up a burst of dust, obliging him to put a hand up and steady his wide-brimmed hat. When the stranger spotted Andrew, a twisted smirk wiggled onto his lips. He walked a wide and circuitous route around the courtyard, slipping into alleys between cottages and going into the various shops. He pretended to browse, but his eyes scanned the village rather than the wares he held.

His eyes would flit around, settle on Andrew like a mosquito on flesh, and then roll around the courtyard area again. He took note of the cart he knew belonged to the traveling duo, and that Maeryl was nowhere to be seen.

He made his way out of the general store and walked slowly towards the cart parked in front of the barber shop. He tried to watch Andrew without being obvious, but his excitement grew with each passing moment. *It has to be him. That's the one they want. I can already taste the women and wine that bounty will bring. Got to be sure, though. Gotta find something.* He circled towards the cart. He walked up to the cart and glanced around again, daring a look inside the barbershop itself. Just some old man in a chair, asleep. No sign of the long-haired man with a pointed cap around. He surreptitiously lifted flaps on the cart and peeked into bags.

Andrew saw none of this. His concentration was purely on the ball as it flew around the courtyard, his head full of laughter and the company of other children. It felt so good to run and play! His enjoyment was slightly muted, however. The other children, used to games, wouldn't let him get the ball for very long. He often tripped over his own feet and lost control, or sometimes they would work in pairs to get it from him. His inexperience began to frustrate him. Until he saw a dog lying under a porch, fast asleep. He smiled as it gave him an idea. Andrew slipped out of the mad rush of crazy children and walked over to the porch. The dog lifted its head to look at him, and its tail began tapping a slow tempo against the ground.

"Good doggy. Friendly doggy!" said Andrew, reaching out a hand. The dog stretched its neck out to give his hand a sniff, and then licked his palm. Andrew laughed and began to pet the dog. He glanced around. Maeryl's still inside the shop, I guess. Heck, this can't hurt anything. He put both hands on the dog's neck and got it to look him in the eyes, and then he was in its mind. Searching...*ooh, what's that smell! This spot is warm. This boy is nice. I'm kinda hungry. Where's my boy? I hope he comes by soon.* A rush of friendly canine thoughts flooded Andrew's head, and he was almost overpowered by the sensations. He took a deep breath and remembered the sessions he and Maeryl had done using smaller mammals. Dominating a squirrel proved much easier than a more capable animal. Still, Andrew dug around in the dog's mind until he found what he was looking for: *chase! And follow! MY boy*! He borrowed the feel of those emotions, the intense drive of dog-kind to love and follow their own special people. Andrew concentrated hard, sweat springing out on his head, and began jogging back towards the tide of children. It was hard to keep it all in his mind and try to get to the ball, but at last he managed and said the words he needed.

The ball quivered as it rolled on the ground, and then flew through the air as one of the bigger boys kicked it out from in front of Andrew. The mob rushed to get to the ball before it landed, but even as it arced through the air it seemed to strain and landed on something of a curve. When the boy kicked it again, it spun around him and came towards Andrew. The other children were agape as the ball rolled back to Andrew and stopped at his feet. He smirked at the flabbergasted crowd and kicked the ball in front of him, going around the maypole. He got one rotation in before the other children rushed back in, but it was rapidly clear that the ball had no intentions of leaving Andrew's close vicinity. No matter how clever the steal, no matter how hard they kicked it, the ball came rushing back to Andrew as loyal as a doggy-boomerang.

When Andrew spoke the words of the spell, the stranger's head jerked up and he stared at the small boy speaking to a rough leather ball on the ground. *It's him! My god, the* power *of it!* The bounty hunter slipped the bag from his back and reached in. He pulled out a length of rope and began to curl one end around his hand. *If I can get him tied and run, there's a chance I can just get out before they can react. Get him on my horse and ride like lightning for Aethero. My worries are over!*

Maeryl awoke with a start and sat up in the barber's seat in a state of total panic. *Magic! Someone is working magic! ANDREW is working a spell! My God!* He ripped the sheet off and began to rush for the front. His foot caught in the rest at the bottom of the chair and tripped him up, sending him to the hardwood floor with a great crash. Anni ran from the back of the store.

"Oh, I'm so sorry! You must have gotten tangled up, let me help you—" said Anni as she tried to help free Maeryl from the chair and sheet.

"Off, off me, woman! I have to get out now!" He wrenched the sheet from around his leg and pulled his foot hard enough against the rest to snap the wood.

"Well! You've turned out to be quite rude after all! And to think I was going to set you up with my good friend Roose!" said Anni, the very picture of affronted hospitality. Maeryl stared at her for a moment, then found his bearing.

"I'm sorry I broke your chair. I'll pay extra. I just have to go now, so sorry to leave like this. I just remembered something important," said Maeryl as he scrambled to his feet. He kept up the steady stream of apologies as he fished in his purse for some gold coins. He grabbed a handful and thrust them into Anni's hands without even counting them.

"There, I hope that covers everything." He turned quickly and ran for the door. Anni stared at the glimmering heap in her hand.

"I can't take this, sir! This is far more than—"

"Don't worry about it!" yelled Maeryl as he raced out the door. "I can always make more!" the door slammed behind him as he nearly fell down the steps. Anni looked at the coins in her hand again then shrugged. She walked into the back and dropped them through a slot in a stout looking oak chest bolted to the floor.

"Those traveling traders. Here one moment, gone the next! I hope that Andrew gets on well," she said.

Maeryl barreled down the steps in time to see the bounty hunter staring at Andrew from around the cart and holding a length of taut cord between his hands. Without a moment's hesitation, he muttered the words of a spell and leaped at the bounty hunter. With his back turned, he had no way to stop Maeryl from seizing onto the ropes.

"Hey!" yelled the man. He tried to yank the rope back from Maeryl but it came alive in his hands. The man's eyes grew wide as the rope snaked around his wrists and began to grow. It moved with fluid grace, a viper made of twisted fibers that wrapped him up. The bounty hunter tried to scream but the rope cinched tight, turning his yell into a squeak. Maeryl pushed the man under the cart to hide him, then ran toward Andrew. Maeryl pushed through the children like they were nothing but wheat and grabbed Andrew by the ear, who shrieked. Maeryl dragged the youngster to the cart.

"Ooooooow! Maeryl, what are you doing?!"

"I should ask you that same question!" said Maeryl. He picked Andrew up under the armpits and thrust him onto the cart seat, then clambered up himself. Andrew's face was bright red as he turned to yell at Maeryl, but he stopped when he heard muffled screaming coming from under the cart.

"What's going on?"

"You're performing magic in public is what's going on! Giyaa!" Maeryl flipped the reins at the startled horse and they took off down a side street. Andrew looked behind them to see a writhing cocoon of rope rolling around on the ground. Townspeople began shouting and running towards the strange shape.

"What was that?"

"That looked like someone who had intentions of kidnapping you, is what that was."

"How do you know?"

"He was coiling rope, hiding behind the cart, and watching you quite closely," said Maeryl. They rounded a corner and they both were forced to grab the seat as the cart lurched and slid along the dusty road.

"I was just having fun, I'm sorry, Maeryl!"

"This is why we have to live out amongst the wilderness, Andrew! Who knows how long that man has been tailing us? What he's after? What he'll do! We're in danger every second of our lives, Andrew. I've told you this time and again," said Maeryl. He didn't look at his nephew, he was afraid he'd turn him into something unsavory if he made eye contact. *A newt would be too nice*, he thought. They rode in silence for a long while, eventually slowing so the horse could get his breath. Its flanks were wet when they came to a walk. Maeryl couldn't believe how stupid Andrew had been, and how angry he was at himself. *Be fair. He's a young man, with no friends. It's natural he'd want to play with the other children. How could I be so stupid to fall asleep like that? I put us both in danger, doing that. I'm old enough to know better than this! Stupid! Reckless! And I yelled at him to top it off, so add unfair and unfeeling to that, too.* Maeryl felt every bit the fool. *Just like my own father, really. You can do better by this boy.* Andrew was watching the other side of the trail as the trees rustled by.

"Andrew, I'm sorry I yelled at you. And for grabbing your ear like that. You scared me, and you made a foolish mistake using magic out in the open like that. I've told you time and again that certain types of people, and certain types of creatures, can sense the presence of magic either by natural inclination or by training. Just because we're the only wizards in the world doesn't mean that magic is unknown to these people."

"You said no one can ever know what we do, because we're the only ones. That doesn't make sense."

"You're confusing the types of magic present here. Aethero is flush with natural magic. The animals can talk, gods walk the Earth. For God's sake, you've seen trolls, same as me! Some of these creatures hunt each other by senses other than the five we are normally given. Those senses can be trained to smell out magic."

"You said it was a man. He can't have any magic."

"No, but he can be trained to sense and to see as well as anyone else. You don't have to be a wizard to see a ball come rolling back to you!" said Maeryl. His face was flush, as was Andrew's. They lapsed into their own thoughts for a time. He looked at Andrew from time to time and saw that the boy looked positively miserable. To his credit, he was right. Andrew felt wretched for causing such a mess, but he was also angry with his uncle. *He goes off and falls asleep and he blames me for making a mistake. It was just a little magic. I know about all that stuff that can find us. We were in the middle of a town! It was just a stupid ball.* Andrew frowned, deep in his thoughts. The cart rocked them gently as late afternoon yawned and turned to dusk. Maeryl cast about with his senses, as subtle as a whisper, and found a place that would be safe for them to pull off the trail. The icy truce continued as they stripped their equipment off the cart and Maeryl walked Andrew through the ritual that formed a magical barrier around their camp. Maeryl could see Andrew was still angry; he flung the salt on the ground as if it had wronged him somehow. In their emotional state, neither of them saw when Andrew flung the salt too far out and left a gap in the circle.

Setting up camp, Maeryl sighed inwardly and beat himself up some more. The truce broke after they ate a small meal of salted beef, hard bread, and Maeryl sliced up the last of a somewhat stale wedge of yellow cheese.

"How did you even get the ball to do that?" said Maeryl around a mouthful of chewy food.

"Do what?" said Andrew.

"Come back to you like that. It wasn't a simple bind that would have stuck it to you. A tension spell would have made it yo-yo. So...how did you do it?" he asked. Andrew failed to suppress a grin.

"I turned it into a dog."

"What?"

"I found a dog and delved to find the parts that make a dog loyal and want to follow a person. Then I gave that to the ball, and made it want to follow me," said Andrew. He took a big bite of the hard bread and chewed around a big smile. Maeryl started laughing.

"That's good! That's very good! Intuitive and resourceful! But...that was quite a delve, wasn't it?" he asked. Andrew swallowed his too-big bite of bread and nodded.

"Almost lost it early. Dogs are more complicated than I thought," said Andrew. He took another bite of the salt beef.

"That was dangerous in and of itself, Andrew. What would I have done when they came to me to say you were running around on all fours barking like a dog?"

"You didn't have to."

"That's not the point, the point is that you put yourself in needless danger. Twice! By doing one thing!" said Maeryl, his voice tense.

"Well, I'll just never do magic again, okay? Is that fine?"

"No, Andrew...it's just...Again. You worried me! You did something dangerous! I couldn't live with it if something happened to you. If you did something, or someone found us...."

"Or if you fell asleep?" said Andrew, not looking at him now. Maeryl felt a stab of guilt in his heart.

"I deserve that. I'm sorry. It's very hard, being on our own. You know that just as well as I do," said Maeryl. "I was trying to find us a place to stay. You need to be around children your age. Just, you know. Without the magical show boating. You have to learn some discretion," said Maeryl. Andrew looked into their fire a while longer.

"I'm sorry, uncle. I guess I was showing off. A little."

"Maybe a bit more than a little, but I forgive you. There's more than one small village around here, after all. Just...be safe. I love you, Andrew," said Maeryl. Andrew looked up at his uncle.

"I love you too, Uncle Maeryl. I forgive you too. For pulling my ear. That hurt!" he said, with a reproachful tone of voice.

"I beg your forgiveness," said Maeryl.

"Granted again. See? You had to apologize twice. That's two to one! I think we're even," said Andrew.

"Wretched child!" said Maeryl with a warm smile. A shadow lurched up behind Maeryl. Before it registered with Andrew, before he could even say anything, the bounty hunter fell on his uncle. He wrapped the rope around Maeryl's neck and savagely yanked the cord. Maeryl's eyes bugged out and he fell back against the bounty hunter.

"Use your magic now, old man! Kill me with my own rope!" he yelled as he drug Maeryl away from the fire and tightened his grip. Maeryl's hands came up to the rope around his neck and he tried to pull it away, but he couldn't get his fingers between the rope and his skin. The coarse fibers burned his skin, and his lungs screamed for air. The world was getting dark. The fire seemed far away. His heart fell, for he knew he had failed his sister. *I'm so sorry I failed you. You and Andrew....*his thoughts became fuzzy....

The bounty hunter unwound the rope from around the old man's neck, laughing cruelly when he saw the dark red furrows the rope dug in the skin. He kicked the motionless form.

"Serves you right. Now come here, you little shit," he said to Andrew, rewinding the rope around his hands. Andrew was pale and still. He looked like a ghost. The whole world lay shattered before him in the form of his still uncle. He was alone. He looked at the furious bounty hunter as the man stepped closer to him. He felt his heart bottom out, and with it, a deathlike calm. A stillness. A willingness. Andrew began to chant, his eyes intent on the bounty hunter. The sound of the spell brought the man to a halt.

"You stop that chanting now! I'll put this rope away and we can go quiet, but you don't do no damn magic!" he said. Andrew continued to speak, his eyes shark-like in the reflected light. The bounty hunter felt a chill go through him. Them eyes are lifeless. I'd better— But his chain of thought was interrupted when Andrew thrust both hands into the fire and drew out a double fistful of coals.

"Hey! Y-you'll get hurt! Don't you come near me!" said the man, now backing away. Andrew brought his hands up and flames shot into the sky like geysers. The roar and heat made the bounty hunter yell and fall backwards over Maeryl's still form. Andrew approached the man as he backed away over the ground, lamely trying to crab-walk away from the nine-year-old boy holding living flames and coals in his hands.

Andrew spoke another word and the wind kicked up in a sudden screaming banshee wail. The campsite was torn by a gale of hurricane winds, and the crimson flames gushing from Andrew's clenched fists swirled into a twister of burning heat and rage. Andrew stood in the eye of a tempest of gusting winds and roaring fires. The bounty hunter's bowels and bladder let go, and he began to whimper. He was too terrified to even move. He closed his eyes against the blazing heat, feeling his hair begin to singe and his clothes smoke. The smell of burning hair and flesh filled his nostrils, and for the first time in his life, the bounty hunter prayed.

Maeryl was so confused: first the world went black and he was floating in a sea of stars, and then a deep, sonorous voice spoke in the dark:
It is not yet time. A huge form moved in the dark: graceful, ancient, gentle.
I am tired. I failed the boy.
You are no failure. What seems best is sometimes worst, what is worst is sometimes best.
How can I fix things?
Take this song in your heart. You will see him again. Remember the music. Music filled him, seemed to start in his chest and radiate out to his limbs and his mind until he felt he could no longer stand it.
This gift is not for you, but it will help you while you have the keeping of it. Goodbye.

A world of whirling flame and debris greeted Maeryl when he opened his eyes. His throat and lungs burned worse than anything he ever felt, and he began coughing and retching at the same time. A song, haunting and beautiful and simple filled his mind for just a moment, and his strength flowed back into his arms as he was able to breathe. He looked around to see a furious roar of flame and wind. He saw his nephew, wreathed completely in writhing flames, staring past him and down. Maeryl rolled over and saw the man who had choked him lying on the ground, his eyes shut tight, tears streaming down his cheeks. He realized what was happening and struggled to his feet, his lungs still full of burning sharp points. He stumbled to his nephew and fell to his knees.

"Andrew! Stop this, or you'll be consumed!" he screamed to be heard over the howls of the winds and fire. He looked into eyes of solid black and tried to find the little boy he knew.

"Andrew! You can't do this! You can't kill with your gifts, it's forbidden! Come back to me, I'm safe! It's Maeryl, it's your uncle!" he screamed at the boy. Andrew seemed lost to him. With nothing else to do, he wrapped his arms around the burning form. The flames consumed his robes and ignited his hair.

"Andrew!" he screamed one last time, in agony as the flames ate at him. Eyes of black turn ed back to brown, and the flames and wind died so fast the sudden silence seemed even louder than the inferno.

"Maeryl?" said Andrew. The man holding him didn't have any hair, or a beard, or eyebrows, and angry burns rippled across his scalp and on one side of his face. His robes smoked.

"Uncle...I'm...so sorry," said Andrew, tears welling in his eyes. The burning pain of the fire was totally gone from Maeryl as he looked into the eyes of his scared nephew. His child had come back to him. He hugged Andrew tight to his chest.

"It's okay, it's okay. I'm okay," said Maeryl. They held each other close, the leaves and woodland debris settling around them in the now stilled night. After a while, the birds and insects began calling again. Maeryl let go of his nephew. The heat and pain from his burns was starting to throb through his body. Andrew looked at the burns and choked back a sob.

"Uncle! Is there anything I can do to help?"

"Y-yes...Andrew....go, make a salve of...aloe, beeswax, and tea. Make sure to boil the tea! Go, be swift," he said. Andrew turned and ran to the cart, which had been overturned. The horse stared at him from behind a small grove of (now leafless) trees with a look of perfect disapproval. Andrew sorted through the jars and packets and got another little fire going as he started the salve. Maeryl dragged himself to his feet and turned around. The bounty hunter was still on the ground. He couldn't tell if the man was awake or not, or even if he was alive. He didn't care. He limped over to an oak tree a ways out of the clearing and cast about the ground until he found what he was looking for. He limped back to the unconscious man and began to speak the words of a spell. Roots crawled up out of the ground like rough worms and wrapped themselves around the man's limbs. The movement caused the man to stir. He tried to break free of the bonds, but the roots proved too strong.

"Hey! Let me go! I'll forget this ever happened and I'll just leave! I'm sorry! I needed the money! I'm sorry!"

"I know you're sorry," Maeryl told him in a rough voice. He bent down and shoved something in the man's throat, who gagged and choked. Maeryl turned away and limped toward the camp, going very slow.

"Hey! What did you do? I'm sorry! Don't kill me!" he screamed. Maeryl turned.

"I didn't kill you. I gave you eternal life," he said. The man screamed some more, but Maeryl closed his ears to it and lay down by Andrew. The screams continued for a while yet, and then silenced. The only sound was a meaty, creaking sound, and rustling. Andrew tried not to think about it as he dipped bandages in the solution and wrapped them around Maeryl's burns. Maeryl helped his nephew with the relevant spells, but neither of them spoke. Bandaged up, Maeryl pulled Andrew to him and gave him another long hug.

"Thank you for saving me, uncle," said Andrew.

"I...you saved...you're welcome. Please promise me, Andrew, you'll never let go like that ever again."

"I...just thought you were gone, Uncle. I couldn't stand to lose anyone else, and when I thought you...you...it all fell out."

"I understand. It's a temptation every wizard feels, if they lose someone they love. The desire to give in to the magic and to sow the world with your suffering. You must not do this. You must be strong."

"I will, uncle. I hope I never lose you, too," said Andrew. Maeryl held his nephew tight.

"I hope so too, Andrew."

"What did you do to...the man?"

"Something I shouldn't have."

"Did you kill him?"

"That depends. Go to sleep, let me worry about what's on my heart. You've had enough for one day," said Maeryl.

Despite his wounds, he carried Andrew over to the cart and made up a place for him to sleep. Andrew was out cold when he laid the boy down. That much magic would leave him unable to help for a few days, at least. Maeryl rested for a minute, then cast about looking for their salt. He found it, and with a weary heart, began casting another protection circle. When this was completed, and double-checked, Maeryl made himself a place to sleep as well, but it was a long time before it came to him. The events of the day kept running through his mind, underpinned by a melody that would haunt him for the rest of his life. He thought about looking into Andrew's eyes, black and bottomless. He shuddered. *A more powerful wizard there may never be. Certainly not, but if things were different....*he turned over, and in the small hours of the morning, he fell into the blessed arms of unconsciousness. No one was awake to see a small leather ball, about the size of a volleyball, come rolling into the camp and stop just at the edge of the salt barrier. Not even the new oak tree that now overlooked the camp. The one with a knot in the center that looked like a man's horrified face.

First Interlude
Eight Years Ago

ASHNA WANDERED THE CASTLE. Her father was dead. Her lover was in iron, being broken to the training of the court. She was alone. The only time anyone talked to her was when they had to, and even then, with reluctance. The guards especially avoided her, and she couldn't figure out why. Asking, of course, was almost impossible. But there was one man who would talk to her from time to time. She knew he wasn't one of the men who were there when her father died. Maybe she could get Will to talk to her today. Ashna held the title and post of Guard Captain, officially, but she let her second in command, a terrified little man named Triin, take care of the training and duty assignments. Even so, she couldn't make people talk to her on a personal level. She got a lot of stoney stairs and a lot of awkward silences. But Will was young, handsome. She knew she was beautiful. That's…what had gotten her here.

First, she ran by the kitchen and grabbed a honey bun. Then she stalked the castle, looking for Will. She found him guarding the armory, which gave her hope. The armory was relatively isolated, and most often a punishment detail. It was perfect for her designs.

Will was sullen, slouching outside the locked grates and trying to ignore the other guard, a young female named Leelu. They came to attention when they Ashna.

"At ease," she said. They relaxed a modicum.

"Leelu, I need to speak with Will alone for a moment."

"We're not to leave our post, Guard Captain."

"I'm *telling* you to leave your post. I am relieving you. There will be two guards on the gate as per my precious instructions. You are to return in fifteen minutes, and not before. Here," she flipped the girl a coin, "go get something from the taco cart in the courtyard."

"I-"

"GO! Or you'll be guarding the royal privy with a sponge for a weapon!" Leelu squeaked and disappeared with haste. Ashna smiled. She could get used to command, one day. She turned to Will. The scary commander worked for Leelu, but Will required something else. Now she had a bright, winning smile. A stage smile. She'd seen men in the audience stop breathing when she smiled that way. Will started to sweat.

"Hi Will."

"Hello, Guard Captain." Ashna tossed her dark hair back and produced the honey bun.

"Hungry?"

"No, Guard Captain. I ate before I came on duty."

"Oh, but this is a real treat, Will. Go ahead. Take a bite. I know it's your favorite." She held the pastry under his nose. She could see Will's weakness. He licked his lips.

"Come on. We're alone. It's fine to take a little bite. It'll be our little secret."

"I...suppose. Thanks." Will took the pastry from her hand and took a big bite. He closed his eyes with pleasure.

"No one makes these like the girls in the kitchen. No body."

"Oh, I know, I know. That's why I brought it for you."

"Thanks, again."

"You're welcome. Say," she leaned against him, backing him into the wall, "can I ask you a...question?" Will swallowed his mouthful of bun.

"Uh...yeah. Sure."

"You know Jean pretty well, right?"

"Yeah."

"He was there when…I came to the castle. When my father died." Will's eyes narrowed.

"Yeah, I think so. Why?"

"I just want a little talk with him."

"Then go talk to him."

"You know he won't talk to me. But he'll talk to you."

"I don't think I-" Ashna pressed harder against him.

"If you don't talk to him for me, I can think of a lot of interesting details to assign you to." Will grew smug.

"You don't write the schedules."

"Not yet. But Triin does."

"And Triin doesn't listen to you."

"I know someone who can make him listen to me. Better yet, I can replace him. I won't have to find someone to do it. I can do it. I'm the Guard Captain, remember?"

"You're just a girl."

"With a knife."

"What?"

"Amend that to 'girl with a knife,' and you'll be a lot closer to the truth, Will." She whipped a dagger out of her belt fast enough that Will gasped in terror.

"You can't-"

"Oh, but I can. The King has a special interest in me, you know that? And that special interest, while I think it's something I could do without, is certainly something I can use to my advantage. You know how jealous the King gets when he thinks ambassadors are looking at me? Those are men he can't have tortured to death. Between you and me, there's just a little space right now. If you wanna make a move, you've got a bit of room. But there's nothing between you and the King, unless I want there to be. And if I decide you've been showering me with attentions I don't want, why…Your Majesty! Your Majesty! You won't believe what one of my guards tried to pull today!" She tapped the dagger against his chest. "I'm gonna be honest, here. Do you want the King taking a close, jealous look at you? Or do you want to go ask someone a question for me? Is it this hard?" Will gulped again.

"Okay. Tell me what you want to hear."

Chapter 7
The Wizard Maeryl

MAERYL STOOD BEFORE THE FORMATION of quaking royal guards. He looked up at the wax man and began laughing.

"What are you going to do? Smother me with wax? That thing looks ridiculous!" he said. He looked at Andrew.

"Well, there you are. All grown up. How have you been in the last, what? Fifteen years?" said Maeryl. Andrew was shaking so hard he could barely stand. Ashna put her hand on his shoulder.

"Figured out some new magic? Started a family? Found some parents? Oh...too soon?" he said with a wicked grin. His eyes, somehow cat-like, took in Ashna and he snorted, sizing her up in an instant and dismissing her. He turned and waved away the guards.

"Off with you. I need some time to speak with my nephew alone. I assure you he is not at all dangerous," said Maeryl. He turned and gave Andrew a significant look, and then brought his right hand up. Watching the wax man, he muttered some words and drew his hand down, as though closing a blind. The wax man slumped forward and melted, turning into a huge puddle of semi-molten mush. The mandrake root at the center poked up and out of the mass. Maeryl laughed derisively.

"You couldn't even stop a simple unwinding. You've turned out to be quite pathetic. I'm glad I changed my mind about using you."

"Wh...using me for what?" said Andrew.

"A vessel. I really have no intentions of explaining, it's all far more complicated than I think you could handle. For now, anyway. You look dreadful, have you been getting enough sun?" he laughed again. "You know,

I spent a long time looking for you. I just...couldn't figure out where you were! Even with you performing magic left and right you're remarkably subtle. That tower falling was a good bit of luck for me. Without that big 'mud-hand' performance I might not have felt your magic at all," said Maeryl. He casually waded through the wax on the floor and bent to pick up the mandrake doll. He looked at it closely and snorted.

"Not bad for a last-minute focus. You didn't bother with any protective runes, I see. Makes sense if you think you're the only wizard in the world," said Maeryl. He looked up at his nephew. Andrew was paralyzed. He hadn't seen Maeryl in so long, had imagined meeting him again and telling him how much leaving hurt him. Had imagined screaming and Maeryl begging to be forgiven. Had imagined reconciliation, in the end. Something to patch up the years that were left to them. All that was gone in a flash of painful mockery from a man he once loved. Maeryl searched Andrew's face for something and shrugged, dropping the doll.

"Well, I suppose it was nice to see you. Goodbye," said Maeryl. He gave Andrew a piercing look, and Andrew's blood went cold. His heart, pounding a panicked rhythm, began to slow. His uncle's gaze held him locked in futile motionless. He knew he was waiting to die. All the while, the dread silence permeated the air like the stench of a rotting body. *How can he cast a spell without speaking?* Andrew wondered through a slowly descending fog of darkness. His breathing slowed. His heart thumped once, sluggishly, and then stopped. He began to slump to the floor. Just before he hit the ground, he looked up to see Ashna standing over him. She was whirling something around her head, but he couldn't see well enough to make out what it was. With a sure, quick motion, she loosed whatever it was. There was a meaty smack and a scream, and suddenly Andrew's heart pumped back into life. He drew a great gasp of air and his whole body shuddered as it came back from the brink. His eyes focused and he saw Ashna reloading a sling with a small iron bullet. He smiled weakly.

"You saved me again," he whispered.

"Not yet. Get up!" she said, whirling and loosing again. There was another smack and Maeryl howled with pain. He opened his mouth and spoke a terrible word that Andrew and Ashna felt in their bodies, cracked the walls, and blew them both flat to the ground. Huge red welts lifted on Maeryl's face and temple. He touched the spots with a look of incredulous indignity.

"You struck me! With *iron*! How *dare* you!" he screamed. Maeryl spoke another word and the flames from the torches on the walls rolled down like poured milk and gathered in the wax on the floor. He drew his arm up and a wave of burning wax rose, and he flung his hand out. The spitting fiery wall rolled down the hallway in a rush of heat and splashing wax. Andrew had only seconds to come up with a plan. A flash of inspiration and he bit down hard on his tongue, drawing blood. He reached for Ashna and covered her with his arms as he mumbled the words of a spell around the blood in his mouth. Ashna shivered as a heart-chilling blast of arctic air froze around her. The air was filled with the sound of cracking stone and blistering cold. The peculiar silence of frigid winter night was conspicuous after the roar of flame and splash of wax. Ashna waited for the rush of molten wax but it never came. She opened her eyes, and the cold sent shivers through her. Andrew felt like stone beneath her hands. The wax wave, preserved perfectly mid-crest, loomed over her. White frost lined everything in the hall. Andrew shivered violently under her hands. She looked to see where Maeryl lay and saw a molten puddle of stone.

"Andrew..." she tried to gasp, but the air was so cold

it stole her voice. She felt ice in her mouth and closed it quickly, before the cold froze her tongue and throat. Andrew shivered again. Her breath making little clouds in the stillness, she wrapped her arms about him. He was so cold, her heart raced with fear that he had gone too far, had drawn too much of the power he commanded to him. She saw no trace of Maeryl. She tried to warm him with her arms and pulled a blanket from the packs they carried and wrapped it around them to share what little warmth they still had. She rubbed at him frantically, fearing the return of the guards or Maeryl. He stirred under the blanket and she raised him up.

"Come on, Andrew. Come on, we have to go," she insisted, encouraging him to his feet. The cold was dissipating. Ashna could still see her breath but it was not as thick as before.

"Come with me, Andrew! We have to get Salim and run. I don't see Maeryl, now is our chance," she insisted. Andrew looked at her and nodded. She saw dark circles under his eyes and the frost in his hair. She pulled him towards the door that led to the prince's bedchamber, skirting around the still-cooling stone of the floor. Andrew stumbled before it, wrapped in the blanket. He sat with his back to the wall.

"Salim!" called Ashna. She put her hands on the door and tried to draw it open. It would not budge. "Salim!" she called again, panic rising in her voice.

"Salim, open the door, it's me!" she yelled. She tugged at the door. It didn't even rattle against the lock. She ran to Andrew and pulled against him.

"Andrew, get the door open. It won't open for me." Andrew's head lolled about, senseless. She slapped him, and his eyes fluttered open.

"W…what...did I do?" he whispered, frost melting as water streamed down his face. She shook him.

"Get the door open! Salim is trapped inside!" she

said. Andrew slumped to his feet and put his hands against the door. He withdrew them as from a fire with a cry.

"What's wrong?" Ashna asked, fear rising. "Get it open."

"It's burning hot. It feels like the wards my unc...Maeryl and I used on the road. But...I probe at it with my mind and hands and it feels as no ward I've ever laid or encountered," he said.

"So what? Get it open!" said Ashna. Andrew splayed his hands over the door but did not touch it. He closed his eyes. A moment or two passed and he cried out again, falling back.

"It's too strong. I cannot open it or break it, not right now," he wheezed.

"Why can't you open it? I thought you were some powerful wizard!" she lashed out. "I thought you had this great otherworldly strength that would let you do anything! Summon dragons and mend broken hearts and open a fucking door!" she screamed at him. She pushed him aside and began kicking the door. The stone in the frame showered dust, but the door itself never moved, never made a sound like she was kicking a door. Her strikes were muffled, as though she kicked a wooden plank through a pile of wet grass. Hot tears streamed down Ashna's face as she tried to break down the door. Andrew tried to put his arms around her to stop her but she threw her elbow and caught him in the face, knocking him to the ground. She began to scream an inarticulate howl of rage and frustration, her face red and eyes streaming. Andrew struggled to his feet, blood streaming from his nose.

"Ashna, stop! You're going to hurt yourself!"

"I don't care! Nothing will keep me from Salim! Nothing!" she yelled. Andrew watched her fruitlessly assault the door a second longer, then put his arm on her and muttered a spell. She dropped to the ground, rendered unconscious. Andrew sighed a deep, weary sigh from the center of his soul. He stepped over her and studied the door for as long as he dared. He felt a powerful enchantment, nothing like he had ever been taught or worked out on his own. He just knew it tasted....old. Like the way books in libraries buried in the stacks might smell.

He knelt and got Ashna and their packs on his shoulder, and a flash of inspiration hit him as he touched Ashna's skin. He set the packs back down and probed into her mind with as much care as he could. He'd never delved a human. He went slow, as slow as he could. Ashna was full of emotions, and the innersphere of a person was so complicated, he thought he'd get lost right away. But he knew her, from the years they spent together. He navigated her mind, her heart. There was a great pain inside her, and he felt hurt himself as he saw parts of him in it. Warmth drew him along a path inside her heart, and there he found Salim. The line that connected them was as bright as staring at a noon day sun, and he basked in her love for her child. Then he touched that love, drew it into himself. He stood and walked to the door sealed shut with a strange wizard's magic. A pang reminded Andrew that his uncle felt no such love for him. He pushed the thought out of his mind and plied at the ward on the door. It fell away like butter in a fire. Even an ancient, powerful spell could not stand up to a mother's love.

The door creaked open and he stepped inside. He saw Maeryl and froze, but his uncle was as unmoving as he was. He let a slow breath out. The wizard looked as if in a trance. Andrew sensed a gathering of strength. He hurried past the man and found Salim in his bedchamber, shaking and hiding under the blankets.

"Salim, it's Andrew."

"Andrew?" The little boy peeked out.

"Yes. Come with me, we have to go."

"Where's my...where's Ashna?"

"She's outside. She's been...injured. She'll be okay, but I need your help to save her, okay?"

Salim gasped and got out of the bed. Andrew helped the little prince throw some clothes into a bag and then they rushed out. Salim gave Maeryl a worried and questioning look but Andrew shook his head. When they got outside his rooms, Salim cried out and ran to his mother.

"Mom!" He cried. Andrew knelt next to them.

"Come on, Salim. Can you carry these bags? We're going to take her where we can help." Andrew had to tug the little boy to get him going, but then he followed without question. Andrew got Ashna into his arms and they struck out towards the courtyard. As they turned the corner away from the royal quarters, he heard the first timid challenges from guards. Andrew felt like he was walking on his heart, his spirits had sunk so low. He found a cart in the courtyard and felt another pang of remorse flash through him. He ignored it and put Ashna in the back, along with their things. He sat Salim on the bench.

"You want to see a little bit of magic?" Salim nodded, his face worried.

"You must be still and quiet, though. No matter what you see, you must be like a stone, okay?" Salim nodded again. Andrew knew he didn't have time to get a horse and attach it to the cart, so he said the words of one last spell and a horse appeared in the traces of the cart, along with a small boy and an older man. He stepped into the horse, which shimmered as he passed through, and grabbed the empty harness. He heard a little gasp from behind him. With one, ponderous step, he got the cart rolling, and began to pull it from the yard. From the outside, one saw a farmer and his son on their way to market, pulled by a tired and weary horse of no interesting color. Ashna, in the back, looked like sacks of potatoes. Andrew gasped for air, and then set his teeth in a grimace of determination. He searched the night sky and saw the North Star shining bright. Adjusting his hold on the harness he pulled toward the flickering light, the last hope he had in the world.

 The night was cold, but not unbearably so. Once the cart got rolling it wasn't so bad, either. Ashna and Salim didn't weigh much, and the bit of luck breaking his way was the road had a slight downward slant. Andrew trudged along, glancing up from time to time to take bearing from the star. He walked into the streets of Aethero. Tall skyscrapers soared on his right, and ancient castles slowly dwindled behind him. He passed arcades and open air markets. Magic shops, bookstores, and groceries rose and fell on the sides of the road as he kept his steady pace. The sounds of crowds came and faded as he passed dance halls, cafes, and taverns. He stuck to the lesser used streets and alleys, sometimes drawing a zigzag across the cobbled streets of Aethero. Gas lanterns lit the street, giving it a warm glow. The star appeared to grow in the sky. He passed a blacksmith's shop where a wolf wielded a blacksmith's hammer with familiar purpose. Andrew was grateful for the blast of hot air coming from the roaring forge. He laughed to himself at going from cold to hot to cold to hot, back and forth since Ashna waked him in his cell. The wolf looked up from the iron it was hammering and watched him pass. His practiced wizard's eye told him it was a creature that could see through his illusion, but as it did not bother him, he moved on.

 After two hours' trudge, the North Star hung almost directly over him, shining brighter than he had ever seen. He was grateful to let go of the leather harness, and looked about him. When he saw where he was, he laughed aloud again. Before him stood Yonston's Theater, boarded up and abandoned. It was a two-story building, the bottom story and basement containing a theater and stage, and the upper story being a living space.

"Perfect," he said to the building and the star. "No one's been here for a decade at least." He stumbled on the steps as he came to the front doors. Exhaustion washed over him, made his limbs heavy and his head thick. He tried the door. It hitched, then gave way. The old iron hinges squealed with rusty protests. He tenderly reached out with his senses, and found no other living things inside.

"Even the rats have moved on," he said. He went back out, slung the packs over his shoulder, and picked up Ashna. Her breathing was steady, and her body was warm against his chest.

"Come on, Salim. We're here." He waited for a moment, and then walked back to the cart. Salim was asleep on the bench. He sighed and carried Ashna over the threshold and into the theater. The door closed behind them, the hinges loud in the night. Andrew stood in the quiet darkness of the foyer for a long moment. Ten years... He adjusted Ashna in his arms, and then walked into the room where he had taken tea with her the first time they met. It was also the last time he saw Maeryl. Andrew set Ashna carefully on a couch that still haunted the study like a ghost's memory. He tried one little spell for light, and was gratified when he was able to catch a spark and brighten it to about the level of a candle. He went back and got Salim, holding the little boy close to his chest. Andrew took Salim into the same parlor and laid him next to Ashna. He watched Ashna sleep on the couch for a long time, trying to regain his strength and energy. *How did he cast a spell without speaking?* He wondered. The sight of Maeryl's malevolent gaze, the shuddering horror of his heart slowly stopping...his spine grew cold. When Ashna and Salim did not wake, he walked out of the room, quietly shutting the door behind him. He wandered down the hall that led through the center of the house. He peeked into the kitchen. It was empty save for an old pot-bellied stove that was too heavy to steal, he reckoned. Kitchens held practical things. He chuckled when he thought back to the study where Ashna slept. The books still lined the walls, though no doubt they were rotten and moth-eaten.

 He walked down the hall further and opened the door to Ashna's old room. He looked inside and saw the frame for her big, four-posted bed still dominated the room with its presence, but the curtains and mattress were gone. Eaten or looted, he wasn't sure. He was surprised to see other bits of her furniture and even a small hand mirror on a vanity. Perhaps the last time they had been in the house had scared all but the boldest of thieves away. Or, perhaps, they just never owned much worth taking. Andrew looked at the bed and the memory of the first time he and Ashna made love filled his mind. They were so young, just seventeen. He smiled at the children who had made so many grand plans so long ago. The lovers who were so enamored, so invincible. So foolish. Suddenly, the memory made him sad, and he closed the door on the room. He wandered down the hall until he came to the door that led to the back stage of the little theater they performed in to pay the bills. He rested his hand on the doorknob, thinking back on the last performance. The one the king attended. He opened the door and stepped through, holding his spark so that he could see in the pitch black of the backstage. The heavy velvet curtains were still there, though tattered and dry-rotted. He walked to the front of the stage through a thick coating of dust. He looked around, then held his spark high and whispered a word. The light grew and pierced the darkness, revealing the empty seats of the house, silently regarding him with ancient reproach. *Why were you gone?* asked the chairs. Andrew ignored them, instead walking a little along the backstage to the prop chest where Ashna had first taught him to juggle. He ran his hand along the top of the box but didn't open it.

Tiring of the theater, he turned and walked back into the house proper. He was about to go check on Ashna, but something stopped him in the hallway outside the door that lead to Yonston's private study. It was the barest tickle on his cheek, light as a peck. He turned and looked at the door. He frowned. *Was this door here before?* He shook his head. *Of course it was...I just walked past it.* Still, he was certain there was more to it than all that. He blew gently on the spark and it fluttered into the air like a startled beetle, then hovered over him. He took his hands and ran them along the dark, dusty wood of the study door. He smiled to himself. *The simplest, smallest, meanest of wards. A little touch of magic to say "I'm not here."* He placed his right hand against the door, palm flat, and carefully teased apart the ancient ward. It gave him a pang in his heart as he unraveled the spell. It was a work of beautiful craftsmanship, for it to last throughout these years and to be so subtle. *Maeryl knew how to work a ward, that's for sure,* he thought. The ward finally slipped away subtle as a ripple, and Andrew opened the door. Unlike the front, this one made not a sound, and Andrew took a curious step into the room. His spark followed him, ducking under the uppermost part of the frame.

The room, like the rest of the house, was covered in a thick layer of dust. The room also seemed riotous after the touring the rest of the mostly-empty house. Everything that had been placed here ten years ago still sulked where it lay, forgotten. A narrow bed lined the far wall, blankets and pillow still neat. His gaze drifted left. A large desk sat underneath a massive bookcase that was shaped like an arch. The desk stood inside the legs of the arch, and was crammed to full with volumes. None of these had the look of decay like the ones in the study. As Andrew gazed around the room, another whisper of a spell caught his attention. At first he dismissed it as the stillness of an untouched room of many years, but it began to nag at him. He walked over to the desk and examined it. An old inkwell, a pen, some paper...a pencil box, perhaps. He ran his hands over the leather topper on the desk, enjoying the softness of it as the dust gave way. His hand bumped the pencil box, and a little spark leapt between his skin and the dusty wood. Ah, there we are...he took the box in his hands. The wood was warm, as though it sat in the sun all day. Andrew glanced at the lone window above the bed and saw it faced south. No sun coming in there, then. He closed his eyes and felt the box with his magical sense, feeling out the ward. *More intricate, this one...almost like a puzzle, or a knot.* He worked the ward in his mind, his hands clasping the box gently in his hands. He teased out the last little bit of the ward as sweat beaded on his forehead. The top of the box clicked open on a spring, and at that same moment a hand fell on his shoulder.

"Gods!" he screamed. He dropped the box and whirled around. Ashna stood behind him, her right hand outstretched to him, a haggard look on her face. Andrew hesitated, then reached out to her. Ashna fell into his arms. She was sobbing.

"Thank you for saving him, thank you."

"It was you that saved him, Ashna. I just helped." She looked up at him with a question in her eyes.

"I tapped into your love for him. Used it. Where I could not batter or sneak through the ward, it simply fell away at the touch of you." She smiled up at Andrew and put her head on his chest. He held her for a long time.

"Thank you," she said.

"You're welcome." Andrew turned back to the box and took out a dusty piece of folded paper.

"What is that?"

"I'll read it aloud."

Andrew,

I know you have many questions about why I left you. One day I hope to answer them, but for now I must keep those secrets to myself. I asked Yonston to hold onto this box for you. You untied the wards on the door to this study and to the box—good, that means you're getting better. Wards were never your best magic. I hope this letter finds you well. If things are not, then this letter may help. Remember the night when I was attacked by that bounty hunter, and how you said you thought I'd died? I did. Or at least, I think I did. I was in the black, the Ocean of Stars the people of Aethero talk about, and I saw a huge shadow in the night. A Whale. He gave me a song to keep for you, and brought me back to give it to you. It is your right. I don't know why or how, but that's what I was compelled to do. Events and powers beyond my control have forced me to leave the music in the only place that I consider safe enough: the Moon. Go to Anastasia's Tower and see the Silver Lady. Tell her you're Maeryl's nephew. She'll know why you've come. I am sorry that the last thing I can leave you is this letter, mere words to try and comfort a confused and broken heart. I will never forgive myself, but I must remind myself that the only reason you're alive to read this is because of the choices I've made. Consequences come home to roost more faithfully than any bird, and sadly they were on the wing when I left you with Yonston. Please forgive me, and know that I loved you as if you were my own. I wish you were.

All my love,
Maeryl

"But he attacked us not an hour ago!"

"I know."

"How does he go from this letter to the man we saw today?"

"I don't know." Andrew pulled away from Ashna and set his hands on the desk.

"I'd like to be alone for a moment, please." Ashna nodded and stepped out of the room, closing the door behind her.

Andrew read and re-read the letter a few more times, then folded it and put it in a pocket. He pulled the chair out from under the desk and sat down, the light of his spark hovering over his head. It bathed the room in gentle yellow light. The words of the letter ran through his mind over and over. *Go to Anastasia's Tower and see the Silver Lady.* He knew where that was, but other than the king he had never met one of Aethero's Pocket Gods. The king, the god of the Sun, was a mighty one, but the Moon was no small god of flowers or crickets. She drove the water and the night. Andrew ran the letter through his mind one more time. *...I loved you as if you were my own.* He stood and reached out for the spark, leaving it in his hand and he left the room behind him. He sought out Ashna, who was sitting on the couch he had laid her on earlier. He sat down next to her. Salim was curled up on the other side of her, his head in Ashna's lap. She was stroking the boy's hair.

"What are we going to do?"

"Go to Anastasia's Tower, I suppose."

"And get a Whale's Song?"

"Yes."

"What does that mean?"

"I don't know."

"I hope it's good."

"I hope so too," Andrew sighed. They sat together for a long time, and finally Andrew snuffed the spark, leaving them in darkness. He felt Ashna slide against him, snuggling up to his warmth.

"Will you hold me?"

"Yes."

"Will you help us?"

"Yes."

"Do you still love me?" she said, barely whispering.

"Yes."

Chapter 8
The Magician Yonston
15 Years Ago

"THIS IS IT," said Maeryl as they pulled up outside a building of mean and somewhat shameful demeanor.

"This is it?" said Andrew, dubious. He stood and looked up at the building. It was made of red brick, familiar to his eyes born in 1883. Dirty windows sulked in the face of the building, and the whole place gave an aura of being decrepit and grumpy.

"Are you sure?" Andrew asked.

"Yes, Andrew, I'm sure," emphasized Maeryl as he hitched the horses to a rail out front. He took Andrew by the arm and led him to the front door, where he knocked sharply. A few moments later a man opened it and peered out at them. He was older, but not so old as Maeryl, putting him about fifty or so. He had a kindly face, was balding, and wore a vest, shirt, and trousers.

"You must be Andrew!" the man said. He opened the door and shook Andrew's hand.

"Yessir," said Andrew. Maeryl took the man's hand after he let go of Andrew's.

"Yonston, nice to see you again," said Maeryl.

"You too. Come in, my daughter has some tea on for us," said Yonston, who led them deeper into the house. The inside was surprisingly clean and snug, completely turn-coating Andrew's initial impression and leaving it for dead in an alley somewhere. It was filled with odds and ends, beautiful objects, art and sculptures, paintings and wall-hangings; swords hung over the odd fireplace and a suit of armor stood in a corner. Other things, more fantastic, filled the many shelves, tables, and glass cabinets. Andrew identified no less than sixteen varieties of volatile chemicals and powders in one such cabinet.

They even passed a large cage from which came the soft cooing of doves. Andrew glimpsed the white birds as Yonston opened a door and ushered them into a fine sitting room. It had rich wood paneling, dark reds and browns of ancient trees, and one wall was lined with a bookshelf creaking under the weight of many, many books.

Andrew and his uncle took seats next to the fire, and Yonston sat across from them next to another empty chair. A little coffee table was between them, and a merry fire chuckled in the fireplace. The chair was plush and comfortable; Andrew was certain he hadn't felt anything so pleasant in his twelve years.

"Now, how can I help you, Maeryl?" said Yonston. Maeryl gave him a grave look and then turned his attention to Andrew. Andrew began to feel uncomfortable when Maeryl broke eye contact and spoke.

"Why don't we do some catching up and chat a bit before we get to that business? How have you been?" said Maeryl. The older men began to talk about things that quickly bored Andrew: aches and pains of being older, the various prices in the market, the weather, and that sort of thing. Just as Andrew thought he could stand it no longer, he saw something that caught his attention indeed. A young woman entered the room from another door. She was carrying a tray with a teapot and several bowls and saucers and other accouterments for tea. She was concentrating on not spilling everything on the (admittedly fine) rugs that helped to warm the room. Andrew was entranced with her. She had fine, delicate features and beautiful dark hair that flowed past her shoulders. She was sticking the tip of her tongue out while she stepped carefully with the heavy tray. The two older men noticed Andrew staring and shared a mutual chuckle.

As she neared them, Yonston spoke:

"Are you going to stare all night, son, or are you going to give my poor daughter a hand?" he said. Andrew jumped and stammered.

"Oh, I, oh, oops! Ha. Okay! Yes." He stumbled as he tried to stand and knocked his knee against the coffee table. The two elders broke out in raucous laughter as he tried to rub his knee and help Ashna with the tray. Her laugh was pretty and light, however, and she gently shooed Andrew away as she deftly set the tray on the table and arranged tea for everyone. Andrew stood behind her, trying to reach for things to help, but she seemed to be one step ahead each time. Finally frustrated in his efforts, he blushed a fierce color of red and retook his seat. He crossed his arms and put his chin on his chest, trying to hide his blush from the two older men and the girl, who was introduced as Ashna. Maeryl and Yonston laughed a while longer and began to calm down as they sipped the tea.

"Wonderful tea, Ashna. Thank you," said Maeryl, holding his cup up to her. She smiled.

"Thank you! My father insists I make the best tea in Aethero," she informed the newcomers.

"Try to be a little modest, Ashna," said Yonston. She nodded at her father and sipped her tea. Andrew, still red, took a swallow from his own cup.

"And how do you like it, Andrew?" said Ashna with a winning smile. Andrew grinned and looked at his cup.

"It's...quite wonderful," said Andrew.

"You're so sweet!" she replied. Andrew grinned some more but found he couldn't think of anything to say. As Maeryl watched the two young teens bat eyes at each other, he suddenly felt very old. *It is a crime we are too young for the wisdom to find joy in such moments.* His heart sank when he thought of what was coming next. Andrew caught his uncle's expression, and it seemed that the room became a little darker.

"What's wrong, uncle?" said Andrew. Maeryl and Yonston looked at each other. Coming to silent agreement, Maeryl sighed and set down his cup.

"It's time we told you why I brought you here, Andrew."

"Why?"

"This is to be your new home."

"You mean *our* new home?"

"No. Just you."

"Why do I have to move here? Why can't I stay with you?"

"I will not be...around much longer. I have to leave you."

"What? Why?"

"I can't tell you right now. It's better this way."

"How is it better? Tell me how it's better!"

"Andrew, try not to make a fuss. Yonston has proven to be a reliable and wise friend, and...."

"I don't want to stay with Yonston! I want you!"

"It can't be that way, Andrew. I'm very sorry." Andrew's face was getting a dark shade of red, and tears began to stream down his face.

"I'm so sorry Andrew."

"Tell my mom you're sorry! Sorry you abandoned me here. I trusted you!"

"This is hard for me too, Andrew."

"I've lost everyone. Who have you lost?"

"Andrew, that's not fair."

"Life's not fair, isn't that what you said, Maeryl?"

"Stop acting like this. Yonston is putting himself in not a small amount of danger by agreeing to watch you."

"Oh, sure, for how long? Six months? A year? How long before he puts me off on someone else?"

"He won't do that, Andrew. He's made a very solemn promise."

"Like the promise you made my parents?" Andrew

countered.

"Listen to me, young man. You're not old enough to understand what you're saying, or what it really means."

"I'm old enough to know you're bailing on me. Leaving me behind. Am I slowing you down, huh?"

"No, Andrew, that's not it and you know it," Maeryl told the boy sternly. His heart felt like it was ancient, with a deep, swelling ache that cut right through him. He opened his mouth to speak, but no words came out. Andrew's chest was heaving and his face was soaked. Ashna was staring at her hands, crying a little herself. Maeryl moved to touch Andrew's shoulder but Andrew wrenched himself away.

"Everyone I've ever loved has left me. Why, Maeryl?"

"This is how things came to be. One day, when I return, I can explain it all. I promise."

"We've seen what your promises are worth," said Andrew, looking at Maeryl with burning eyes. Maeryl felt his reassuring words die in his throat. He was truly at a loss. Andrew started when Ashna stood and walked over to his chair. She knelt next to him. Andrew had forgotten she was even there. She put her hands on his arm and looked up at him. He saw the tears in her eyes.

"Please stay with us, Andrew. It gets lonely in here without anyone my age to talk to, as nice as Dad is," she said, turning and giving her father a grateful smile.

He nodded.

"There's plenty to learn and to do. You could join our show...would you like that?"

Andrew wiped his eyes with the heels of his hands.

"What show?"

"Dad is a magician. He...," began Ashna, but the look of contempt on Andrew's face killed her words.

"A magician? Me? I know real magic, not kid stuff," said Andrew. Ashna took her hand off his arm. Maeryl stood up.

"You will not insult our hosts that way, Andrew. A magician's trade will help you blend in."

"I remember what you had to say about magicians, Maeryl," said Andrew, his eyes dark and angry. "Do you? 'Child's play. Foolery and trickery, a stain on the noble arts.' That's what you said."

Maeryl gave his hosts and embarrassed look. "I know what I said, Andrew, and I suggest you forget it. I regret those words, and I think you'll find later that you'll regret your own. There's real skill involved. I don't think you'd find it as easy as all that," said Maeryl.

"Like you would even care what happens to me when you're gone."

"I do care about you, Andrew. Deeply. Sometimes we have to do things we don't want to do, and at the time it looks bad but later on you gain a better understanding...."

Andrew cut him off. "Just go. I'm sick of your excuses. You're disgusting," said Andrew. He turned from his uncle and tried to bury his face in the high-backed chair. He tried not to cry, and let out a few piteous sobs. Maeryl reached out again, but Yonston motioned for him to stop. Ashna put her hand back on Andrew's arm, and used her other to stroke his back. He didn't look up, but he didn't push her away. Yonston motioned for Maeryl to follow him, and the two older men left the room silently. Yonston pulled the door to behind him, making no sound at all. When the other two departed, Ashna turned her attention fully to Andrew, who descended into deep, heart-wrenching sobs. His whole body shook with each one, and he sounded sick when he tried to draw his raspy breaths. Ashna took a napkin off the table and tried to wipe his face some, but he pushed her hand away.

"Just leave me alone."

"I don't want to, Andrew. I want to be here for you."

"W-why? You'll probably leave me too, one d-day."

"I won't. I promise I won't! We're here together, and this way we can become friends."

"Whatever," said Andrew. When Ashna reached up again to wipe his tears, he didn't turn from her.

"Why...why are you being so nice?" said Andrew, looking at Ashna. She stroked his arm.

"My mom is dead, too," said Ashna. She stood and began to clean the tea dishes

"I didn't know that. I'm sorry," said Andrew.

"Don't be. It was some time ago."

"What happened to her?"

"She died in an accident. It was just a few years ago," said Ashna.

"That's terrible," said Andrew.

"Yeah. It still hurts," said Ashna.

"Does it ever get better?"

"Bit by bit, day by day," said Ashna.

"So...um...tell me about this show?" said Andrew. Ashna smiled and sat down again in her seat.

"Oh, it's so much fun! Right now father is teaching me tumbling and juggling and sword play!"

"Wow! Swords and everything?"

"Uh, huh. He says 'Every young woman should know how to use a blade, whether in kitchen or in battle.'"

"That's neat!"

"And he does magic tricks, and I help him," said Ashna. "He says I'm the most capable assistant he's ever had."

"What kind of...tricks does he do?"

"Well, he can make me disappear in a box. And he saws me in half."

"No, he doesn't! You can't saw someone in half with magic!"

"Maybe not with magic, but my father the magician sure can."

"I'd like to see that!"

"Come to our show tonight, and I'll make him promise to do that part of the act," said Ashna. "If you're not too good for us, that is," she added.

Andrew blushed. "I'm...sorry I said all that. I'm just so mad at Maeryl. He's supposed to be taking care of me, and he's...he's...just leaving me!" said Andrew.

"I'm sure he has reasons," said Ashna.

"Maybe," said Andrew. They both fell silent for a while. Andrew brooded in his chair and Ashna wracked her brain for ways to make him feel better. Her face lit up.

"Hey! Want to see the stage? I'll juggle for you!" she said. Andrew smiled and sat up.

"Okay!" he said. Ashna jumped up from her chair and grabbed Andrew's hand. He smiled broadly as she led him out of the room and through the house. He looked around as she took him down a long hallway. A number of doors lined the halls, and Ashna told him what each was as they walked past.

"This one is a closet. This one is the bathroom. Another closet. This leads into the kitchen!" they poked their heads in to see a nice-sized kitchen, with a merry fire burning in the stove. A pot bubbled on top of it.

"We're having lamb stew tonight. It's been cooking for a while now, sure smells good, huh?" said Ashna.

"Sure does," said Andrew, licking his lips. She started dragging him down the hall again.

"This is my room. You can't go in there!" she practically pulled him over when he tried to stop.

"And this is father's room. I almost never go in there," she said. They continued on.

"Library. And the door to the back of the stage!" she said. She twisted the knob and the door opened inward. It was dark. Andrew could only see the vague outlines of things he supposed to be sandbags and ropes and so on.

"So the stage is attached to the back of your house?"

"Yep."

"Is that weird?"

"Nah. You get used to it, for sure. And it's nice 'cause you don't have to walk very far when the show is over," said Ashna. Her pace slowed, but she led Andrew through the darkness with an ease that could only have come with a lot of practice.

"Wait here," she said. Andrew's eyes felt like they were growing in his head. The black was complete, now. He turned around and supposed that he could see some light leaking from the doorway where they had just come, but he wasn't sure. He was starting to get nervous. How long had Ashna been gone? What if she had left him, too?

"Ashna?" he called, quiet, nervous. A light flared in the darkness, and he heard a gentle fwoof as gaslights in front of him caught one by one. Suddenly, he found himself center stage in a modest theater. About two-dozen rows of soft chairs were his silent audience. He saw Ashna waving out a long, lit taper at one end of the stage. She ran around to in front of him. Now his audience had one.

"You look good up there! Very regal, as my father would say," she said with an approving smile. Andrew smiled in spite of himself and turned about. A little upright piano stood in the corner.

"Do you play?" he asked, pointing. Ashna shook her head.

"Not yet. Father hires a nifty guy to play for us when we're performing from time to time. He said he'll give me lessons, sometime," said Ashna. Andrew liked the way his voice carried in the little space. He tried to imagine an audience of people looking up at him.

"Don't you get nervous?" he said. Ashna shook her head again as she climbed the little steps on the left side of the stage.

"You get used to it. I'm usually so focused on helping that I don't even notice the crowd half the time anymore," she said. She ducked behind the curtains and Andrew heard a few wooden bangs, and she reappeared with juggling clubs. She was walking backwards as she tossed them hand to hand, making a neat little arc over her head.

"Wow! Backwards even! That's terrific!" said Andrew, applauding. Ashna laughed.

"Backwards took a little while. Juggling with clubs is easy, they're weighted just right," she said. Andrew watched her with appreciation for a moment as she went from a basic cascade and through a number of different patterns, finally dropping the clubs as she tried to cross her arms over each other while keeping the clubs in the air.

"You want to try?" she said as she picked up the dropped clubs.

"I don't know. I've never been really, whoops!" he said as she tossed him the clubs. He struggled to keep them all in his hands but they seemed to leap about of their own accord and he dropped them all. Ashna laughed in a good-natured way.

"Pick 'em up, I'll show you," she said. Andrew picked up the clubs.

"Okay. It's easy. Toss one up in the air kinda toward the other hand, while your two hands move in circles towards each other. Like wheels. Yeah! Oops. Try again." She walked him through the basic steps, and soon enough Andrew found that he was able to keep the clubs in the air for longer than a few seconds. He even managed to go for thirty seconds before slipping up and letting them fall.

"You're not bad!" she said.

"Thanks. You're really, really good though. I don't think I could ever be that good."

"It's just practice, that's all. Father says anyone can

get good at something as long as they try hard enough."

"I bet. That's like with magic. Real magic, I mean," said Andrew. Ashna gave him a look. "I'm sorry! That's just how it is. I have to learn the words of spells and how the elements fit together...you see Maeryl do it and he just whispers some words and suddenly there's blue flames crawling out of his hat, but it's a lot harder than that."

"Will you show me some magic?" said Ashna. Andrew grew serious.

"I'm not supposed to show anyone. Uncle Maeryl says someone might want to take me away and use my magic in a bad way, if they found out."

"I won't tell anyone. And you'll be living with us, so it's not like I don't know already." pointed out Ashna. Andrew's face fell.

"I want to show you...I just wish we could be friends and me....stay with my uncle. This is hard."

"I understand. If you'd rather not, that's fine. They're probably wondering where we are anyway," said Ashna. She took the clubs and was putting them away when Andrew spoke up:

"Hey. I'll show you something. Just a little something," he said. Ashna smiled and walked back onto the stage with Andrew. He was looking around the stage.

"Can I look in the box?" he said, indicating the chest where they kept the stage props.

"Sure," said Ashna. She tried to look over his shoulder as he dug through the chest, finally coming up with some orange-sized crystal balls.

"May I use these?"

"Yes. I don't think we've ever used them in an act. There's a lot of old stuff around here," she said. Andrew nodded and walked back onto the stage. He was looking into the crystals and muttering under his breath. As he worked, he walked towards one of the gas lamps on the stage. With the crystals in one hand, he reached into the lamp.

"Andrew!" gasped Ashna. Her legs threatened to go weak when he brought out a handful of fire, flowing through his fingers as though he held a bit of sand. The flames winked out as they hit the stage. Beads of sweat stood out on his face and he continued to speak in his low, even tone of voice. Ashna thought of a horseman she once saw talk down an angry stallion that had broken loose one day at market. It had reared and kicked out of its stall, and suddenly there was the horseman: whispering and talking to the stallion in a calm, even tone of voice. His eyes never left the horse's. The great, raging beast snorted and pawed, and slowly, slowly, the man was able to stroke its mane and lead it back into a stall. Ashna felt as though she was watching the same thing, as Andrew now turned his focus on the fire he held and spoke smoothly to the dripping flames.

He cupped the crystals in his right hand, the fire in his left, and held one up. He tilted his hand and the fire flowed out and into the crystal, as from the top of an hourglass to the bottom. The fire slewed about inside, and slowly rose until it was about halfway full. Andrew then tapped the glass with his wrist, and set it on the ground. He performed this act three times, until there were as many crystal balls on the stage. When the he put the last one down, he sat heavily and gasped for air. He was soaked with sweat, and had a huge grin on his face. Ashna couldn't find anything to say. She stumbled over to the glasses and slumped to the ground, staring at the bright balls of fire. The yellow light played over her face, and as Andrew looked at the wonder on her face his heart became as warm as the flames he had held for her. Ashna reached out a hand to touch one, then withdrew it.

"May I?" she whispered.

"Of course," said Andrew. She gently wrapped her fingers around one of the little globes, and giggled.

"It's warm!"

"I would think so, it's full of fire," he said. She picked it up and held it at eye level. The crystal bent the firelight across her face in a fetching way, and Andrew felt something stir in the pit of his stomach. Ashna rolled the ball back and forth between her hands, watching the fire slosh about inside the glass.

"But these glasses were solid."

"It's magic," he said. Ashna looked at the crystal for a long time, content to watch the flames dance inside the glass.

"You tamed a fire for me," she said.

"Or lit one, however you look at it," Andrew murmured softly. She smiled at him. They looked into each other's eyes for a long moment, the soft firelight flickering in the silence and semi-darkness between them.

"Ashna? Andrew? Where did you two get off to?" the sound of Ashna's father calling for them broke the silence.

"Oh my! I forgot the time. You'd better put these out or something, before they find them!" said Ashna. Andrew gathered up the other two and walked over to a gas light. Speaking quickly, he tapped them together with a gentle touch and drew them apart like cracking an egg, and the fire poured out of the glass balls like egg yolks into the gas lamp. The glasses returned to their mundane state: clear, beautiful, and cold. Ashna brought the one she was holding over to Andrew.

"What about this one?"

"Keep it. Just keep it secret. And safe," said Andrew. Ashna smiled again and slipped the warm little globe into her pocket. They both jumped when Yonston clumped onto the back of the stage.

"What are you two doing?"

"I was just showing him the stage and the theater," said Ashna. Yonston smiled.

"How does it suit you, Andrew?" he said.

"I dunno," Andrew responded quietly, suddenly reminded of his uncle leaving.

"Well, if you decide to stay with us, you may find you like performing. Just think about it," said Yonston. Ashna and Andrew shared a look and they began laughing.

"What's so funny?" he said.

"I think it'd be a lot of fun. I guess," said Andrew.

Yonston smiled. "Do you think you can say goodbye to your uncle?" he said.

Andrew's face grew hard. "No. I don't want to see him again."

"Don't you want to say goodbye? That you love him?" Yonston pressed.

"He broke a promise. To me and my mom and my dad. I can...I can make it here, I guess. But I don't want to talk to him. Not ever again," said Andrew.

Yonston's face fell. "It's up to you."

"That's the way I want it," said Andrew, turning his back. Yonston looked at the young man for a long time.

"Then that's how it'll be. We'll take your stuff to your room. We'll be a bit, if you want to wait in the library or somewhere," said Yonston.

"Fine," said Andrew. Yonston turned and walked away. Ashna looked at Andrew's back, unsure of what to say. She reached a hand out to his shoulder, but he shrugged it away.

"Leave me alone. Please. For a while," he whispered. He sniffled, and hated how the theater made it sound loud and empty. Ashna hesitated, then followed her father out of the theater. Andrew stood center stage, the only sound the quiet flicker of gas lights, and his gentle, pained sobbing. The chairs made the silence heavy. Ashna went to her room and locked the door. She wiped away some tears of her own and tried to think of ways to cheer Andrew up. She climbed onto her bed, a big four-poster with curtains, and drew them around. She took out the little glass with the fire inside and sighed. The flames were blue and low, like a fire dying at the end of night. She cradled it to her chest and hummed tunelessly. She fell asleep with the glass in her hands, her long dark hair falling over it. It slid out of her hands and rolled a little ways on the mattress. The low flames warmed her through the night, and the gentle blue light caressed her face.

    The two older men found themselves back in Yonston's sitting room after the two children went to bed. There was a tense, pregnant silence. Mearyl's face was a shadow of pain and remorse. They sipped the tea though it had gone cold. Yonston could hold in his thoughts no longer.
    "If it upsets you both so much, why do you leave the boy?" he said.
    Maeryl started, as if he had forgotten there was someone else in the room with him. "I have my reasons."
    "They must be pretty good to leave your nephew behind after he lost his parents."
    "They are."
    "Dammit, Maeryl! What's so important?" said Yonston, slamming his tea cup down. Maeryl sipped his own and seemed to look off into the distance. When he spoke, he kept that distant expression.
    "There are forces at work that mean him harm. Their only route is through me. When they get to me, I must not be where he is."
    "What forces?" asked Yonston, suddenly afraid.
    "I must say no more. If you ever see me again, Yonston, run. Do not speak with me, do not get my attention, try not to even be seen by me. If Andrew is with you, do whatever you can to prevent him from doing the same," said Maeryl. His looked so tired, so worn

down. "Promise me you'll do this. You have to protect him from me if I ever return," said Maeryl.

"I...I promise, Maeryl," he said. Maeryl looked as though a little of the massive weight on his shoulders lifted.

"That's good. Now, I must take my leave. I mean to be far away from here in the morning," he said.

"Where will you go?" said Yonston.

"As far as I can. I will try to get lost somewhere in the wilderness. Maybe onto another world, if I can manage it. I will stop by Anastasia's Tower, first. There is something I've meant to give her for a long time now," said Maeryl. "Speaking of," he drew a little box of polished wood from his cloak. It was about eight inches across and two or three deep. "Put this in your office. One day Andrew will want to learn why I've left, same as you. I hope perhaps it is sometime soon, but I understand if he has no desire to learn my motives. Nonetheless, should he ask, this is for him," said Maeryl. Yonston took the box and set it in his lap. It was warm to the touch. Maeryl set his pointed wizard hat on his head and left the room without further conversation. Yonston held the box in his lap for a long while, thinking on what was said. Then he cleaned up the tea, turned down the gas lights, and retired to his own room.

Chapter 9
The Silver Lady

THE NEXT MORNING DAWNED with no fanfare. The sun came up as He does (though He was extremely angry about losing Andrew) and the Moon went to her rest. Sunlight reached out with pale orange tendrils and stirred in the old theatre where Andrew, Ashna, and Salim slept. Andrew stirred first, the light playing over his pale skin with gentle caresses. He woke, and looked at the two sleepers till beside him. Sometime during the night Ashna had changed places with Salim at the other end of the couch, and he had snuggled up next to her, their arms wrapped tight around one another. Andrew wondered if they'd ever been able to sleep that way before. He leaned over and stroked Ashna's hair. It was silky and smooth under his hand. A smile crept onto her face. Andrew stood and began twisting and turning, muttering under his breath as the aches from last night set up shop.

Ashna stirred, and Salim yawned, his mouth in a wide jaw-creaking gasp. Salim started when he looked around, and then saw Ashna.

"Mom!" He threw himself into a hug around her neck. Ashna laughed with joy and hugged him back. Andrew couldn't help but smile.

"You two look glad to see each other."

"Andrew!" Salim turned to look. "You saved us!"

"With help from your mom. She's a strong woman."

"Thank you, Andrew." Salim and Ashna stood up from the couch. Despite the meanness of their bed, Andrew couldn't think of a time he'd seen either so happy. Not in a long time, for Ashna.

"You're welcome. You're both welcome."

"I'm hungry!" said Salim. He looked at the adults.

"Oh! I guess I'd better go out and get something for us to eat," said Ashna.

"Is that wise?"

"Well, it's me, you, or the prince. I can tell you who I would pick."

"Are you calling me indiscreet?"

"Yes."

"Well! That's fine. The prince and I will enjoy a chat while you're gone."

"Don't go without me!" Salim's face was pained. Ashna knelt next to her son.

"It's okay, Salim. I'll be back in a flash. Keep an eye on Andrew for me, okay? He's not as wise or well-behaved as you." Salim giggled.

"I will!" He turned to Andrew. "No funny business!" Andrew held his hands up in surrender.

"No, your majesty, I wouldn't dream of funny business, and trouble is right out of the question." Ashna hugged her son one last time and drew Andrew in for a hug and a peck on the cheek.

"Take care of my son. We'll think of a plan when I return." Andrew kissed her back.

"Of course." Salim and Andrew watched her slip out the door with sad expressions.

"Well, Salim, what shall we do?" Andrew sat back down on the couch and patted the cushion beside him. Salim hopped up next to him.

"What is this place?"

"This is the famous Yonston's Theater."

"A theater! I've been to the Royal on Carp Street."

"That's a fine venue, no doubt, but when it comes to the finest performances, there was nowhere better in Aethero than this here theater."

"Wow! Did you know the performers?"

"Quite well. Your mom and me both performed here."

"Wow! Wow! Mom in this theater!"

"That's right. She's a talented juggler, as well as actress, acrobat, and other various arts."

"And I bet you did magic!"

"Some. I couldn't perform real magic, you know."

"Why not?" Andrew felt a pang of sadness.

"That's a long story, Salim. Let me put it this way: I didn't work for the King yet, and I didn't want people to know my talent."

"I would want people to know. Magic is so cool."

"Thank you! I'll tell you more about it when you're a bit older. There're…scary parts."

"Oh! How scary?"

"Terrifying! I don't think your mom would thank me for scaring you that bad."

"I bet it's not that scary."

"Let me tell you something, Salim. I once knew a young boy like you who was too curious. One day I told him just a little about my adventures, and do you know what happened to him?"

"No…"

"His hair turned white."

"No way!"

"Yes. Very serious. It could happen to anyone."

"Why isn't *your* hair white?"

"Maybe it is. I am a wizard, you know."

"Where did you learn to be a wizard?" It struck Andrew that he'd lived in the same castle as the prince for almost a decade, and yet they'd never had a chance to talk before.

"My uncle taught me. His father taught him, and his father, until a long time ago."

"Why not your father?"

"My father died when I was a little younger than you are now."

"Oh! I'm sorry." Salim reached out and took

Andrew's hand and squeezed it.

"I…well, thank you, Salim. It was a long time ago."

"Do you remember him? Your dad?"

"Not much. I remember him as a big man. I think most little boys think their dads are giants."

"Was he nice?"

"I think so. He was always nice to me, and taught me to be kind to everyone around me. That's especially true for wizards, but I think princes should remember that too."

"Why? For wizards and princes?"

"We're very similar, Salim. Very similar, because we have a lot of power."

"I don't feel powerful."

"That's because you're a prince, and a boy. One day you'll be a man, and king. Kings are powerful men. They have the ability to change people's lives."

"I'll be a good king!"

"I hope so. So, kings and wizards, we can change people's lives. We can have a direct effect. Do you remember the other day when I held up the tower?"

"Yes! That was so scary!"

"I agree. That's why I have to be careful Salim. If I can hold up that big tower, think about how easy it would be for me to hurt a person." Salim nodded solemnly. Andrew had to smile at the serious little boy.

"And for Kings, while most couldn't hold up that tower, they can declare war, or raise unfair taxes, or have people executed."

"I wouldn't want anyone executed."

"Me either." Andrew sensed a change in the air.

"Let's talk more about that another time. I bet you'd like to see the house and theater, eh?"

"You bet!" Andrew and Salim stood together and Andrew showed him the house. He showed Salim Ashna's bedroom, the meager kitchen, the rest of the library, and finally, the theater itself.

"There ought to be a little gas for the lights, let me check." Salim felt like he was floating in space, or underwater, in the darkness. It felt wonderful. It felt scary. A faint hiss filled the air as the gas lines came on, and a *fwoomp* as the lamps caught. Salim closed his eyes, delighting in the lights coming on in front of him. The lights adjusted, and Andrew said:

"Go ahead, take a look." Salim opened his eyes and smiled wide. The gas lamps threw off wonderful light, and he felt a million feet tall standing in front of all those empty seats.

"Wow!"

"You're saying that often enough."

"Yeah! It's awesome in here!"

"I'm glad you think so. Your mother and I made a lot of fond memories here." Andrew thought back to the night where it went wrong. "Some sad ones, too, but mostly happy."

"It seems impossible to be sad in a place like this."

"It can happen. We brought the audience to tears one night, performing 'The Turtle's Tragedy,' have you heard of it?"

"I have, but I fell asleep when we went to see it."

"I think like a lot of things you'll grow to appreciate it when you're a bit older."

"You say that a lot." Andrew's mouth turned in a wry smile.

"I don't mean to repeat myself. There're a lot of things to appreciate when you're older, and some things you don't. It's just life, ignore me, Salim."

"Okay," said Salim. The sudden silence was blessed short, as they heard the front door close and a voice calling from the back:

"Salim? Andrew? I've got breakfast!"

"Race you back!" said Salim, breaking into a run.

Andrew laughed and chased after him. They pounded into the library, where Ashna was setting out food.

"You beat me you little devil!" said Andrew. Salim beamed.

"Did you boys have a good time?"

"Andrew showed me the theater!"

"Did he tell you we used to be actors here?"

"Yep! He said you were one of the best." Ashna smiled at Andrew as Salim tore into the repast. The food Ashna brought was hot and delicious. There were boiled eggs, fire peppers, egg toast, jam, cold slices of good ham, iced juice for Salim and coffee in a bottle for the adults.

"Real coffee! I rarely get such a good meal," said Andrew.

"Well, I got used to drinking it mornings and…well, anyway, I thought you'd enjoy some. There's honey and cream to go in, too." They ate in silence, each ravenous and concerned not at all with decorum as they tore into the food. Salim announced the end of the meal with a mighty burp.

"Salim! Excuse yourself!"

"Sorry, I ate too fast."

"It's okay, just try to control that in the future. "Yes'm." Andrew poured a fresh cup of coffee for himself and Ashna and leaned back in the couch.

"What next?" said Ashna.

"The Tower, I guess."

"What tower? Anastasia's Tower?"

"That's right, Salim."

"How are we going to get there?"

"Is it even safe for us? Salim and you are easy to recognize, and I'm not totally unknown outside the palace."

"I have to. It's the last thing my uncle left me."

"He attacked us last night. What if it's a trap?"

"Maeryl was a smart man, but I doubt he set a trap ten years in advance."

"Yesterday you would have said he wouldn't try to kill you."

"Yes, but I don't think the Moon would go in for a plot."

"Still, is it safe? Is it worth it?" Andrew looked at Ashna.

"Please. Maybe the Song has something to do with what's going on. Maybe it can help us, even."

"I don't see how."

"Ashna! I have no family now. I need to know what this is about, if it's about anything at all." He reached out and took her hand. Ashna looked at her lap.

"I'm sorry. I'm just so scared we'll be caught and taken back to the castle."

"I don't want to go back!"

"I know Salim, I'll protect you both. None of us are going back."

"Please," said Andrew. Ashna squeezed his hand and thought for a long moment.

"Yes, of course. If it's important to you, it's important to me."

"Thank you. Now we have to figure out how to go." Ashna smiled.

"You know, I have an idea! I'll be right back, I saw something on my search for breakfast." Ashna hopped off the couch and strode out the door. Andrew and Salim looked at each other in bewilderment, but in no time Ashna was back with an armload of clothes.

"Good idea! A disguise!" Andrew smiled and began sorting.

"A dress, a cloak, another dress…and a little girl's skirt and blouse…" He eyed Ashna.

"What gives?"

"They'll be looking for a woman, a man, and a little

boy, not two women and a girl doing their morning shopping." Andrew groaned.

"I concede the logic." Salim looked even less convinced.

"It's just until we get out of Aethero, Salim. Okay?"

"Okay. Fine." Andrew knelt next to the little boy.

"You know Salim, I had to dress up as a woman many times for our theater."

"Really?"

"Yep. It can even be a little fun. See the world from a new perspective, eh? Try to spot how people treat you differently."

"Okay!" They got dressed, helping each other into the clothes and making adjustments. Ashna stood back and looked them over in satisfaction. Andrew was wearing a sensible dress, dark blue, with a floral bonnet. Salim wore a skirt with a paisley pattern and a brown blouse.

"Thank goodness you didn't work in a quarry or something. We didn't even need to alter the dress." Ashna smiled as Andrew looked down grimaced. "I'm glad I've got such a good eye for fashion." Andrew sighed. Ten minutes later, two women emerged from the theater and set off in the direction of Anastasia's Tower along with a little girl. One woman kept her face down and hunched her shoulders while the other strode forward with a confident grin and a skip in her step.

"Didn't even need to alter the dress indeed," muttered Andrew under his breath.

****

The King raged around his room, throwing chairs and smashing precious lamps.

"How could you let them escape?" he screamed at Maeryl, whose face was a neutral mask. "Is Andrew so powerful his own teacher can't defeat him? You told me you harbored no warm feelings for him, yet he is gone, and with my guard captain, too! I'll have them killed when I find them, burned on coals and suspended from chains. Drawn apart by horses! I'll grind up iron filings and force-feed them to that wizard while my guards beat Ashna to a pulp. Death is too good for them! I'm humiliated in front of my own court, in my own castle! And you!" he said, turned to Maeryl.

"You couldn't even keep them in the building. You disgust me. You said you were a great and powerful wizard, from the same fantastic land Andrew claims as a homeland, but I've yet to see YOUR amazing powers," said the King. Maeryl said nothing, just picked up one of the few remaining unbroken items in the room and turning it over in his hands. It was a delicate glass sculpture. He didn't react when the King snatched it out of his hands and shattered the figure against a wall.

"I'm talking to you, you impudent magician!" said the King. Maeryl looked up at him.

"What do you want? I told you I thought he wouldn't be a problem. He surprised me, that's all. It's been almost ten years since we last met, I didn't think he would adapt to magic he'd never seen before so quickly. He's really quite the virtuoso," said Maeryl.

"If you're done licking his feet because of what a wonderful wizard he is, are you going to explain to me why you let them get away? Are you going to help me track him down, or should I have you broken on the wheel for failing me like my guards?" said the King. Almost as if on cue, a faint scream echoed up from beneath their feet. Maeryl shrugged. The King, breathing hard, clenched his fists. He loomed over the wizard.

"You'd better come up with something good, and fast, before I have your tongue ripped out and give it to a dog," he said. Maeryl laughed.

"You could do no such thing, unless I allowed it,"

said Maeryl. He knelt and picked up one of the many shards of glass in the room left over from the king's rampage. He spoke a word and all the glass in the room rose into the air, tinkling, chiming, shining fragments of razor-sharp glass. They made scratching and plinking sounds as they pulled into each other, forming a large circle of arrowheads pointing in at the king. They hovered in the air, and somehow managed to convey their own sense of menace even apart from the fact they were deadly sharp.

"N...now, let's not be hasty," said the King. Maeryl looked at one of the shards of glass and watched as it drifted across the room to rest on the King's shoulder, the wicked point right at his neck.

"I'm never hasty. I can make my own time. What we should making is a plan," said Maeryl, who turned from the king and walked to a liquor cabinet (carefully untouched during the king's tantrum). Maeryl browsed the bottles until he found something he liked the look of and poured himself a drink.

"I'm listening," said the King, trying to lean away from the glass at his neck.

"Did I tell you the original reason I left Andrew?" said Maeryl, swirling a brown liquid in his glass.

"No, you never did mention..."

"Hm. Of course. I'm not really Maeryl," said the man. The king's eyes widened, then narrowed.

"Who are you, then?"

"When I was home on Earth, I was called Oberon," he replied. He spoke a word to his glass and the liquor inside turned clear. The smell of honeysuckle and fresh spring apples filled the room. "I was worshiped by all living things for most of that disgusting planet's history. I watched as humans came up from the seas as nothing more than up-jumped fish with stumps. I thought nothing of it when it happened. The world was a paradise. Trees and groves and swamps and glades as far as the eye could see. You could have walked the world over from branch to branch and never need step foot on the ground. There were flowers, exotic and huge, bigger than a man. Bigger than you, some as big as houses. The smells were intoxicating. My court and I would get lost in the jungles, cavorting in the warm rains of the tropical sun. We knew no pain, no fear. There were only dancing and drinking and love-making," said Oberon. He looked deep into his glass. The King was silent.

"The sky fell one day, and the sky turned from blue to gray. It was cold for so long, a long time even as counted by one who will never die. So many of my people froze. The jungles were gone. The flowers all died. The only living things were thick with fur and stank hideously. Humans, how they ever made it through is anyone's guess. They were there, though, even after the masters of the world fell, their reptilian hands grasping for life. They were there."

"I knew on that day I should have stomped them out, but they seemed so inconsequential, such little things, that I paid them no mind. I had to rebuild my court, had to rebuild the civilization we made. Without even turning around, there they were again. Pushing us out of our lands, pushing us back until there was to be no more pushing and it came to war. I thought I had them when I crafted a sickness so devastating it killed almost half of all living humans, but they came on harder. They fought us to a standstill, and a truce was made. I gave them magic. Such a fool. And from there I was pushed off my throne by a metal man, a god of wheel and cog and steel. I thought I would be lost forever, but I found someone. A man, a wizard named Maeryl. You see, without magic wizards die. My presence is to them as air is to humans, and worship is to you or me. They were dying like flies, and I felt a little glad wandering the world as at least my loss would hurt my old enemies."

"Yet, as I was displaced I had no one to worship me. The days of magic were forever gone. But this man, Maeryl, he knew of a land where magic was the way of things. Gods walked amongst the people, and magic was not performed but simply was, all things we could think of on Earth were here in the flesh. A world of magic, on the back of a turtle. It seemed absurd, but at the time I was desperate. I bargained with him: life for life. Give me his body or another's, and I would be able to keep him alive if he took me to this world, to Aethero. He agreed, and told me his nephew had been given to him by his brother, and I could have the boy when I awoke. I needed to rest so desperately, I entered the man's soul and merged with the magic and wizardry inside him. I slept these many years, waiting for him to awaken me and give me my payment."

"He was going to give you Andrew?" said the King.

"Yes. That was the agreement. A new body for me, one that I could shape to my desires as my own was destroyed by the machine god. The disgusting ape lied to me, hid Andrew away and used his magic to erase the memory of where Andrew was. When I finally clawed out of my prison, I found the truth. I was furious," said Oberon. He sipped his drink and smiled.

"Ambrosia nectar. I have not had this in I cannot tell you how long; Earth lost the will for such things many hundreds of years ago."

"What did you do with Maeryl?"

"Oh, he's still here. I trapped him in his own cage, his own body, where I was held. He is awake where I was sleeping, however. His reward for betraying me is to get to watch me hunt down his nephew and kill him."

"Good. That will teach him to betray me, as well," said the King. He took a step toward Oberon. "We are much the same, you and I. The humans, and even my own wizard, too, betrayed me. If you get revenge for yourself, my own need for vengeance will be satisfied. I will give you anything you want, if you require it, in this," said the King with a dazzling smile. His muscles strained and sweat poured down his face. He had not forgotten the shard of glass nested on his shoulder.

"Anything?" said Oberon, looking at the king over the rim of his glass.

"Oh, yes."

"Your son. He's a firstborn, no? An only child?"

"I...yes, he is. But...he's to be king after me."

"Then I shall not find and kill Andrew. Your shame will live on. I'll try not to mention to anyone you lacked the resolve to answer a grievous insult in your own home. I would not hesitate to destroy one such as he, in my own world and court. Still, monarchs have their own way of doing things, no?" said Oberon. He tossed back the rest of the drink and set the glass down.

"No! No, wait. You can have him. He was not born of a queen, he's just a bastard, anyway. I don't need him, I can always make another son," said the King. Oberon smiled, his teeth bright and sharp.

"Oh, good. Then we shall both be happy," said Oberon. The glass shard lifted from the king's shoulder, and it floated off in a trail with the others to settle in a neat pile. He closed his eyes.

"Andrew left a neat trail of magic. It will be nothing to track him," said Oberon. He opened his eyes. "I will return. What of the guard captain, shall I bring her to you for justice?"

The King smiled, and this one was in no way pleasant. "Please do. I have another son to make, after all."

*****

Andrew, Ashna, and Salim stood at the base of

Anastasia's Tower. There was no door of which to speak.

"So, how do we get in?" asked Ashna as she ran her hands along the stone of the tower. There weren't even seams in the alabaster stone.

"Uh, well. You know, Maeryl was not so forthcoming as I thought," said Andrew. He adjusted his bonnet.

"There's no door!" said Salim.

"You two look fetching," said Ashna.

"Thanks. If you're not careful, I'll have a young lad on my arm before long, and then where will you be? An old spinster knitting by the fire, that's where," said Andrew. Ashna stuck her tongue out at him. Andrew laughed as he walked around the base of the tower.

"What's so funny?"

"I remember the first time you did that."

"Did what?"

"Stuck your tongue out at me."

"You do? Why would you remember that?"

"Have you ever noticed that we're the only two people who do that? It's not a gesture native to this land."

"Nuh uh! I do it too, and some of the kids I play with." Salim stuck his tongue out at Andrew and laughed.

"I never thought of that. Now that you mention it, I've never seen anyone else do it but us."

"Yeah. People here wag their eyebrows. Freaks, the lot of you," said Andrew. "The prince excluded, of course. Royal prerogative." He finally stopped and shrugged. "I have no clue as to how to get in. Maybe we should knock?"

"Worth a try," said Ashna. She took a step and tapped politely on the stone of the tower. Nothing happened for a long while, and just as Andrew was about to knock himself they saw a faint, pale green light fluttering down towards them in lazy arcs.

"What's that?" said Andrew.

"Looks like a moth," said Salim. The pale light did

indeed resolve into a moth, but it was about as big as a hawk. It was a luna moth, and it flew down to them as silent as still waters. Ashna started when it landed on the back of her right shoulder, but managed not to scream or jump. It yawned audibly.

"Oh, goodness. What time is it? The sun makes it hard to see. Good morning, I suppose," said the moth. It had a light and friendly voice, almost like a little sister.

"Good morning," they all replied. The moth fluttered a little to get a better grip on Ashna's shoulder and it looked at them.

"How can I help you?" it said.

"Well, first let me make introductions. I'm Andrew, this is Ashna, and this is Salim," said Andrew.

"Charmed. You may call me Lauria," said the moth. Andrew inclined his head.

"Nice to meet you. I need to speak with Anastasia, if at all possible," he said.

"Oh, my, no. It's very late and she's in bed," said Lauria.

"It's very important I see her. Will you be kind enough to at least let her know I'm here?" said Andrew. "My name is Andrew Dale. Here, take her this letter. My uncle left it for me a long time ago, and told me to come to her." He pulled the letter out of his pocket and held it up to the moth. Lauria's long, lustrous antenna sagged a little, but she dutifully flapped over and took it in her feet and flew to the top of the tower. They stood at the base of the tower for some time, waiting nervously. They jumped when a seam appeared in the side of the flawless tower, and Lauria was waiting on the other side of a door with no visible hinges that swung out.

"She'll see you, and thanks for waiting," said Lauria. She turned and led them into the tower. After they stepped over the threshold, the door swung shut silently. They looked up and saw a huge spiral staircase made of moonstone, ranging in color from the palest white to the darkest blue. It glowed with faint internal light. They climbed the stairs as Lauria led the way, lazily flapping her wings and yawning often. The stairs seemed endless. Andrew was about to suggest a break when they came to the final landing. A door, carved with thousands of depictions of the moon, stood at the top. There were crescent moons and full moons, moons with faces both friendly and brooding, moons wearing sleeping caps, cats sleeping on moons, cows jumping over moons, and a cat with a broad smile whose teeth were, in fact, the moon. Salim laughed with delight and ran over to the door. He ran his hands over the bas relief, the texture delightful.

"Look, mom! The rabbit in the moon is here, too!" Ashna knelt next to Salim and looked. Lauria fluttered up to a shelf set into the wall, with dark velvet curtains that were pulled back, and landed. She settled herself on a pillow and the curtains closed around her.

"Nice to meet you, go on in if you would. Good morning, good night," she said, somewhat muffled by the curtains. Andrew looked at Ashna and put his hand on the door, seeking a handle. It opened under his touch without a sound, and swung open. They walked through the door together. Andrew slipped his hand into Ashna's as they looked around the room. It was dim, with faint light coming from nowhere and everywhere. A large, luxurious bed dominated the room. It looked like you could sleep there for a mere moment and be refreshed the rest of your life. Ashna nudged Andrew and he looked. She pointed toward a desk, and his breath was taken away. A beautiful woman sat at it, dressed in simple white gowns that cascaded from her shoulders and flowed across the floor in a long train. Her hair was black as raven feathers, and she glowed faintly. The room was so silent even whispers tiptoed. She was holding Andrew's letter, apparently reading over it. When she looked up, her beauty took them in. Her face was smooth and full in a healthy and attractive way. Her eyes were dark pools, and her hair fell across her face so that half was covered. Even when she gathered her hair in a loose pony tail, the hair over her face didn't move. Salim slid behind Ashna and peeked out.

"Welcome. I'm sorry if Lauria was at all rude—she likes to sleep, does my Lauria," said Anastasia.

"T-thank you, uh…" said Andrew.

"Just call me Anastasia. All that 'm'lady' and other nonsense would be fine for public occasions and all that, but here in my bedroom I believe we can be less formal. Don't you think?"

"Of course," said Andrew. There was a pointed silence until Ashna kicked him. "Sorry! This is Ashna, and her son Salim." Ashna curtsied.

"I am glad to have met you. Before we get started, may I inquire as to your pretty dresses?" she said. There was a twinkle in her eye. Andrew turned red and began climbing out of the dress as fast as he could, and Salim followed suit.

"There's a perfectly reasonable explanation, which Ashna will be happy to provide," he said. Ashna took a deep breath and filled in Anastasia as to what had happened up to their meeting as Andrew slipped out of the dress. He had on trousers and a loose shirt. When Ashna was finished, Andrew added, "That's what brings us here. When I went into his study, I found the letter you've just read yourself, telling me to seek you out." Anastasia nodded.

"I remember when he came to me those years ago. We were introduced by my husband, Bart. They met in the wilds, and Bart brought him to our home to share a meal," she said. Salim was wide-eyed.

"Bart the Bard!" Anastasia smiled.

"That's right." She looked at Ashna. "If he is the son

of the King, how is it we've never met?" Ashna looked down at her son.

"I think, perhaps, the King is ashamed his son is half-mortal. He is also a wicked, proud man. It doesn't surprise me at all he never took Salim to official functions. He's barely met any of the gods." Anastasia shook her head.

"While the peers meet infrequently, it's customary for a child to be brought to visit. After all, I may work with him one day." She smiled at Salim, who blushed.

Ashna looked at Andrew. "Did your uncle ever say anything about meeting Bart?"

"No, not a word. We spent a lot of time in the forests, avoiding towns and Aethero proper and such. If Bart was wandering the wilds, then it's entirely possible they met some time when I was asleep."

"It was at night," said Anastasia. "My husband and I usually converse at night, for reasons that are obvious. Your uncle didn't stay for long, but I got a good impression of him. He was very concerned for you."

"That's why this is all so difficult. Why would the same man who left me the note attack me after ten years?" said Andrew.

"Perhaps he is not the same man," Anastasia hazarded.

Andrew paused in surprise. "I...I suppose. I don't know." Anastasia stood up from her desk and walked over to an armoire, which she opened. She found a long leather cylinder and pulled off the cap. Inside was a flute made of pure silver.

"He left me this song for you. He gave me the keeping of it since there are so few of us who remember the Whales, and because he knows I would be happy to do so. While I am going to play it for you, it may be sung or hummed or played on any other instrument. It is important to remember something about Whale songs, though," she said, and now she regarded them both with a very stern and uncompromising expression. "With the songs of the first ones, there is no half. There is no trying. They are pure beyond anything you can imagine. They cannot, *cannot*, be played for a selfish reason. They are the songs of creation, of birth, of womb and of child and of hatching egg. Do not, for any selfish reason, ever use a Whale song," she said to them. She looked at Salim, who nodded, serious as a small child could ever be.

Then she put the flute to her lips, and began to play. The song haunted them. It flowed through the flute and into their souls. Andrew closed his eyes and floated in a sea of music unlike anything he ever heard before. He would never hear anything like it again. The song flowed like the water of the oceans, the deep currents moving them, hinting at ancient things in the deep. The melody struck Andrew right through his heart, and when he opened his eyes, when the last note of the song hung in the air like a missing friend, he saw tears on everyone's faces. Anastasia took the flute from her lips and slipped it back into its case. She set it in the armoire and returned to her seat. The room held its breath. Ashna knelt and hugged Salim.

"Wow..." Andrew breathed out. Anastasia nodded.

"You must be a good shepherd of this song. It must not be used lightly."

"I understand. I don't think I could ever use it. I can't think of any reason."

"It is perhaps better that way. They say the mercy of a Whale is large and crushing. I would not want to meet one without a good reason." They stood together for a long, quiet moment. Anastasia stirred, stifled a yawn.

"I must bid you a good night. It is well past my bedtime." She smiled for them again, a beautiful, cool smile, and showed them to the door.

"I wish you luck on your future. Do you know where

you will go?" Ashna spoke:

"There are said to be as many worlds on the backs of turtles just like this one. Perhaps we can find one where we can live in peace."

"I hope so, for your sakes, and for Salim." She knelt next to the little boy. "I sense a sadness in you, Salim. Be not sad, for here are two that love you very much." She hugged the silent prince, and then stood.

"Farewell," she said. They walked through the door and back down the stairs, the mood too somber for talking. When they stepped outside, they were amazed at the sun in their eyes. A whole day had transpired during their talk. When they adjusted to the light, Salim gave a frightened yell.

Maeryl was before them, sitting on a horse.

"Andrew, nephew. You really need to learn to tie a more subtle spell! I could follow you from miles away."

"But..I thought..."

"Oh! You did. However, that little prince there reeks of magic. When you tied that illusion around him you must have been so tired. Which reminds me. How did you break that ward on the prince's door?" Maeryl looked interested, but Andrew refused to answer.

"Very well. Hand over the child and the woman, and you can go free."

"No! Never. How could you think I would betray my family when so many have left me before?"

"That's just it, Andrew. The people you love are the most dangerous around us. They all leave you, in the end, isn't that right? Your parents died, your uncle abandoned you, and your girl there, why, she betrayed you and turned you into a slave! Don't be so stupid and noble to think that it won't happen again. Those that love you, that love, makes you weak." Andrew's mind reeled under the assault. His misgivings and fears roared in his heart, making him feel weak and confused.

"They would never..."

"I bet you thought the same thing about your uncle, and now look where I am." Maeryl laughed with derisive scorn.

"I..." Ashna stepped in front of Andrew.

"I won't leave his side again, and you will never take my son."

"Quiet, bitch, this is between me and Andrew." Ashna's sword appeared in her hand, her draw so fast as to confuse the eye.

"Call me a bitch again and we'll see what's between your ribs soon enough," she growled. Maeryl sighed.

"Guards!"

A troop of royal guards appeared from a nearby alley and marched over to them.

"Give yourselves up, or I will put the guards on you." Andrew bristled.

"We'll never give up!"

"Be silent, Andrew. Your words are as weak as your magic. I know you will not kill."

Andrew quailed under the verbal onslaught.

"He may not kill. But nothing prevents me from doing so. Any more of your evil words and I'll cut the hate out of your mouth and jam it down your throat."

"Enough of this. Guards!" The guards lowered their spears at the trio.

"Do not harm the prince. The other two you may kill." Ashna set herself in a fighting stance and waited.

"Guards! Now!"

Chapter 10
The Show
10 Years Ago

A GREAT CLASH OF SWORDS shattered the otherwise quiet theatre. The audience, captive to the action, held their breath. Ashna and Andrew (dressed in fanciful costumes to make them ant-like) crossed shining blades on the stage. Their choreography was beautiful. They seemed to float and to fly and to flow like water all at once as they pursued each other across the little space, lit by gas lamps. Above the pounding of their feet and slicing rapiers, they yelled their lines with undeniable conviction.

"You stole my princess!" screamed Ashna, the red ant.

"I love her!" yelled Andrew, the black ant.

"You only wish to take her from my people, to deprive us of a queen and to shame us!" accused Ashna, with a vicious kick at Andrew's torso.

"No! Never! I love her with all my heart and antennae, and I wish us to be wed!"

"No daughter of mine will ever marry a black ant! Never!"

"Try to see past your anger at my father and forgive the son! I have no wish to be your enemy!" said Andrew. Ashna snarled and snapped the blade at his face, forcing him to jump back.

"You killed my son!" accused the red ant queen.

"I'm sorry! He attacked me in the dark and slew my best friend. I had to defend myself, I had no wish to kill him!"

"Lies! All I hear are lies and filth from your mandibles. No more!"

"This is too much for me! I will not fight the mother

of the ant I love!" cried Andrew. He threw down his blade and knelt on the stage, his hands clasped before him in abject supplication.

"Give us your leave to be married! Let us be happy! I will trouble you no more!" pleaded Andrew. Ashna screamed with incoherent rage and rushed across the stage, her sword held high, and swung it with all her strength at Andrew's head. He bowed low and awaited his inevitable death. Just at the last moment, a figure leapt in front of Andrew. The blade rang against an armored shell.

"Alexander! I thought you were dead!" said the red ant queen. A wise figure turned to the crowd, and there were cheers and energetic clapping as the turtle was revealed. It was Yonston, dressed in a large shell and green clothing.

"It is not so easy to kill a turtle," said Alexander.

"Then stand aside and I will show you how easy it is to slay a rogue!"

"I'll do no such thing. Lay down your sword and listen, child, for you are acting the fool."

"I will not rest until that vagabond ant is brought to justice!" cried the ant queen.

"I await your judgment!" the black ant called out.

"There is no need for this," said Alexander. He nodded his wise head. "No need at all. Lay down your sword and listen, child, I say to you again." He looked at the ant queen hard with his wise old eyes, and reluctantly she lowered her weapon.

"I have for you three minutes, no more," said the ant queen. Alexander nodded.

"If that is your wish. Please stand, youngster. There's no need to kneel while I speak," said Alexander. He helped the young blank ant prince to his feet.

"As I understand it, this young man slew your son?"

"He murdered him!"

"I was defending my friend!"

"Liar!"

"Stop, stop. Do you deny killing her son?"

"...No."

"Hear his confession and let me take vengeance!"

"It is true he killed your son, but I was there, watching with my wise old eye, and I saw your son attack his friend. This young man tried to step in to stop the fight, and in the struggle your son fell on a sword. Nothing more," said Alexander.

"You take his side? I heard the great Alexander was impartial! Well! We see your reputation laid bare for all to see the lies!"

"I am not finished. Since the death of your son was tragic, and untimely, the young ant prince will be beholden to you for a year and a day. He will willingly, and without complaint, do any task you set before him. If, after a year and a day, he has done all that you asked with a glad heart, and if he still loves your daughter and she him, will you grant them your blessing?" Alexander finished speaking. The ant queen wavered, debating with herself.

"Anything? Any task?" she said.

"Anything that one could ask of an ant fairly," Alexander amended.

"I will ask of him only one task, then," said the queen. The ant prince, hoping against hope, ran and fell to his knees before her.

"Name it! Any task, I will do this thing for you if it means your blessing!" said the ant prince.

"Discover for me the name of the wind," said the queen with a smirk. Alexander, frustrated, was about to speak, but the ant prince cut him off.

"I will discover its name for you, and bring it to you in a sack," said the ant prince. The queen laughed.

"Only a fool would take such a burden and agree to

more!"

"Then I am a fool, and you will have for your son-in-law a fool as well," said the ant. He bowed to Alexander, an elaborate bow only ants of royal descent can perform. (It helps that they have three sets of legs.)

"Do you think you can do it? Surely you see this is insane," said Alexander.

"I am a madman of passion, a lunatic of love, a demented of devotion, then, my good turtle. Trust me." The ant prince set off with a purpose to the west, and the curtains fell to much applause.

Ashna, Andrew, and Yonston ran back onto the stage and took a bow.

"The second act will begin after a short intermission! Thank you! Thank you!" they all cried, and then ran backstage. Ashna and Andrew rushed to their shared dressing room. Andrew helped Ashna strip out of her ant queen costume (she was to play a witch in the next act) and stopped when her costume revealed her bare shoulders. He kissed her right shoulder, wrapping an arm around her waist, between the bobbing fake ant legs, and trailed soft kisses up the side of her neck. She turned her head and met his mouth with hers. They opened their mouths and kissed deeply, tongues dancing, passionate and fierce.

"I need you," said Andrew. Ashna kissed him again and turned so they were pressed together.

"We don't have time before the curtains rise, you know," she replied. He put his hands under her costume and slid it off of her the rest of the way, leaving her without clothing except tights and a thin cloth top. Andrew slid his hands up her sides and Ashna gasped.

"We really don't have time for that," whispered Ashna. Andrew grinned as she put her arms around him and pulled down his own ant costume.

"We'll have some time after the show, I just wanted

to give you a little taste," said Ashna, sliding her hand down the front of his ant suit as she kissed him deeply again. Andrew gasped against her lips, hot and wet, and they might have forgotten they were in the middle of a play at all if Yonston hadn't started banging on their door.

"If you're doing what I think you're doing I'm going to drown you both in a freezing cold river! Ashna, get dressed for your witch act, and Andrew, your legs and antennae better not be bent all to hell again!" There was a pause as they untangled themselves from their respective ant suits and limbs and Ashna began dressing in the traditional whites and veil of a witch. Andrew straightened his costume and gave Ashna another passionate kiss.

"Soon," she said in a throaty whisper. Andrew put his hand on the door handle and turned to look at Ashna.

"I love you," he said.

"I love you, too. Now get out there before Father has a fit!" she replied. Andrew winked and slid out of the door. He turned and nearly ran into his adopted uncle. Yonston still wore his Alexander costume, and even though he was shorter than Andrew by half a head nowadays, he managed to loom over the teenager.

"I remember being young, young man, sometimes perhaps all too well, but you need to show some restraint and respect to my house. I know I can't stop the two of you, perhaps I don't want to since you seem happy, but I wish you would take it out of my home. There's only so much my old heart can bear." Yonston reached to put his arm around Andrew's shoulders and drew him towards the curtains.

"It's not time for me to go back out yet, Yonston."

"No, I wanted to show you something in the crowd. Come, look through the peep here." Yonston lifted a little flap in the curtain, which was covered with a sheer cloth on the other side. Andrew leaned down to look out. The seats were about half empty, with some patrons stretching their legs or buying food and drink from the vendors who set up just outside the theatre doors.

"What am I looking for?" said Andrew.

"Do you see a tall man, very dark in skin, with a long red cloak near the back?" Andrew scanned the crowd for the man Yonston was describing, and finally saw him in the back of the theatre. He was as described, and when he shifted his cloak would open a little. Andrew thought he saw the hilt of a sword poking out before the man shifted his cloak back over it.

"Yes."

"That's the captain of the Royal Guard."

"Wow!"

"Think, Andrew, why would the captain come here to see a show when the man he protects can command the finest players in all of Aethero to come before him?"

"Maybe the captain likes a simpler venue."

"The captain is of noble birth, I would wager this is perhaps only the second time he's been in our theatre."

"You're being oblique, Yonston."

"Think. I saw him at last week's show. He came thirty minutes early and walked around the theatre. He was checking exits and corners."

"Maybe he's a fan of architecture."

"Andrew, you're being a toad. He was examining places where assassins and other low sorts could hide. Muggers, kidnappers, highwaymen. He was checking our theatre's safety for a royal visit."

"The king is here?!" Andrew dropped the peephole cover back in place and turned to Yonston. The older man nodded.

"Why would he come here?"

"That's a good question, Andrew. While you and Ashna are wonderful actors, you're not formally trained. I don't know why he would come, but I'm almost entirely certain he's out there, watching our show."

"Why did you tell me this? Now my nerves are all shot!" said Andrew.

"I tell you this because it may mean better things for us. If word got out that the king himself came to see our show, we might be able to attract more and better patronage. Richer customers. We could fix the theatre up and hire some more actors and maybe even an artist to paint backgrounds. Our luck may be changing, and I wanted to share this with you."

"Does Ashna know? Have you already told her?"

"No, I haven't yet. You can, if you like. I just wanted to let you know so that you're both at your best for the second act. My original writing of the Ant Prince's adventures is where you both really shine, so do your best, and pray that we may all three do well."

"We'll be as our characters, so real the people will come up to touch our feet in disbelief!" said Andrew with a huge grin. Yonston returned the smile and turned his back to Andrew.

"Help me out of my costume, I have to get into my incognito Alexander disguise," said Yonston. Andrew helped the older man out of the costume and into a bushy costume (from when Alexander would whisper to the Ant Prince when he was asleep, to help him in his quest.) Just as Yonston was ready and the curtains were about to rise, Ashna joined them in the backstage, her white robes flowing. Andrew grabbed her hand and pulled her close.

"Careful! You'll rip my sleeve," she said.

"Sorry, I'm just so excited! Yonston gave me some wonderful news!"

"What is it? You know you have to be on in just a minute."

"He said the king may be in attendance, and we're to do our best because a royal endorsement means we'll all be famous."

"The king!? *The* king? Oh! I've heard he sometimes dresses as a commoner and goes amongst the people," said Ashna.

"The same. Do your best witch and ant queen, because it may mean great things for us!"

"I will, and you do the same. Have you seen him in the crowd?"

"No, Your dad pointed out his guard captain, though. Here, look through the peep. You're looking for the tall dark man in the red cloak in the back of the theatre."

"I see him! I wonder where the king is! I've heard he's tall, and strong, and just gorgeous," said Ashna, eagerly scanning the crowd. Andrew felt a pang of hot jealousy flash through his heart and stomach.

"I'm sure he's just as any other man."

"Oh, he's better, I bet. Kings are all the best-looking men in the stories."

"Well, this is real life and not a story. He's probably fat and old and bald since he doesn't have to work or anything." Ashna turned from the peep and regarded Andrew with a critical eye.

"Are you jealous?"

"No. You're just getting all weird and girly, fluttering over a king. He's no better than anyone else."

"Oh, that's good to know. Except his being a Pocket God, you know, the sun and all? The thing that gives life to all Aethero?" Andrew flushed a deep red.

"Well, if that's what you go for, then maybe you don't want a nasty mortal jerk like me. Excuse me, I hear Yonston calling. My part is up," said Andrew, who shoved past Ashna and onto the stage. The crowd applauded and settled into the second act. Andrew, flushed with young anger and jealousy, acted his heart out. The crowed oohed when he challenged an ogre to a wrestling match, and ahhhed when he won. His emotions poured across the stage and over the crowd, and to them he was no mere actor, but the Ant Prince himself come to life. He fought for months across hostile lands into the Mountains of Wind, tricking the gods that lived there into giving him what he sought, and they cried with him when he let it out of the bag halfway home. A year had passed when the Ant Prince returned from his adventure, skinny, broken, and depressed. He had nothing to give after all his efforts. The crowd wept when the two young ants, together for the last time, decide to take poison rather than be denied their love. The theatre was utterly silent when the last speech was over, Alexander admonishing the Ant Queen for her harsh, unforgiving nature, and urging the crowd to learn to forgive one's enemies.

    The three players came back onto the stage amidst cheers and accolades. They all bowed deeply. Yonston shooed the two teenagers off the stage and addressed the crowd.

    "Thank you for coming to enjoy our show! As a special encore tonight there will be a mystifying, indescribable magician's act from my ward, Andrew. Then, my lovely daughter and I will thrill you with feats of juggling and dexterity you will not see at any other show house! We're staying open late tonight, so please enjoy the expanded show! We will begin after another intermission, so don't lose your seats to the eager crowds outside!"

    Andrew was changing into his magician's outfit, a garish affair of blue robes covered in stars and moons with a big hat covered in multi-colored metal discs, meant to catch the light of the stage. Ashna came to him, standing a little ways off. He didn't say anything to her, and when she finally came up and tried to kiss him, he turned his face away. Ashna stepped back.

    "Andrew, I'm sorry about what I said before. About the king. I love you just the way you are." Andrew turned to her, his hat jingling.

"Sure, just good enough, right?"

"Andrew! I'm trying to apologize."

"I don't want your apology or your pity. Just let me do my stupid 'act' and get this over with. I don't want to talk to you," he said. Tears welled up in Ashna's eyes, but her voice was fierce.

"If you're too stupid to understand when someone is trying to apologize to you, maybe I deserve better."

"Whatever. You're just like my uncle," said Andrew. He turned from her and strode onto the stage, taking with him a little table. He waved a wand in the air and Yonston, backstage, struck a sheet of metal with a hammer, making the theatre rumble with thunder. Without speaking to the crowd at all, he tapped his wand on the table, which turned into a cabinet. From the cabinet, he withdrew a tall round hat and turned it up so the crowd could see it was empty. He flourished his robes, set the hat on the table with the band up, tapped it with his wand, and stuck in his hand. He yelled suddenly, and the crowd jumped. He picked the hat up and said to the crowd:

"Anyone fancy some crabs?" He held it so they could see inside, and it was filled to the brim with snapping orange crabs. The crowd laughed and applauded.

"You, sir! You look like you would enjoy a crab dinner!" he said, and slung the hat like a bucket of water. The front row screamed and ducked, but when the crabs fell on the crowd they were made of streamers and thin crepe paper. He took a bow as they applauded. Andrew glanced backstage to see Ashna staring out of the peep, no doubt trying to locate the king in the crowd. *She wants the king. I'll give them a wizard.* Andrew picked up one of the crepe crabs that didn't come out of the hat and spoke some words. To the crowd's delight, the paper crabs came to life, scuttling under seats and painlessly nipping grabbing hands. The crowd applauded uproariously. Andrew watched out of the corner of his eye as Ashna whipped her head back from the curtain and stared at him, eyes wide.

"What are you doing?" she yelled at him in a stage whisper. Andrew smirked and raised his hands for quiet, then brought them together and blew against the crab he held. The other crabs in the audience drifted up from the floor and danced about over their heads on drafts of air, now turning a step in time together like a dance routine, now forming up sides and fighting mock battles. Andrew ignored the desperate pleas for him to restrain himself coming from the backstage as he worked greater and more elaborate magics. The crabs turned into elephants, then to elegant swans as he refolded the paper in his hands. They danced and cavorted above the audience, and Andrew folded and whispered to the paper again. The swans turned in a giant flock together, then began flying into each other, forming into a single, large swan. It was regal and intricately detailed. Its feathers fluttered in an unfelt breeze, and everyone jumped then laughed when it trumpeted. Andrew gestured, and it turned and knelt in a royal bow in the direction of the king's guard captain. He then beckoned to his giant swan, which flew over the heads of the audience with another great trumpeting, ruffling hair and hats. It shrank as it came to Andrew, until at last it alighted in his outstretched hand, no bigger than the crabs from before. He unfolded the paper and revealed the blank white sheet to the audience. Amidst cheers and vigorous clapping, Andrew bowed his way off the stage. Yonston grabbed him by the arm when he got behind the curtain.

"What the hell are you thinking?"

"I'm thinking that I'm done with a petty magician's show and two-bit theatre. It's time to show off my stuff and try to get somewhere, unlike you."

"Andrew, why are you acting this way? "

"I just love performing for royalty I suppose."

"What does this have to do with the King? I understand wanting to impress him but what you did is dangerous. You've jeopardized everything your uncle worked for, and the life we've all been building together here."

"Maybe. It's not much of a life, since Ashna wants the King more than me."

"Is that what this is about? What did she say?"

"Something stupid about him being charming and handsome. It's stupid."

Yonston grabbed his own hair in exasperation. "She's a young lady, Andrew. You have to understand that while she lost her mother the same as you, she was not on the run for the most of her life. She's not as worldly as you."

"It sure shows."

"I know it does, to someone like you. You, however, have to be a better person and forgive her for that. Does she kiss the King? Does she tell him she loves him? Or is it you she does those things for?"

"If she's happy with me then she shouldn't even care about the King."

"Maybe, Andrew, maybe. That's not the way it works, though. Just because she is with you, and yes, I'd say she seems quite happy here with us, doesn't mean that she's going to stop being young, or a woman, or alive. Just because the thought of the King is thrilling doesn't mean she wants to leave you."

"Everyone leaves."

"By death or another way, yes, in time. I know up until now things have been that way for you, but that is not the normal way of things."

"So I'm not normal?"

"You are normal, Andrew. Your life until now? That's not the way it usually works. Most people don't spend the first half of their lives running from something. It's changed you, affected the way you see the world, and why wouldn't it? You have to understand, no one who left wanted to. Do you think your parents wanted to die and leave you behind?"

"...No."

"And do you think Maeryl honestly would have left you with me if he thought you would be better with him?"

"I don't know."

"I didn't know him as well as you, but it seemed to me like he cared about you very much and leaving you was a very difficult thing for him."

"Then he shouldn't have left! I have no one left!"

"You have us, Andrew. Give Ashna some time, apologize if you said something harsh, and things will look better," said Yonston. Ashna ran up to them.

"It's time for our act, uncle," she said. She was carrying a multitude of colorful juggling clubs. She didn't spare Andrew a glance.

"Think about what we've been talking about, Andrew."

"Fine."

Yonston squeezed Andrew's shoulder, and then put his hand out to lead Ashna onto the stage. Andrew watched them from the wings of the stage. Their juggling act was thrilling. They started with the typical clubs and balls and gradually worked their way up to juggling fiery torches and knives and swords. At the climax of the show Ashna would put on a blind fold and start by catching blades that Yonston threw, seemingly at random, from various parts of the stage. She never interrupted her intricate juggling pattern of glittering weaponry, even as he threw knives at her as many as two and three in a row. They were brilliant. Andrew felt his anger subsiding, and being replaced with a heavy gut full of guilt. As he watched her moving across the stage with grace, her face beautiful and arresting while the lights reflected off the tumbling blades. He could see the faint sheen of sweat on her skin as she struggled to make sure she didn't lose control of her waterfall of weapons. He admired her youthful body and grace in her juggling costume. *Maybe I overreacted.*

Yonston and Ashna wrapped their juggling show with Ashna hurling all her knives in the air, whipping off her blindfold in a courtly bow, and then holding out her hands and catching the hilts of the spinning weapons. The theatre-goers surged to their feet in a tumult of exalted applause. Andrew, Yonston, and Ashna knew it was the best show they'd ever done. If the king was in the audience, he was sure to give them a formal patronage. Andrew hurried to the side of the stage to close the curtains. The ropes were heavy and it was difficult work for one man, but he managed them all the same. Flushed with excitement and not a little remorse for his fight with Ashna, he hurried back to where they would be waiting behind the curtains. An excited tumult of voices slowed his eager steps, and as they came into view his heart leapt into his throat. The King of Aethero, the Celestial Light, Serapis II, and many other courtly titles, was already speaking to Ashna and Yonston, both of whom were on their knees.

"Rise, rise and let me see the famous players of Yonston's theater!" boomed the giant. He stood over seven feet tall, with skin black as murder, and a generous, winning smile full of teeth white as purity. To Andrew's dismay, the man seemed everything a King should, handsome and kind-seeming. *No doubt he is just and strong, with an eye for kindness towards little children and puppies,* thought Andrew with a scowl. His scowl deepened when he saw Ashna's face, flushed and grinning, which made her all the more beautiful. Andrew growled inwardly when he saw the King sizing up her figure, his eyes roaming her frame, no doubt as intoxicated by the sight as he was. He walked up quickly and cut a bow, formal and fitting for his first meeting with the King. At least I have etiquette to rely on, he thought.

"Ah! And the prince of the ants! A wonderful performance, lad, and a magician to boot. You'll go far with your flair for the theatre, both in drama and in spectacle. I could not help but notice the swan, the emblem of my family. Did you have word of my secret attendance?" said the king. Andrew rose from his bow.

"There was a rumor, sire, and I felt the gesture would honor you, whether or not you actually attended. With you close in our hearts, it was as if you are here regardless."

The king laughed. "A honeyed tongue off and on the stage. Good, child! With your magician's tricks, I have half a mind to make you my court magician," said the king with a smile. Yonston and Ashna gasped, but Andrew had ears only for being called a child.

"I am not a child, majesty," he said. The king stopped smiling, and a hush fell as before a storm. The king eyed Andrew critically, who held himself to his full height and looked the king dead in the face.

"And tell me, young magician, how did you perform those feats of wonder?"

"I am not a magician," said Andrew. His face burned and his heart raced. Ashna covered her mouth, her eyes wide and unblinking. Yonston's palms were slick with sweat, and his heart was fit to burst. Yonston broke into the conversation, putting an arm around Andrew.

"I'm afraid the wonder would be lost if you knew the technical details, sire, and Andrew, I am sure, is loath to reveal them lest the magic of the show disappear. He takes our work here very seriously," he squeezed

Andrew, "Sometimes too seriously, I fear. Pray, excuse him, his nerves make him bold after the show. I am sure later he will be better fit for such lofty company."

Yonston bit his lip. The king regarded them both with a murderous eye, and Yonston worried for a moment that all would be lost, but then the king laughed, a great booming that echoed throughout the theater.

"Of course, of course. I know myself the feeling of boldness after a great performance. You may leave us, Andrew, to sort yourself. I am sure your master and this lady will have much to occupy my time, until you are ready." He turned from them, and Yonston let out a silent breath of relief. The king turned to speak with Ashna, whose eyes managed to get wider still, and her blush deepen further. Yonston lead Andrew to the door that lead to their home.

"I didn't need your help," said Andrew, throwing off Yonston's arm as they reached the door.

"You sure didn't, you were hanging us all just fine by yourself. What got into you?"

"I saw him looking at Ashna."

"He is the king, Andrew. Should he wish to look at any of us, it is his right."

"Not the way he looked at her, the lecherous pig."

"You're going to get yourself killed with that mouth, and she and I with you if you're not lucky!"

"I did not mean to put either of you in danger."

"Well, you certainly did! We're lucky he's forgiving, Andrew. You're lucky, I should say. I doubt you'd find much satisfaction in getting put in a cold cell under the castle."

"I can defend myself, Yonston."

"I know you can, Andrew, that's the danger. It makes you reckless. Your lip with the king, the magic, *real magic*, during the show. It's as if you want to die."

"I don't want to die, I just...I just...."

"I know, Andrew. We talked earlier, I know how you feel about her. Please go upstairs and take some time to find your wits, or I fear we'll all pay for your jealousy. It's perfectly normal, and natural, but right now it is a deadly emotion. You used real magic in front of an audience, the king no less!"

"They didn't know it was real magic."

"And if there was a hunter in the audience? Someone with the training your uncle mentioned? What then?"

"Don't talk to me about my uncle."

"I am just trying to help you, Andrew."

"Likely so you'll feel no guilt when you abandon me."

"Andrew! Why would you say such a thing?"

"I see where this is all headed. I am putting you and Ashna in danger, I see that now. Better if I just disappeared, right?"

"That is not what I am trying to tell you! You know that!"

"I don't see how it's different."

"You don't see any difference in avoiding bears and wearing raw meat for a dress in the forest?"

"Stuff your stupid analogies. I'm going upstairs. Tell his majesty the performance has left my stomach feeling queer, should he ask after me." Andrew turned to open the door. Yonston stopped him with a hand on his arm.

"Andrew. Since you have lived here with us I have come to think of you as my own nephew. Please know that I care for you, and Ashna does too. She would be devastated if you left us, okay? I know you're angry. Take some time for yourself; we'll be here for you. I'll let you know if we get that patronage." Yonston took his hand from Andrew's arm, who paused a moment then shoved the door open. Yonston let out another deep sigh. A jealous teenager with unpredictable temper and magic. Who did I offend to get such a child under my roof? Gods love him. Yonston turned and walked back to where the king was speaking with Ashna. He almost paused when he saw that the king had his arm on her shoulder, caressing it gently. Ashna's face was still flushed with excitement, but her stance was defensive, with her captive shoulder pulled far from the king.

"Your majesty, I must beg your indulgence. He is high spirited, and meant no offense with his behavior," said Yonston. The king smiled at him but did not let go of Ashna.

"Don't trouble yourself with apologies. We were all young once, even if it was a very long time ago. I would like to speak with your daughter for a while...alone, if you don't mind." Yonston hesitated.

"It wouldn't be proper without an escort…" said Yonston. The king looked at him levelly.

"As king, my behavior is always beyond reproach, you have my royal word," said the king. Yonston looked at Ashna. She was flushed and still seemed excited. She nodded her head slightly, eager for the chance. He thought about the large, powerful hand on her shoulder. Dread filled his stomach, but the weight of the king's gaze was upon him. Even the strongest oak bends before the storm.

"Of course, forgive me. Do take care of her," said Yonston. He forced a smile, but it did not reach his eyes. The king nodded graciously and indicated with a wave of his hand for Yonston to leave them. Yonston kept the painful smile, and turned to clean up the stage. The dread in his stomach weighed him down, as if he had eaten a meal of lead shot. He put the props and knives away from the show, and began sweeping the theater of the peanut shells and other trash left by the crowd. He chased not a few paper crabs around the theater. All the while his mind was separate of the task, and always on Ashna.

Ashna felt flattered and overwhelmed by the king's

attention. He was listening closely to her every word, asked her engaging questions, and showed genuine interest in what she had to say. They were walking through the back of the theater as Ashna gave him a tour, the king's personal guard a respectful distance behind them.

"Do you enjoy the lifestyle, here? Performing shows?" asked the king.

"I love it! It's all I've ever known, since I was young. Father takes such good care of me that I don't mind the work at all. I owe it to him."

"A woman as beautiful as you owes the world nothing, your grace and radiance is payment enough. Like the songs of birds, pleasing to the ears and offered freely for all to enjoy."

"You flatter me!"

"It is not undeserved, I feel. I came tonight to see your play when I heard about how the beautiful queen of ants drew men like bears to honey."

"You came to see me?"

"Yes, my lady. What I heard did you no justice. You are a thousand times more beautiful in the flesh."

"Your majesty, you honor me far more than I deserve."

"I would never do such a thing, for it would cheapen what I say."

"Words are free, majesty, but actions have weight and value," she said with a coy smile. The king boomed his huge laugh.

"I love it! She is beautiful and sly of tongue! What other talents do you possess? I have seen your skill with juggling, but I feel there is much more beneath the surface."

"I make a wonderful pot of tea."

"I hope you would so indulge me." Ashna led the king through their meager home, embarrassed at the cracked walls and dusty floors.

"I'm afraid it's a bit more common than perhaps you're used to, majesty."

"The décor is rich enough," said the king, looking at her. She didn't think it possible, but her flush deepened. She held the door for him into the meager kitchen and bowed her head as he swept past, ducking low to get under the frame. Their kitchen was a simple thing, with a small brown table with chairs for three, a little pot-bellied wood burning stove merry with fire, and a sink with faucet and knobs. The floor was stone, well worn with many years of feet and brushes. Pots and pans hung from a rack over the stove, and a few ratty cabinets were all they had for storage. The king walked over to the sink and turned a knob, letting cool clear water flow out. He grimaced and closed the tap.

"I suppose we should be thankful for running water, at least. Why do you use wood instead of gas?" said the king. Ashna's face stayed flushed, but her tone altered.

"Beg pardon, majesty, but the building is older and we...we don't make enough to pay for piping to be laid. The gas merchants want an outrageous fortune for pipes and product. We do not want for hot meals, and the stove heats the house nicely, we find." The king turned to her, his winning smile back on familiar ground.

"I apologize, of course. It is cozy, and makes a fine home, I do not doubt." The huge man was crouched in the little kitchen. Ashna felt her embarrassment growing each passing moment.

"Please have a seat, sire," said Ashna. She held her breath as he sat in one of the aging chairs, which creaked like a ship at full sail, but thankfully did not collapse. She put a kettle on to boil, and got out the tin of tea leaves they kept in the cupboard.

"How do you take your tea, majesty?"

"I am fond of a bit of milk and sugar," said the king,

adjusting his robes. Ashna looked at the guard captain, who had come into the room, swept it with his eyes, and then put his back against the wall near the door and said not a word. The king noticed her look.

"He will not need any tea; his mind is solely on keeping me safe."

"Oh. I assure you, majesty, you are safe with me," she said.

"I am sure that you could do me no harm, unless of course to steal my heart," said the king. Ashna turned from him and got out of the sugar. She could think of nothing to say until the kettle began singing, so she placed cups on the table with sieves and the leaves, and then poured the tea for them both. She added milk and sugar to the king's, watching him for the correct amount, and then added only a single scoop of sugar to her own. The kitchen was filled with the almost sweet smell of tea. They sipped it hot, and each felt the soothing warmth spread through their bodies. Ashna looked over the rim of her cup, watching the king obviously enjoying the tea she made. After they both had sipped some, the king set his cup on the table.

"You were right, a most enjoyable cup of tea. You will have to tell me where I can send someone to get the same leaves," said the king. Ashna cradled her steaming cup in her hands.

"We get them at the market, majesty. A stall run by a man named Ios. He has all the best teas! I think this one was a special blend he called 'Homestead', but there are so many and they are all so good that you couldn't go wrong with any of them," said Ashna. The king smiled and took another drink.

"Tell me about your life here, Ashna," said the king. Ashna waited for a moment, trying to gather her thoughts, and then she began to speak. She told him about her early life, before she lost her mother to an illness and moved in to the theater. Her father was a kind and gentle man, and though they were poor she did not lack for the things she needed. She spent some time learning in the schools of Aethero, which were more like daycares or crèches than other, more formal schools, but he found it difficult to maintain the house and earn money with their theater without her. Before Ashna was old enough to help, Yonston had done a juggling and comedy routine with mild success, but only with the lower classes of Aethero, such that he never made enough money or a big enough name to move up in the world. She talked about learning to juggle and to act, and how Andrew came into their lives. She shied away from telling the king about how she felt about Andrew, how they had become friends, learning to lean on each other in a way only those who have lost loved ones can. She didn't tell him they had become lovers, that they held each other in passion and fervor. Yet, she sensed that the king could see this in her, could see how she felt. And she did not like how he became even more attentive when she mentioned Andrew in the first place.

"Tell me more about him. Where does he come from? His accent is quite unlike anything I've ever heard," said the king, watching Ashna closely. Their teacups were set to the side, empty but for a few leaves that slipped the sieve. Ashna's heart began racing.

"Ah...um, he's from far away. I've never really understood where exactly...there are a lot of, um, rural towns and villages in Aethero, I'm sure you know, uh, and I think he's from one of those," she said, the attempted obfuscation ringing loud in her voice. The king leaned forward in his chair alarmingly close.

"Ashna, we both know that's not true. Where is he really from?" He pressed close to her, his eyes suddenly feral.

"He's...he's from another world. I don't know how he

came to Aethero, just that this is not where he was born," she said, voice small. The king leaned back, the smile back on his face.

"There! Was that so hard? I suspected as much, but I wasn't sure. I don't know why you would try to hide that from me, so many people come through here from other worlds it's not such a strange thing, is it?"

"No, uh, sire, I guess not. I'm sorry, I hope you'll forgive me!" she said.

"No apology needed, as long as you are as accommodating in the future."

"Of...of course, majesty," said Ashna.

"Now, where did Andrew learn those wonderful magic tricks? Is that something your father taught him?"

"No, sire. He came to us with that knowledge."

"Ah! So a natural, is he?"

"It would seem so, sire."

"And how did he perform those feats?" said the king, looking right into her eyes. He leaned forward. Ashna gulped and tried to think.

"I...I admit that I don't know, sire. He is very secretive about his trade," said Ashna, looking down. The King put his hand under her chin and forced her to look at him.

"We both know that's not true, Ashna. Will you lie to me twice in one night?" He held her face firmly. Ashna's eyes began to water.

"N...no, sire, it's just that—"

"Just what?"

"J-just that...that he's afraid and alone, and he's had to protect himself for so long. I can't tell his secrets, I just can't..."

"You will tell me," said the king. Menace was thick in his voice, like smoke on the wind.

"He's...he's..."

"What! Spit it out!" He took his hand off her chin and

put his hands on her shoulders, shaking her.

"He's a wizard," she whispered.

"A wizard? He knows how to do magic?"

"Yes." Ashna started to sob. The King pulled her gently to him and hugged her, the tension in the air seemingly gone.

"There, there, now. Don't cry! That's a wonderful thing! He's the most special man in the world right now!"

"You're...you're not mad at me?" said Ashna, relief flooding her voice.

"Of course not. I had heard there was a wizard wandering Aethero, and I've spent many years trying to track him down. He was always moving around so much! I'm glad I've finally found him," said the King. He continued to hold Ashna, and began stroking her hair.

"Why have you been looking for him?" said Ashna.

"Why? To hire him! A real wizard in my court would make me the toast of all gods. Especially here! How does he do it?"

"I don't know sire, I've only seen a little magic in all the years he's been here. He's very secretive, you must not tell him I told you!" said Ashna. She pushed away from the King's embrace and looked up at him, her eyes wide. "If he knew I told you he'd be very angry at me. I can't believe I told his secret, but...but maybe he'll be happy to be a court wizard! He would finally be able to perform his magic in public for all the world to see," said Ashna.

"Not just the world, dear girl, my court! All the most famous and rich of all people, all gods, all beings in the whole of the world will come to see such a thing! It's just that..." He trailed off, and for the first time since meeting him, Ashna thought the king seemed shy, even sad.

"What is it?" she asked.

"I am without a wife, and it would mean a lot to me if...I could find someone who would add the touch of a lady to the castle, the laughter of a woman, perhaps even a child," said the King. He looked at her with soft eyes, eyes that had been as steel just moments ago.

"A...a child? With me, majesty?"

"In time, but first I would just want to invite you to court, let you get a feel for living in the castle."

"What about Yonston and Andrew?"

"They could come too, of course. Yonston could be put in charge of my players and Andrew would come on as my court wizard," said the king.

"I don't know if they would want to go. Yonston loves doing shows here, and I can't speak for Andrew...and...there is something...between us...."

"You love Andrew?"

"I do, majesty. I am so sorry, I do love him, so much, I just...."

"I understand, Ashna, I do. It seems like he is the only one in the world for you, the only person you could possibly be happy with from now to forever. Just give me a chance, let me win you," said the King, his hand reaching out and taking hers.

"I don't know...."

"Only come to the castle, and let me show you what it would be like," he said.

"May I talk to my uncle and Andrew about it?" she asked, after a long silence. The king took his hand from hers.

"I am offering to take you away from all of this. Away from a life as a show monkey and living day to day scrabbling in the dirt, trying to feed yourselves! You live in the dirt in rags and perform for hours for yowling dogs who do not even understand the grace of your performance! You would *discuss* this? There is nothing to discuss! I have made you an offer, and whether or not you take it is your decision. I have room for a boy and an old man, yes, but I am making you the offer, not them.

The choice is yours," said the king.

"Sire, please don't be angry with me! I am just inexperienced and scared and young, please, please don't be mad at me," said Ashna, leaning forward to take the king's hand back. "Let me go to my room and pack, I will go with you," she said, her heart sinking. Andrew won't have to run anymore, and we'll all be fed, and maybe even happy, one day.

"Do not go upstairs for rags, girl, just come with me."

"Oh, but what about Andrew and my father?"

"My carriage does not have room for them, and I would like to have you all to myself for the ride back. I will send it right back to get them and to share the joyous news," said the king. He stood and helped her stand as well, so small a woman next to him. He smiled wide, seeming to light the room with the sun's own rays.

"This will be wonderful! You will not regret it, Ashna!" he gave her a hug and leaned down for a kiss. Ashna hesitated, then leaned on her toes to give him a quick peck on the cheek. He frowned but seemed to be contented, and led her through the kitchen door.

"Can we leave the house on this side, or do we need to go through the theater?" said the king.

"There is a door in the back that faces the street, sire," said Ashna. He nodded and grabbed his guard captain's arm, pulling him close.

"Have my carriage brought around back," he said. He turned to Ashna.

"Dear one, pray go wait outside for the carriage and your new life. I am going to make arrangements with my captain," said the king. Ashna bit her lip, but nodded, curtseyed, and hurried to the front. *I hope they will forgive me,* she thought. The king watched her disappear down a hallway and the door open and shut.

"Kill her father, take the wizard captive. Instruct your men to be careful! I do not want him damaged," said the king.

"It will be done," said the captain. The king turned and followed Ashna's path out front. The guard captain hurried through the back of the house, through the theatre, and told the carriage driver to pull around to the other side. They had brought four other guards with them, left outside to watch the carriage. He motioned them over.

"The king has instructed me to kill the old man inside and to bring the boy, the magician with us. He is not to be harmed!" said the captain, looking each man in the eye.

"But he knows magic!" protested one. The captain turned to look at him. "I heard the people talking about it as they came out, said he summoned a great giant bird that swooped over them." The captain shook his head.

"It's all tricks, you stupid shit, tricks and lights! You think people can do magic, eh? Think he'll grow horns and give ya a gorin'? Eh?" He mocked the guard into submission.

"In and out real quick, and the king promised us a good reward, okay men?" They nodded and hefted their pikes, but the captain shook his head.

"Those'll be no good inside, leave them out here. Cudgels and daggers work for tonight's business," said the captain. They stacked their pikes outside and crept into the house. They found Yonston at the foot of the stairs, just outside the sitting room where he had taken tea with Maeryl years ago. He started when he saw the soldiers, but recognized the captain at their head.

"Captain! Forgive me, but the king and my daughter seem to have gone, do you know where? I wish she had said something before she left," he said. The guards prowled towards him. Yonston took a step back, his face creased with worry.

"Have they gone for a stroll? I don't mind, I just—" He was cut short when the guard captain stepped forward and stabbed him in the gut, the knife flashing in the yellow lamp light. Yonston looked at the blood pouring from his wound, and tasted the hot copper coming up in his mouth in great heaves. He fell to his hands and knees, vomiting crimson, the world getting cold and wavy. Colors began to fade.

"Where...Ashna..." he muttered through the blood. The guards fell on him, knives and clubs rising and falling. The work was messy but quick, for he was an old man. The captain wiped his blade on an unstained portion of Yonston's dressing gown.

"Now for the boy," said the captain. He looked up to the top of the stairs, and Andrew was standing there, his mouth open, his eyes wide and white.

"Come with us, there's no need for more hurting tonight," said the captain, holding the knife close. Andrew couldn't take his eyes off of Yonston's body, blood spreading in a thick pool around his old gray hair. Tears welled up in his eyes, and vengeance in his heart.

"The hurting for tonight has just begun," said Andrew, his voice low. He turned and punched the wall beside him, the thin brittle wood splintering. At the foot of the stairs, the wall burst out in an explosion of splinters, showering the guards in razor sharp wooden spikes. One man screamed: a foot long splinter had gone through both temples, blinding him. He fell to the floor, writhing and screaming. The other guards cursed and swore, splinters stood out from exposed skin and between joints in their leather armor. The guard captain yelled and ran up the steps, his knife before him. Two guards managed to get up the steps behind him. Andrew knelt and grabbed the shabby rug that went up the center of the steps and spoke a word. The rug snatched itself up the steps, pulling out from the two guards near the bottom and knocking the guard captain off his feet. The rug crashed into Andrew, knocking him back. His head made a hollow cracking sound against the wall. The guard captain was able to gain his balance first, pulling himself up with the stair rails and leaping the last few steps. Andrew lay on the floor dazed, water in his eyes.

"You... you killed him...bastards..," said Andrew. The guard captain lifted his foot and tried to stomp Andrew's face, but Andrew regained himself well enough to catch the boot with his hands and shove up against the captain's attack. Unbalanced, the man fell back down the stairs and into the guards who were now recovering from being showered with deadly splinters. The man with the jagged piece of wood in his head had passed out, blood oozing around the shard. The captain cried out with pain when he tried to stand and fell back to the floor, his leg twisted under him terribly. The few men remaining looked up at Andrew, who now held living flames in his arms from one of the gas lamps on the wall.

"Get out," he said. He began to descend the stairs, taking them slowly, the flames wild and high above his head, licking at the ceiling and walls. Black soot smeared across everything, and thick smoke billowed around Andrew like a dark cloak. Two men grabbed the captain under his arms and drug him out as fast as they could. He screamed, each hasty step and tug jerking his leg. The other men were close behind, in a near panic. They abandoned the man on the floor as they fled. When Andrew sensed they were all out of the house, he let go of the fire, which roared over his head and disappeared in sudden silence. He knelt and touched Yonston's face, but he knew that the man was dead. Tears poured down his face, making streaks in the soot on his cheeks. Andrew turned to the man on the floor, blood flowing sluggishly now, mingled with Yonston's on the floor. Andrew looked at the pooled blood. One of the men had dropped a dagger in their haste, and Andrew took it up in his hands. He wrapped both hands around the hilt and held the blade high over his head, but he hesitated. A moan escaped from the lips of the dying guard. Crying out, Andrew threw the dagger away and put his hands on the man's face.

He concentrated, still crying, and slid his left hand into the blood on the floor. He took a deep breath, and the jagged splinter began sliding out of the man's head. The guard screamed but Andrew's right hand held him down as the splinter clattered to the floor. The wound closed up, knitting together, but was red and angry. The scar would be huge and puckered. The guard struggled to breathe, so Andrew pulled him up so he could sit with his back against a wall. The man coughed, and turned his head to and fro. He spoke hoarsely.

"What happened?"

"You killed a man who was more important to me than any in the world, and took my love away from me, is what happened," said Andrew. The man stiffened and tried to scuttle away from Andrew, but he didn't have the strength.

"You blinded me, you bastard!" he coughed and heaved.

"I did. I could have left you to die, too, but I didn't. You'll live because of me. *Because of me*," said Andrew.

"I'll never see my wife again," said the guard. "My children." Andrew knelt next to Yonston and closed the still-open eyes.

"Neither will he, but you may at least hear them, may yet feel their arms around you. You will eat dinner with them, and kiss your wife, and tell your children stories. Yonston is beyond the vale, and the only things he will hear are the shrieks of the dead," said Andrew. He picked the limp body up and walked out of the house, seeking a place to bury another loved one. He spared what thoughts he could for Ashna, for now Andrew was alone again, but he knew he could not go to the castle. The only thing left for him was to bury the dead, and to run so that the living may stay so.

*****

"How *dare* you show yourself to me without completing what I sent you to do!" roared the king. His guard captain, wrapped in bandages and on a crutch, could not raise his head.

"He used his magic against us, sire. It would not matter if you had sent a hundred men."

"I don't want your excuses, I want the only person capable of doing magic in the whole world in my court! Following my commands! How will I do that with him on the run? How will I do that with such an incompetent fool for my guard captain?" The king picked up a lamp and hurled it against a wall, shattering the delicate crystal, denting the precious metal. The captain flinched and kept his mouth shut.

"The king of Earth has a creature he calls a *dyed-no-sir*! It's at least as tall as this palace and knows tricks! Have you ever seen a forty-ton beast *sit*? What do I have? Guards who can't capture a child."

The king opened his mouth to continue, but a demure knock, really just tapping, at the door cut him short.

"What!" he bellowed. The door creaked open and Ashna stuck her head around.

"May I come in, majesty?"

"Of course, of course. We were just discussing the captain's duties, and how he goes about them," said the king, all smiles. Ashna walked into the room, stepping slowly, her eyes skipping over the shattered lamp and the sweat on the captain's forehead.

"I was wondering if you've told my father and Andrew to come to the palace yet?"

The king and the captain exchanged a look. The

king's face turned soft, mournful. Ashna's blood turned to ice.

"What is it? What happened?"

"Your father is dead. Andrew killed him," said the king, with a significant look at his captain. Tears welled up in Ashna's eyes. Her hands went to her face, covering her mouth. She sank into a chair.

"H…how? Why?" she whispered. Her pain, so palpable, could make rocks bleed.

"The king sent us to…escort your father and Andrew to the palace. Andrew, ah, asked us what happened to you before. I told him you went with the king, but he mistook my meaning. He flew into a rage, lashing out at us with his magic. He injured me and my men, killing one of them I think. We didn't have a chance to explain, so great were his anger and jealousy."

"Jealous? Of what?"

"We didn't exactly have a conversation, if you'll pardon me. What I could hear, he said something about leaving him for the king." Ashna sobbed into her hands.

"And my father? Why did he kill my father?"

"Your father died trying to intervene. He was a brave man, but Andrew was so out of control he struck out against him. I'm very sorry," said the guard captain. His face was a mixture of pity and self-loathing.

"I wish he was dead! Why did he have to take my father? Why?" Ashna sobbed, her whole body shaking with each heaving gasp. The king strode over and sat next to Ashna.

"Let it out, my doll. It's good to cry. We'll find him, and I promise you, we'll bring Andrew to justice. He cannot escape my grasp," said the king. "I'll do it for you. I swear it." Ashna looked up from her hands, her face read and puffy.

"When you find him, I want to talk to him first. I want to be there, so I can see it," said Ashna. Her voice was coarse and fierce.

"Then you shall, my dear, you shall," said the king. He motioned the guard captain over, and whispered in her ear.

"Find him. When you do, watch him and send a runner. We'll want to be there. And if you fail, I will find a new guard captain," said the king. The captain nodded and made an awkward bow on his crutch. He turned and hobbled away. The king focused his attention on Ashna, stroking her hair as she cried and making soothing sounds. Meanwhile, the gears of his mind turned and turned. After her sniffles died down, the king spoke.

"Ashna, this is very important. I know you're upset, but I need to know something,"

"W…what?"

"Does Andrew have any weaknesses? Anything we can use to help get him under control? We don't want to hurt him, we just want to stop him before anyone else gets hurt or killed," said the king, his voice soothing, calm. Ashna buried her face in his robe, and then brought her mouth up to his ear. She whispered, and the king smiled.

*****

One Year Later

Andrew huddled next to his little fire. The winter was freezing cold, and his whiskers, the fine whiskers of a young man, were frosted with ice. The wind kicked up and knifed through his meager garments, chilling him further. His breath coiled in front of him and ghosted away on the bitter breeze. His hands shook as he bit into the barely cooked meat from his fire. His desperate attempt at trapping had finally paid out this morning in the form of a skinny rabbit. Until today, he'd eaten roots dug and chiseled from the frozen ground. He was too weak to use magic, except to spark the fire that barely warmed him now. The meat, pink, stringy, and scorched, was the finest meal he'd ever eaten.

A snap of branches brought his head up with feral quickness. He eyed the darkness menacing the clearing in front of his cave. His face was sunken, hollow. His hands looked like the naked branches of the trees around him. With a last glance around, he went back to gnawing on the rabbit bone. It snapped in his mouth, and he sucked at the hot marrow eagerly. The wind blew, the fire cracked, and Andrew shivered. There was movement in the trees, just outside the ring of flickering yellow light. Andrew looked up again. Snow slumped from the branches of a pine tree. Just as he was about to work at the bone again, the shadows moved.

"Who is it?" he demanded. His voice was weak. It struggled against the cold and darkness. The snow muffled him, creating a muffled silence. Branches at the edge of the clearing moved aside, and a figure dressed in a thick white fur cloak appeared. Andrew's heart raced. *They've found me. They've finally come for me*, he thought. He and the figure watched each other for a long time, the only sounds coming from the fire and the winds.

"Well?" said Andrew. "What do you want? I have nothing. I know no one," he said.

"You know someone," said the figure. The voice was familiar, feminine.

"Ashna?" said Andrew. His heart, already racing, kicked up another gear.

"You never came to see me in the castle. Why did you abandon me?"

"I never meant…the guards attacked me…"

"You killed my father?"

"What? I would never kill any-" Andrew was cut off as an arrow came out of the darkness and slammed into his thigh. Blinding light flashed in his head, along with an explosion that left his ears ringing. Andrew screamed and fell to the ground, his muscles so tense that his tendons and muscles pressed out against his skin, threatening to tear through. Andrew's leg seized violently, jerking and shaking. From out of the trees came the guard captain, a vicious grin on his face.

"How do you like being at my mercy, wizard?" he gloated. He walked past Ashna and knelt next to Andrew. His skin was bright red, and he was sweating profusely, even in the frigid cold. The guard captain grabbed the arrow and jerked it with sadistic pleasure, twisting the metal inside Andrew's thigh. Andrew screamed out in pain, a convulsion rocking his body. Ashna felt her stomach turn over, her powerful resolve melting as she watched Andrew kick and shriek in pain as the guard captain worked the arrow in the thin flesh of Andrew's body. She ran over, grabbing the captain by the shoulders.

"Hey, stop, that's not what we talked about!" she shouted and pulled at the large man. Andrew came out of his haze long enough to see the captain elbow Ashna and knock her to the ground.

"He blinded one of my men and killed your father, what do you care?" he snapped. Andrew saw the rabbit bones on the ground, pale and oozing blood from the cracks, and reached out for it. The captain turned to him as Andrew seized the bone and forced a word out through gritted jaw. Andrew used a thumb to press on the bone, which started to bend like a thin pipe. The captain began screaming as his neck bent over, his bones brutally popping. He sank to the ground, his head canted at a near impossible angle. The sound of his bones grinding and popping grew louder as Andrew pressed the bone harder. The captain choked and wheezed, his eyes squeezed shut as he struggled against the inexorable magic pressing his bones together. He made a desperate lunge at Andrew, grabbing the arrow and driving it further into Andrew's thigh. He screamed and seized up, the bone snapping in his hand. The captain gave one last choke as his head bent past his shoulder and his neck shattered. A purple spot appeared on his neck, and slowly spread like a pot of dropped ink. Andrew vomited, his partially cooked rabbit steaming on the scattered snow. The king appeared at the edge of the clearing, guards at his side. He surveyed the scene, then walked forward to kneel next to the guard captain. Blood was welling out of the dead man's mouth now. The king snorted.

"Serves him right for underestimating the boy, and for his constant failure." He turned to Ashna, helped her up out of the snow.

"And to you, a special thanks for leading us to him. How did you manage it?" Ashna turned from him, pulling her cloak tight about her.

"A little instinct, a little…something. I could feel him, at times, and I followed it," said Ashna. The king seemed satisfied with that.

"I think you've shown yourself to be much more capable than this idiot. How would you feel about being my new guard captain? It would give you something to do around the castle," said the King. He motioned to his men, who wrapped iron chains around Andrew's throat and tied his hands. The king watched them leave.

"Now I have everything I want," said the king. He turned to Ashna. "Thanks to you." Ashna nodded her head.

"I am happy to help, majesty," she said. She felt the king's gaze lingering.

"Yet, there is something more I desire. Something I've wanted since you came to my castle," he said.

"What?"

"You. I've waited all this time, these many long

months, until I knew we had Andrew. Now that I have what I want, and you got what you want, it's time for payment," he said.

"What do you mean?"

"Strip off your cloak. I am more than enough to keep you warm," said the king. Ashna tried to run, but her long cloak tripped her up, and the king was on her in a moment. His skin was blazing hot to the touch. She squirmed and struggled against him, but he was so much stronger than her. Ashna screamed, but the woods were frozen, and all the men and creatures who might have heard her were holed up against the cold. Afterwards, the king hauled her to her feet, and set her cloak about her gently.

"You will stay in the castle, but you must earn your keep. At least until you birth my heir, you will be my guard captain. So that you are close to me at all times," he said. Ashna, her face pale and her hair wild and mussed, said nothing, just stared into the fire.

"So my fortunes rise, as will yours, Ashna. I think this is the beginning of something good,"

Chapter 11
Duel

THE GUARDS HESITATED. They looked at one another and at the still, deadly form of Ashna. She spoke:

"You all know me. You know what I am capable of. I trained each and every one of you. I know your strengths, and I know your weaknesses. Think about what you're doing, trying to do. This is my son. You know how the King treats him. Let us go, and I won't have to hurt any of you."

The guards murmured, several raising their weapons.

"Idiots!" Maeryl was in a full rage. "Kill them and take the prince."

"No!" One man cried out and threw down his weapon. "I will not betray the prince or Ashna. This is not right. Maybe it's time for the King to step down."

"Yomishi is right, men. The King has let this winter go on too long. He is cruel, and hard on everyone around him. It's time for him to retire, to move on." Ashna wove a spell on them. More men threw down their weapons.

"I fight for Ashna, not for you, stranger." Maeryl watched the men abandon their weapons and face him with defiance. He shrugged, took out a knife, and swung out of the horse's saddle.

"Witness the power of magic unfettered, then." Maeryl gripped the knife hard, took a step forward, and then turned and plunged it one guard's chest. The man coughed and crimson blood poured from his mouth. The other men yelled and tried to draw their swords, but he spoke a powerful word and moved like the wind, slashing, stabbing, cutting. Fans of dark blood spewed into the air as arteries and veins were severed. Blood poured into the street and ran in rivulets in the gutters, mingling with filth and dirt. All the while Maeryl laughed, the sound high and insane, the very sound of a man lost in slaughter. The men screamed, the men ran, and the men died. It was over before anyone could really react, and soon they lay on the ground, a mangled heap of gore and flowing blood that steamed in the wintery air.

Where Andrew's heart used to be, there was a howling void, an emptiness that roared and wailed and screamed at the sanguine wizard. Something inside him died with the men who were so casually murdered with the aid of magic. Maeryl spent no effort, had snubbed them out like a candle. He was covered from head to toe in blood. Andrew reeled with revulsion and horror, and that great shrieking maw inside him that refused to believe what he had just seen.

"But…you said…never…"

"Child, fools put limits on themselves. The powerful put limits on others. You never learned blood magic, did you? What you just saw was a prelude. Behold!" At the word "behold" his voice stretched, filling the world with its sound and power. Maeryl shook the skies and heavens with the power of his words, and even Anastasia's Tower shuddered and rocked under the blast. Andrew and Ashna had to cover their ears, and the force of it drove them to their knees. After a moment the roaring passed, and they were able to look up.

Maeryl stood at the center of a writhing mass of offal. Blood and sinew and gore flowed up and around him, as the wax had flowed and turned into the golem Andrew created. They could hear Maeryl speaking words of power and shaping the gory mass around him, and as he spoke and spun his spell he rose into the air. The mass of bones and blood writhed around him and wrapped up his limbs, turning them into monstrous muscled arms and legs, with great boney claws punching through the stretching skin. The flow of the mess moved up his body, bulging out his chest so that it was deep and long. He grew taller, and a pair of great wings, like a bat's, stretched out behind him. His neck snapped and ground as it grew longer, and his face came forward as bloody horns burst from the back of his head. The words of his spell were almost understandable until the end, where his jaw grew with his face and his teeth popped out and were replaced with jagged daggers of bone.

All told, he now stood at least fourteen feet tall, not including tail, and with the added mass of the dead guards and the magical extension of the material, weighed close to a ton. The beast stood over them, stretching its wings and arms as they finished growing out, the bone claws and spurs gleaming with wet blood and gore. The thing's skin was dark and angry red, mottled with black splotches of dead blood. It was perversely covered in bits of skins and hair. It stank like an unkept slaughterhouse, and everyone who ever laid eyes on it shared nightmares for the rest of their lives. It shook itself, showering them with blood. Andrew whipped over and vomited, sick in heart and stomach alike. Salim screamed and clutched Ashna tight.

The beast roared at them, showering them with leftover chunks of flesh and surrounding them with the stench of Hell's own butchery. Andrew couldn't stop vomiting, dry heaving and breathing in high-pitched gasps. The roaring void in his stomach consumed him, drowning out even the will to survive. The monster made a move towards them, lunging with a powerful thrust of its legs and a terrific flapping of wings.

"Move, Andrew!" screamed Ashna as she shoved him aside. The outstretched claws of the beast clipped Andrew's shoulder, rending the flesh open and spilling blood on the ground. Maeryl roared past them and slammed into the base of Anastasia's Tower. White stone exploded around them as the great beast shattered through, leaving a gaping hole. Ashna pushed Andrew as the stone rained down on them, sweeping Salim into her arms along the way. A blinding cloud of white dust settled around them. The tower groaned under the assault. Maeryl swung his head about, seeking out his prey. His blood-red nostrils expanded and twitched as he tested the air. Baleful eyes sought them, and he began to stalk around the base of the tower.

Ashna was the first up, coughing and hacking up white spit. Her eyes were red with irritating dust. She was about to shout for Andrew, but felt the great thuds of the monster's steps, could hear it snuffling the air for them. She put a hand over Salim's mouth, crouched, and felt through the cloud of dust, stepping carefully through the rubble.

"Andrew," she whispered. She crawled through the broken stones, the white dust swirling around her, calling for Andrew. She stopped when the ground shuddering beneath her got stronger. The monster was approaching her, each footstep making her heart skip a beat. Suddenly, one leg impacted behind her. She sank to the ground, trying to hide amongst the broken stones. She clutched Salim tight to her chest, the little boy sobbing and desperate to keep it in. The beast paused and whuffed at the air. Ashna's heart stopped. While Maeryl searched around her, her hand brushed against something warm. She almost screamed, thinking it was one of the monster's feet, but she felt a hand instead grip her fingers. As the dust swirled around her, she saw Andrew, and relief flooded her heart. One of his legs was trapped under a rock, and a dark streak flowed from his torn shoulder. The tower groaned again, and a creeping shadow started to loom over them. The moon rose in the sky, though dusk was just coming on. A great crack shattered the eerie silence that fell when the dust set around them. The tower groaned again, and the sound of grinding stone rose from hesitant cracks to a full-on roar.

Anastasia's Tower was falling. The shadow grew over them.

Ashna got her hands under the rock as Andrew struggled to pull himself out from under its weight. The sound of their struggles drew the attention of the beast, and it spread its wings and roared again as it moved closer. The tower tipped towards them and cast them all under its shadow in the fading light. Andrew stopped struggling against the rock and instead put his hands against it, searching for a spell in his mind that would help them. The tower was falling in earnest now as it tore itself apart. Stone again showered around them. Maeryl leapt with a pump of his wings so he could descend upon them. Andrew's mind sparked, and he spoke a word to the brick on his leg. As the tower fell it drew the stone and all the stones that fell back into it, slowing its fall. Andrew directed his will against the fallen bricks and stones around him, and all the dust swirled up and threw itself against the beast that dropped towards them. Maeryl grunted as the stone on Andrew's leg flew up into his stomach, and screamed as it pulled him towards the tower.

The air rushed out of the beast's mouth as it was crushed against the tower itself, and rocks and stones flew up towards it to form a growing mound. Maeryl struggled against the stones as the tower continued to fall. Ashna helped pull Andrew away from the falling tower with Salim in tow, and the monster screamed one last time as the tower roared to the ground. The impact and blast of air knocked them down and the wind rushed around them like a tornado for an impossibly long time. The roar and impact of the tower hitting the ground could be heard for miles around. The falling tower threw even more white dust and debris into the air, and it was a long time before they could see. Ashna helped Andrew to his feet, and they looked at the rubble. Ashna tore some fabric from the bottom of her dress and tried to bind Andrew's shoulder up. The cuts were long but not very deep. Though the bleeding was slowing Andrew was still pale, and Ashna helped hold him up as they looked at the devastation. Salim was silent, wide-eyed, and pressed tight to her side.

Anastasia's Tower was over a mile tall, and it had cut a path through the heart of Aethero. Sirens called and klaxons banged all over the city as people rushed to help the trapped. Andrew could see smoke rising in some places where the tower had upset cooking fires and forges. Andrew's shoulder pained him, and his leg was strained as well. It would be a long while before he would walk normally.

"Is he dead?" said Salim.

"I think so. At the same time, I wish not. It is not my place to kill with magic. He was a monster. I don't know who that man was, but he was not really my uncle. Something changed him."

"Then perhaps this is for the best, before his evil could spread," said Ashna.

"I hope so."

"What do we do now?" said Ashna.

"I've got to help the people who were hurt by this. It's my fault."

"You're in no shape to go about trying to help, Andrew!"

"How could I not? I caused all this."

"I scarcely see how this is your fault, Andrew."

"I want to go home!" Salim was crying.

"It doesn't matter. People are hurt because of me, because of magic. I can do a lot to help them."

"Andrew-"

"I can't-"

"Go home!"

The tower groaned again. They fell silent.

"Is it about to roll?" said Ashna.

The tower was broken in huge chunks, each taller than the houses around it. The piece closest to them rocked. As they watched it, the stone seemed to bend out as a sheet would with someone pressing on it from the other side. At first it was indistinct, but then as the force from the other side increased they could see it was the shape of the beast's head pressing through. The stone tore with a sound like ripping cloth, and the head burst out of the jagged chunks in mockery of birth. It tore at the ripping stone and roared at them. Andrew's leg ceased to bother him as Ashna grabbed him by his good arm and turned him around. She knelt and hauled Salim onto her back, his legs tucked under her shoulders, his arms around her neck.

"Run!" she said. They took off, Andrew hobbling as well as he could as Ashna tried to support and push him along. The tower gave another loud tearing sound, like the sky ripping open, and they heard the *whoosh* as the creature gathered the wind in its wings and sprang aloft. They were amongst a crowd of people who had gathered to help the survivors of the tower collapsing and had heard the fighting. Now that the beast roared over them in the sky, the crowd panicked and ran as well. Ashna had to fight to both keep Andrew upright and to prevent the crowd from overrunning them. She pushed to the edge of the mob, underneath the shadow of a building. They tried to catch their breath as the crowd surged past, and then the street was clear in a flash. The beast roared overhead and circled, looking for them. Ashna pulled Andrew into an alley and led the way, her arm underneath Andrew's.

"Where do we run from something like that? How can I possibly fight someone so powerful? All I know is parlor tricks and smoke," said Andrew between gasps.

"We're going to the castle. We may both hate the king, but I think he should be powerful enough to stop

Maeryl. If nothing else, the castle is sturdy and if we can get into the dungeons Maeryl will be too big to follow in his present shape."

"Unless he decides to tear his way through as he did just now," said Andrew. His face was pale, tight, and grim. Salim was breathing hard and fast, his breath a hot wind in Ashna's ear.

"We'll stomp that anthill when we get there," said Ashna. The sound of pumping wings hurried them along as Ashna rushed them through the twists and turns of the alleys. They came to one that opened on a wide plaza. They huddled in the shadows and watched as people screamed and scattered as the beast wheeled in the sky. Ashna pointed to an alley that opened up next to two merchant stalls.

"That's the next leg," said Ashna.

"We'll be awfully exposed," said Andrew

"I know, but it's the only way unless we want to take a route that's twice as dangerous. It's be exposed for thirty seconds, or be exposed the rest of the way," said Ashna. "The only other way is down a main road." Andrew looked up as the shadow of the monster fell over them. It was swooping low, and this time it grabbed a pair of people on the run. It hovered over the plaza as it held them close to its face. When it realized they were not Ashna and Andrew, it roared again and ripped the unfortunates apart. Andrew grew even paler.

"Salim, close your eyes." The child pressed his face into her neck.

"People are dying because of us," said Andrew.

"It's not our fault, Andrew. You're not controlling that monster," she said.

"But if I let him kill me maybe it will end."

"You don't know that. He hasn't shown restraint so far. Does that look like someone who will stop killing?" Ashna pointed at the monster, which was screaming with frustration and swooping down on more victims.

"I—"

"No, shut up. You're not leaving me alone. I need you, and Salim needs you, and the people of Aethero need you, dammit. You're the only wizard we've got."

"This land is full of gods and heroes, what am I supposed to do?"

"Be one or the other and help me stop him, Andrew."

"He knows so much more magic than me."

"You knew enough to stop him in the hallway, remember?" Andrew turned from her to watch the monster flying and wheeling about. Andrew thought for a few moments. Ashna put her hand against his face and pulled him to her.

"I know you can do it, Andrew. I know you can." She kissed him deeply. "I love you." Andrew looked into her eyes. He looked at the little boy clinging to her back. He turned back to the plaza, thought for a moment, and then turned back to her.

"I think I've got something."

"Will it work?"

"Only one way to find out, but stick close to me."

"Go!" They ran out from their cover and made for the alley. The sudden movement in the now empty plaza drew a shriek from the monster, which dove at them. Andrew stopped limping and drew in a great breath, grabbing at the air with both hands, drawing in more and more until it seemed it impossible that he could heave again, but he did. The monster was twenty feet away and diving fast. Fifteen feet. Ten feet. Five feet. Andrew could see every detail of the monster, the throbbing veins crisscrossing its skin, the sinews in the outstretched claws, the clots of blood and flesh that stuck all around it. When a second more would have meant his death, Andrew blew out the great breath he took. As the world had shaken when Maeryl had spoken a word of power, it shook and shrieked now as Andrew unleashed one of his own. The breath came out of him like a hurricane, blasting a huge cloud of dust and throwing the monster back as it tore at the thing's wings. It tried to fight the howling winds, and with a sickening tearing and cracking one wing broke and was blown away. Blood spewed out of the stump on the monster's back and it roared with pain. The winds wailed and shrieked, even drowning out the monster's howls, and the wind battered it to the ground as though it weighed nothing. Andrew doubled over, pale and shaking. Ashna grabbed him in her arms and helped him along to the alley. The monster writhed on the ground and shrieked in pain again. Ashna pulled Andrew along the alley as he coughed and heaved.

"I need you to use your legs, Andrew!" said Ashna. Her own lungs burned and she gasped for breath, mouth wide and gulping. Salim's weight on her back was wearing her down. Sweat streamed down both their faces despite the chill air. Andrew struggled to gain a semblance of balance and move with her. Ashna saw his face, strained and white, and with no little despair helped him to the ground in the alley. The beast roared, reminding them he was not far behind.

"Get what rest you can, Andrew. I don't think we have long," said Ashna. Andrew lay on the ground, looking at some unknown thing in the distance, breathing hard and fast. Ashna clutched his hand in hers. The world grew quiet for a moment. The whirlwind had raged out of the plaza and was off somewhere else in the city. The strong winds blew around them, but otherwise all was still. Andrew's breathing slowed. Ashna squeezed his hand. The crunch of stone made her look up as Salim screamed.

Maeryl glared down at them from on top of the building that formed the alley. It was another older stone building, similar in material to Anastasia's Tower of white stone and brick. The stones crumbled under the beast's clawed feet. Blood, thick and black, oozed out of the stump of the torn wing. The head snapped down at them. Ashna rolled herself on top of Salim, pressing him as low to the ground as she could.

The snap of jagged teeth rang her ears. She pushed Andrew to one side, one arm across his chest. The beast's head was but a foot from her face, snarling and snapping. The stone roof crumbled beneath it with each lunge, and it would not be long before it could reach them. Ashna screamed as the monster lunged at them again, raining dust and small broken stone around them. Andrew's eyes cleared, but it took him a moment to take in their danger. When realization dawned, he splayed his hands behind him and said a spell. The beast suddenly plunged into the house, its body yanking its head back over the broken stones and smashing its jaw as it went down. It roared again in frustration and fury as the house collapsed. Ashna struggled to her feet and helped Andrew to stand. Without a word they fled the alley, Salim back on Ashna's back. The beast scrabbled up the side of the house, having to fight for each step as the stone sagged like taffy.

"How many tricks do you know?" said Ashna as they hurried along.

"Less every moment, more every day." The sound of the beast moving along the rooftops behind them renewed their energy. Maeryl tried to get ahead of them, but the missing wing threw off his balance and the rooftops were old and powdery. He would often step through the roof and down into the house itself, or even nearly fall through the ceiling again. He beat his remaining wing to help alleviate his great weight, but the other wing, now a stump, would try to beat too, causing him to roar in pain. Whenever he got a lead, he would try to wiggle into the alley or find a place where he could get down, but the houses in this part of Aethero were very old and were built close together over many hundreds of years, creating a warren where you could lose your own shadow with ease. Through sight and smell he kept their bearing, but could not get the edge he needed to finish them.

"There's the castle wall!" said Ashna. Andrew's leg made him limp more with each passing moment. He was certain he would fall and not be able to stand if they had to go much further.

"Can't wait to see the king. Never thought I'd say that," Andrew panted.

They were fast approaching the palace gates, which were a fair thirty yards from the mouth of the narrow alley they hurried down. The frantic scrabbling and roaring of the monster above them was ever-present in their ears, death riding on their shoulders, a blade at their throats.

"Go save your son, I'll try to stop him for as long as I can," gasped Andrew. They broke from the cover of the alley. Maeryl leapt down from the rooftops and surged towards them like a breaking wave. Andrew pushed Ashna ahead of him and stumbled as he tried to turn around.

"Andrew!" she yelled, turning back for him.

"Just go!" He shooed her away even as he ran his hands over the cobblestones of the street. Maeryl bore down on him, but he was intercepted when stone spikes erupted from the ground. After the spikes thrust into the air, he collapsed on the cobblestones. The stone spines, while sharp, were brittle. Maeryl used his bulk to smash through them until he was only ten yards away from Andrew. Maeryl reared onto his back legs and prepared to fall upon Andrew like an eagle on a lamb, but as he began his descent a huge blast of fire checked him. It crashed into his chest, searing the skin, and knocked the beast back against the broken stone spikes. Maeryl roared a challenge, struggling back to his feet. The king stood in the open gates to the palace, soaring above even his natural height to tower over the beast. He was resplendent, radiant. Light shone from him as from a brightly lit crystal, each movement showering beams of light all around him. The sun rose in the sky, blood red turning to bright yellow, until the air itself warmed and the heat closed in on the cold. Ferocious winds whipped up all around the city, blowing down trees and sending dust and debris flying down alleys.

"You dare act this way in *my* city? This was not our agreement!" thundered the king, heat blasting from his mouth like winds from a desert. The air shimmered around the king as he got hotter and brighter. He turned so bright he was hard to look at, and then any mortals around had to shield their eyes lest the light blind them.

"I am the king of this world! I am the light, the sun, the warmth, and the brightest star. *You. Will. Not. Defy me!*" he roared.

Intense beams of light burst from the star that walked amongst them, from the center of the light so bright the dust on the ground was smoldering. Andrew struggled to breathe the air, hot as an oven. The air shimmered from the heat so much he could barely see what little wasn't washed out by the light coming from the king.

Maeryl roared in reply to the king and found his feet. The beast dug into the ground with sharp bone claws and charged at the shimmering light. The ground thundered beneath his feet, making stones dance. The titans crashed together, the sound of flesh searing against hot metal filling the air. Maeryl grappled with pure light, smoke rising from all over his body as he began to cook. The king, when the light broke long enough for him to be seen, set about the monster with his fists that roared like balls of pure fire. He hammered at the skull of the monster, leaving impressions burned in the red, blistering skin. Maeryl began to give ground as the furious assault of the king continued. He retreated from the burning onslaught, his roars of defiance toned with sharp notes of pain. The king herded the monster with his fury, unrelenting, unforgiving, affronted so totally that nothing short of Maery's death would cause him to cease.

When Salim saw his father, he broke away from Ashna.

"Salim! No!" The boy was heedless to Ashna's cries. He ran towards his father, the bright star, the fiery god that grappled with the monster. Ashna's legs went to jelly, watching her son run towards the brawling gods.

"No!"

"Salim? What are you doing? Get back!" The king turned towards him.

"Papa!" cried the boy. Maeryl flipped around with cunning speed and seized the boy in a smoking black claw.

"Release my son!"

Maeryl, skin burned black and cracked in most places, managed an evil smile.

"He is released," said Maeryl. He dug a claw into the boy's stomach, spilling intestines onto the ground. Salim shrieked once in pain and then fell silent as the beast ravaged his body. Blood spilled down the boney claws of the monster.

The king screamed with incoherent rage and bolted fast as light to save his son, but he was too late. Maeryl smeared the blood on his claws, spoke a word, and the king simply ceased. His light went out as if he had burned out, and he fell to the ground. Maeryl laughed, a throaty, coarse thing, and threw Salim's body towards the king. The little boy landed next to his father, their arms stretched out, hands nearly touching. The sun went from bright yellow to dark red and then faded from the sky. The hot air began to move again as the world grew cold.

Andrew's heart and hope died in him with the fading of the sun's light. He pushed himself to a standing position. The world was silent, already mourning the death of its ruler and young prince.

"Salim!" Ashna ran to her son, tears already flowing down her face. "No! Not my son, not my Salim. Why did you take him from me?" she screamed and bawled and held the broken child in her arms, blood smearing on her clothes. Andrew tried to limp to her but Maeryl slapped him down with the back of a ragged, blood-soaked claw. The beast spoke, its voice raspy and burned.

"I am nearly finished with my work. Andrew, if you will join me, help me find a new young body to inhabit, I will spare you and this woman. We will remake the world together, make it into another Earth, but even better. You can feel the magic in the air. With me in place of that pathetic sun king, the world will teem with magic. We will reap among them, and shape it to our will."

Ashna looked up from her broken child. "You are a monster. This world will not have you for its god. No world will, with the blood of innocents on your hands," said Ashna. She stood and drew her sword, her chest heaving, her long dark hair matted and blowing in the winds. She raised her blade and rushed the beast. Maeryl was caught off guard when she screamed in defiance as she rushed at him. He swept at her with one deadly claw, which she ducked, and then the other, which she dodged. She screamed again, her pain and rage and a thousand-thousand emotions rushing out of her, and plunged her sword into the cracking black hide of the monster. It screamed in pain and swiped at her again, struggling to get her off. Ashna ducked and dodged as well as she could, stabbing into the beast again and again. Black flesh crumbled into powder and flaked off, covering her in soot. Finally, Maeryl caught her in a claw and held her up to his face.

"What will you do now?" roared the angry beast. Ashna spit on the smoldering skin of its face. Maeryl slammed her to the ground, breaking her head open and spilling red across the cobblestones.

Andrew screamed. It had happened so fast he could not react at all in his weakened state, but now he hobbled and fell and crawled over to Ashna's corpse. In death, her face was peaceful. Andrew cried over her. He was alone with the monster.

With his uncle.

"Well," said the beast, blood trickling from more wounds than seemed possible. "Have you made a decision?"

Second Interlude
Seven Years Ago

ASHNA WALKED THE STREETS of Aethero in a deep, hooded cloak. The sounds of a thousand languages sang in her ears, the songs of a thousand cultures tempted her feet, and the faces of a thousand species passed her eyes. But none of these things held temptation for her. Tonight she was looking for one thing. A blind man. Will had asked his friend, and his friend was scared to speak of the night, but the blind man wouldn't be. He'd already lost everything. On the far side of Aethero, within sight of the Mirrorman's Palace, she found the house, just as described. It was small, with white plaster walls, and exposed wooden beams. The roof was made of red tiles. It was snug looking, and homey. She knocked on the door. A little girl answered. She had blonde hair that glowed in the firelight.

"Yes'm?"

"Hi there. I'm a friend of your father's. Is he home?"

"Yes. Papa! There's a stranger asking for you!"

"Who is it?"

"Who are you?"

"Tell him I'm a friend of Andrew."

"She says she's a friend of-"

"I heard the name! Get out of the door Leese!" The little girl disappeared back into the house, her glowing hair leaving a comet's tail of sparkles in her wake. Ashna waited at the door until a man, getting into his middle years, appeared. He had a cruel-looking scar on the side of his head, and his eyes were covered with a rag. He felt around the frame, stepped outside, and pulled the door shut behind him.

"What do you want?"

"I want to ask about the night my father died."

"The night that bastard blinded me, you mean?"

"Yes. The night you were blinded after attacking my family." The blind man bristled.

"Did you come here to gloat over my scars, girl?"

"I came to ask you the truth."

"The truth is in my face, girl. You see the scars."

"Yes, but I want the truth of it! Did Andrew kill my father?"

"The old man? No. That wizard shit attacked us, when he saw the body. We should have stabbed that bastard kid to death instead of that geezer." Ashna felt the world drop away below her. She'd been lied to all this time. She was responsible for Andrew's situation. She'd betrayed him. She sagged against the house.

"Are you happy now, girl? Can I go back to my family?"

"Yes, thank you." She took his hand and pressed a coin into it. He ran his fingers over it. He stuttered a thanks and slipped into the house, leaving Ashna in the street. She leaned against the wall, and started to sob. She whispered over and over while the tears poured down her face.

"Oh, Andrew, I'm so sorry. I'm so sorry."

Chapter 13
Whale Song

ANDREW STARED AT THE bright red that sprayed across the stones. *She was the last part of me,* he thought. Maeryl was panting, blood oozing from his many wounds. The monster looked rough. It was missing a wing, and most of its skin was blackened and cracked from its fight with the king. Pus and blood oozed from the crackling skin. Yet, Andrew could only see the way the fading light shone in Ashna's hair. How her face, covered in blood though it was, looked peaceful. Andrew looked up at the monster looming over him.

"I think we could mutually benefit, Andrew," said Maeryl. The voice was raspy, like a file on a rusty sword.

"How?" said Andrew.

"Think on it. We are the most powerful beings in this world. Not even their petty gods can stand up to us. I can tutor you, teach you secret magics that mortal man never dreamed were possible. Just because you won the war against us, you think we gave you all our secrets? Body-changing, flesh-shaping, blood magic, these were never yours. Look at what I've made myself. If I chose, I could use these bodies to heal myself, as though today never happened. I can take any form," rasped the beast. The effort of speaking was wearing on it. It lay down, hissing in pain as its skin cracked and flaked.

"Then why do you need me?"

"I must have a new body, a young one. A child. The soul in a child is not yet set, and I could take its place. Become a changeling."

"But why do you need me?"

"Truthfully, I don't. Anyone who I could convince to protect my infant form would do. But there is a connection between us. You come from the same world as me. We are the last two, Andrew. The last two wizards of Earth."

"You're not my uncle. You talked about the war as if you were on the elven side."

"That's true. I was. I am Oberon, the king of elves and god of magic."

"What about my uncle?"

"Maeryl? That fool. He gained an audience with me near the end of the war that ended magic on Earth. He whispered of another world, where magic was so thick in the air it could sustain us. Without magic on Earth, we would all die. With his help, we could live on."

"What about me?"

"You were the price. You were perhaps a bit old for a changeling, but I was not about to be picky. I was weak, injured. The fight with the machine god had left me close to oblivion. Then Maeryl came, and I inhabited him, and slept. You were our mutual price. You would survive the destruction of our world, and so would I. Together!"

"Maeryl sold me."

"You could look at it that way, but think, Andrew, what good would your death have served on Earth? This way we both could live."

"You would have replaced my soul, there would have been nothing left of me."

"Ah, well…that's not something I shared with your uncle, is it?"

"And now you think I'll join with you? Help you rape the soul of a child," he looked at the broken body of Salim "Another child, and then raise you?"

"That's the deal. I spare you here, and the lives of however many it takes, and you help me find a body I can call my own. Once I am able to function as myself again, we'll take this world for our own. A few years and I could be a god again, and you…we'll raise you to godhood. You will be a force of nature, my right hand,

and we can turn this world into a new Earth. A paradise, like it was before man, no offense intended against yourself, of course. Think of it: a golden age of magic, lasting forever, with no need to worry about the machines replacing us again. This world is ripe, and it ready for us to pluck," said Oberon. He heaved for breath, the long speech wearing on him. Andrew thought about being alone again. Oberon was right: he was all that Andrew had left of his previous life. Maeryl was most likely dead, Ashna was dead, the king was dead. His parents had been dead for longer than the time he had been with them, that ache was long buried. The people of Aethero, with the exception of a tiny few, were nothing to him. After years of bondage, and humiliation, and servitude, he was now offered the world. His head spun, and his heart ached. He looked down at the shattered corpse of the first woman he fell in love with. He looked at Salim. The light was failing fast now, the wind was kicking up to a howl.

"Make your choice, Andrew. There is only time for action!" Andrew looked up at the monster.

"You said that those around me were my greatest weakness, their love. See how it makes me strong." Oberon roared and reared back to strike him, and then the world seemed to slow down. Everything happened over long, drawn-out, breathless moments. Andrew jabbed his fingers into his cut shoulder, drawing the blood out. From the blood he saw his own family, the severed strands where his parents died, and one meager, weak thread leading from him to the monster. He followed it, past the sick pulsing red and black of Oberon's soul to the tiny fleck of light in the creature's monstrous heart. He found Maeryl there. He found the sorrowful love that his uncle still bore for him. He found his uncle's voice.

"End it," whispered Maeryl.

"Good-bye," whispered Andrew. All it would take as a little push.

So he pushed.

The beast screamed with piercing sharpness, the sound rebounding through Andrew's mind and body and the brightness in the center of his being. The thread snapped. The monster crashed to the ground, as still and lifeless as the stone it laid on. Andrew heaved a breath out, and collapsed to the ground himself. The darkness of dying sun fell, and the world was cold and the wind howled over the bodies. Flurries of snow started kicking up in the maelstrom. Andrew shivered. He crawled to where Ashna's body laid, snowflakes gathering in her hair. He pulled the body up into his arms. His tears froze on his cheeks and he stroked her face, the gory mess of her head forgotten.

He began to sing. The song that Anastasia taught him came pouring out of him. The wind tried to snatch the music away, but he was louder than the wind. The cold tried to freeze his resolve, but he burned with loss. The magic in him amplified the song, until the earth and world shook around him, vibrating in time to the music. The light, weak as it was, began to fade, until Andrew was alone in the black. Stars twinkled around him, brighter and bigger than he'd ever seen before. The howling winds were gone. The cold was gone. All was black, and silent, and warm. A shape moved in the darkness.

You sang a song of creation, and I have come.

"Hello?" said Andrew.

Be not afraid. I am a Whale. I see you. I understand why you sang. It cannot be.

"What do you mean?"

I will not unmake these deaths.

"It's not fair! Salim was just a child, Ashna…she deserved better. This is because of me, it's not her fault!"

It is not death's place to find fault. It is the only thing that is fair. It cares not for youth or age, does not recognize position or station. When darkness falls, we all must sleep.

"Is there nothing? Take me, not them. Take me. I'm alone, I don't want to be alone anymore. Please."

The whale was silent. Andrew could feel it moving in the black, slowly pumping its tail.

A life is rare, a soul precious. There is no price on these things.

"Please. I just saved your world! I stopped a monster from destroying all things!"

If it had succeeded, that would be the way of things.

"You just don't care, then? You create and you abandon? What responsibility do you share with the inhabitants of the world you created? They wouldn't be here without you!"

I came.

"You showed up? That's good enough?"

My obligations are my own.

"Fuck you! This is not the compassion I was told of, when they spoke of the Whales! They spoke of beings vast and powerful and compassionate!"

I grieve as you do.

"Bullshit!"

I understand and accept your anger, but it will not bring them back.

"But…there must be something," said Andrew. His voice was raw, his eyes red-rimmed and puffy. "Please don't leave me alone again."

Perhaps. There is something you have that has no price in this world. A gift.

"My…my magic?"

Yes. If you would give this gift up, for another, that perhaps would bring a balance.

"You said death cannot be stopped."

Do not mistake this for a bargain. It is a gift. There is a difference between a purchase and sacrifice.

"Will I have them all back? My uncle, Ashna, and Salim?"

No. It is sufficient for only one.

"I have to choose between them?"

Yes.

"That's not fair!"

I think you would do well to recognize that nothing is fair. Do not seek fairness, seek comfort. That one life may be saved is...priceless.

"How do I choose?"

That is for you to decide. The act of creation carries many burdens.

"Could I speak with them?"

No. They are dead.

"Damn you and your kind! I saved countless lives on this world!"

I have been since before your world was brought screaming and crashing into this sea. I saw the first stars. I heard the first songs. I was, I am, I will be. A life is a grain of sand on a beach as far as I can see, and I can see very far indeed, Andrew. There are things beyond your life that you will not understand. There is, perhaps, a purpose you could yet realize.

"It seems my purpose is to suffer."

All life is suffering. It is beyond the vale that your kind finds true peace. You may find some aspect of that in your existence, if only you would let go of your selfish pain, and embrace the gifts you receive.

Andrew didn't reply, just sobbed and heaved for breath. He cried for a very long time, his tears dripping down onto Ashna's face, cutting tracks through the tacky blood. The whale waited in the silence, and despite Andrew's anger and pain, the presence was, in fact, very comforting.

You are ready. I may not tarry further. Choose.

Andrew set Ashna down gently, stood, and wiped his

eyes. He looked at Ashna.

"Give me back Salim. And damn you for leaving me alone again," said Andrew.

It is done. Make the most of this life you claimed, for you are responsible for it. Goodbye, Andrew.

The whale swam into the night, the lack of its presence leaving a dull ache in Andrew's heart. The stars began to fade, and the courtyard began to reappear around Andrew. He sat back down, his legs too weak to hold him, and pulled Ashna back into his lap. The courtyard was back, and Andrew braced for the cold, but instead he found the day warm and comforting. A bright yellow sun hung over them, warming the air and the stones around him. Andrew had never seen such a beautiful sun, such a bright blue sky. It did not touch his heart at all, could find no place in him where it could warm him. Ashna's body was heavy in his arms, and all the pain and suffering in the world was in him, tearing him, wailing and screaming and sobbing in him, and he reached out in the darkness to grab the magic that would let him destroy the world.

But it was not there. He fumbled in his mind, trying to find the familiar touch of the magic he had always known. Tried to find the thing that made him whole. The magic that was falling in love over and over, the magic that filled him, the magic that sustained him. It was gone. He was truly alone. He hunched over the still form of Ashna and cried. His sobs were deep and heart-wrenching. He held Ashna close to him, but she did not stir. He rocked in the courtyard and looked at her face, her eyes closed, her expression relaxed. Perhaps there was a peace in death. He fumbled a dagger out of her belt. A hand touched his shoulder. He turned his head to see Salim standing behind him, the ravaged flesh from Oberon's attack made whole and healthy.

At first rage filled Andrew in all his being. He wanted

nothing more than to stab the dagger into Salim and kill the child all over again. Kill the child responsible for his Ashna's death. Kill the child that she died to save.

"Andrew?" said Salim. His voice quavered. His eyes were wide and brimmed with tears. "Is my mom okay?" Andrew dropped the dagger and shook his head. Tears flowed down Salim's face, and he threw his arms around Andrew's shoulders. Andrew put an arm around the young child, and they wept together. Andrew whispered.

"I'm so sorry."

Epilogue
One Year Later

ANDREW WATCHED SALIM playing in the courtyard with the other children. His chest was tight, his heart ached, and he limped from the wound he received in the fighting. Whenever he saw Salim, his throat tightened. He saw Ashna's face in the boy's features. Saw her eyes. He limped over to a bench and sat down, grateful for the break. Tracking down a small boy was no easy feat, even for the Prince Regent. Salim saw his guardian and ran over to him.

"I know a neat trick! Wanna see?" said Salim with a familiar eagerness. Andrew smiled.

"Please show me." He laughed when Salim screwed his eyes shut tight and put his hands behind his back. Andrew was expecting a mud ball in his lap, perhaps a frog in his shirt.

He did not expect Salim to produce a lizard with scales that changed colors in a riotous clash. Andrew stared in amazement for a moment.

"Did you find that?"

"No," said Salim. "I made it." Andrew knelt in front of the little boy, and put his hands on his shoulders. "You made it change colors?"

"Yes, sir."

"How?"

"I'm not sure how to explain it. I just…saw the colors. And then there they were." Andrew felt something in him give way. He pulled Salim into a hug. The little boy looked a little confused, but hugged him back readily enough.

"That's a wonderful gift, Salim. Would you like me to teach you how to use it?"

"I would like that." Andrew stood, wincing as his bad

leg pained him, and then slid back onto the bench. Salim plopped down next to him.

"I was a wizard once, you know," he said to the little boy.

"I remember! You made a cake dance for me."

"I remember that too."

"Why don't you make them do that any more?"

"I don't have my magic anymore." They sat in silence for a long moment.

"Is that…why you couldn't save my mom?" Salim whispered. Andrew turned to look at Salim, who was examining the lizard in his hands.

"I did everything I could."

"I miss her."

"I do too." They fell silent again, until Andrew suddenly brightened.

"Salim! Stay right here, okay?" he said. He stood up and rushed off as fast as his limp would carry him. Salim watched the man he was slowly beginning to think of as his father disappear, and reappear a few minutes later. Andrew had a huge, hopeful grin on his face, and he was carrying something. He sat back down next to the boy he was beginning to think of as his son.

"What did you bring back?"

Andrew showed him: a glass globe with a little fire inside. "I gave this to your mother the first time we met."

The End

Enjoy this excerpt from Jeff Hewitt's debut novel
A Reflection of Glass!

Chapter 1: The Mirror

DEXTER LEVIN WAS LATE. That made three days in a row, and last time he was late his step-father, the owner of McGuinness's Fine Clothing, made it clear he was certain to fire him this time. The sad thing for Dexter was being in a rush only changed how likely he was to make it on time very little. He did not have a car, and thus had to wait for a bus to pick him up at the bus stop like any other fool who was late for work. Judging from the lack of people checking their watches and cursing, he stood alone amongst the ranks of The Rushing. *I'll never read before work again!* He promised himself. *You always do this! You always start reading and look up and it's 'Oh, I've got ten minutes!' And then it's ten minutes until the bus arrives, not ten until you can leave! Moron!*

The bus driver was not late today, and was happy to see his usual gaggle of riders. The bus driver, Leonard Dins, was in his fifties, graying, a bit portly, and very agreeable. He enjoyed his job because he got people where they were going, and often as not he got one or two chatty types in the long mid morning stretch where not many people were riding the bus.

"Late again, Dexter?" he said to the twenty-something young man with brownish, mop-like hair.

"Yes, Leonard. If you speed it up a bit though I should be able to run in time to make it," said Dexter.

"We'll see," said Leonard as the doors hissed shut and he put his foot on the gas. Dexter knew that was an empty suggestion: Leonard never sped up. He more often slowed down, especially when he was talking with a chatty lunatic. Dexter slumped into a seat and stared glumly out a window as the trees rolled by. The bus ride took twenty minutes, and Dexter would sit and possibly overcome his guilt for being late by reading again. I'll spare you those details and just say that Dexter did in fact put his nose back in a book, and the mountains overlooking Chattanooga, Tennessee shook their heads at him. Unlike earlier, Dexter was quite keen on when he would need to stop reading and was ready when the bus came to his stop. He attempted to rush down the aisle, but the other passengers were not late for their various meetings; and Dexter was stuck at the back of a small group of tourists hopping from one foot to the other. After five eternities, Dexter was free from the bus, and bolted towards the store.

"Good luck, Dexter!" called the smiling bus driver. The bus pulled away, and Leonard listened with rapt interest as an earnest woman with a cat in a birdcage whispered to him about great secrets. Dexter hoofed it to work, racing as fast as he could along the sidewalks leading to the department store. He could see it in the distance. It was a fine white building with a gaudy neon sign. Its only problem was that the owner of the business was a self-important twat with absolutely no taste in clothing. Dexter, it could be said, was not a fan of his step-father. He was a loud, broad man with a time-traveling mustache from a '70's porno who liked to yell at Dexter and trick people into buying perfectly hideous clothes. Also...Dexter thought the man might be a voodoo priest or wizard. It was the only explanation for...the Mirror. Dexter knew something was wrong with the Mirror, and not that it was wavy or blurry or anything like that. He pushed through a small crowd of people milling around outside. He bumped into a pair of hooded teenagers, who turned away from him quickly even as he tried to apologize. Confused, he opened the door to the building and slipped in. As it closed behind him, he averted his eyes lest he see the Mirror.

He checked his watch: 11:55, A.M. Five minutes to spare. That was close. He took a moment to adjust the backpack he carried with him to work, heavy with books, notebooks, pencils, and the like, and started walking back towards the security room. Dexter worked as security for the store. The other employees were a pair of sisters who worked the cash registers, set out clothes, and made snide remarks. Sometimes Dexter was enlisted to help, but this was only in the rare emergencies that cropped up in a life of working retail as it was readily apparent that Dexter could no more fold a shirt than a cricket could be an operatic soprano. His main function was to watch the monitors trained on the dressing room doors and mirrors. He made sure no skinny customers went into a room with an armful of clothes and came out empty handed and portly as a politician.

Dexter was decent at this; enough that McGuinness had not fired him yet, anyway. Dexter would glance up from the book he was reading to check. People often wanted the clothes, and that's where Dexter's suspicions of witchcraft or magickry came from. No one wanted the clothes that you could find in McGuinness's Fine Clothing. They exclusively stocked the products of insane clothing designers bent on the destruction of taste, society, or both. The garish colors, awful embroidery, experimental lengths, and other heinous crimes against civilized cloth-wearing cultures haunted the walls and lurked on the racks.

...And all this strange activity centered on the Mirror: the Mirror McGuinness installed a few months before he hired Dexter. He also had ideas as to what broke the original mirror, and it involved a neon-colored animal-print spandex suit. When Dexter first started working there, he boggled at the idea that they actually let customers *see* themselves in the clothes before paying. It just wasn't good business sense. Somehow, this helped rather than hindered the business. Dexter's concern focused on one of those roundish rooms with three mirrors facing at an angle, so you could examine yourself from every angle.

It was *the* Mirror, the central mirror of the dressing room mirrors. It was the one that made Dexter certain McGuinness was a warlock who enchanted the Mirror to make people lose their taste, common sense, or sanity. They looked at the clothes, and you could tell from their expressions they were either eating a rotten lemon or looking at the same clothes Dexter saw everyday. Then McGuinness, for all the world like an eagle swooping down on a miniature poodle, appeared out of nowhere and lead the customer to the Mirror. They would look in the Mirror and turn away, having confirmed how terrible the outfit was. Then they would stop. They'd look back at the Mirror. They turned, and their faces slowly lit up with delight as though they just made the fashion find of the century. At this point, no amount of persuading could change the mind of the unfortunate victim. Enamored, they bought whatever outfit they had on, in their arms, it didn't matter. They bought it, and with a big grin on their face, to boot.

Maybe the Mirror is like a Venus fly trap. Lures you in and then POW! Dexter mused as he walked around the far aisles of the store. He could have walked straight down the middle, but then the mirror was in full view and even looking at it made him queasy. So he would walk around the aisles on the outside, hugging the wall the whole way, and looking at anything other than the Mirror. This route coursed through the women's lingerie outside the dressing rooms. His breath would get heavy and his palms would sweat. One of those things was caused by the Mirror. Finally, and with great speed, he would rush into the hall with the Mirror, unlock his security door, and throw himself into the room. More than once he bashed some part of his body on the partially-opened door in his haste to get inside. The Mirror, it should be noted, always thought it was funny when he did that.

Today he managed to get inside without causing himself bodily harm, and he slammed the door shut behind him. He caught his breath, arranged his clothes more professionally, and then screamed when the chair in front of his security station turned around of its own accord. McGuinness was sitting in it with his hands steepled in front of his mustache.

"Dexter, you were late today," said McGuinness. His voice could oil a car engine. Dexter gulped and looked at his watch. 11:59 A.M.

"Respectfully sir, but my watch says eleven fifty-nine, and we don't open until twelve," he said.

"That's true, Dexter! Quite true! However, you are supposed to be here at eleven-thirty to review the nighttime security tapes. That's what I've been doing instead of getting the store ready to open," said McGuinness. He smiled, and Dexter felt his stomach falling. He couldn't lose his job; he had to pay rent soon and his box of baking soda in the fridge was getting lonely.

"I'm so sorry sir. I know I've been late a lot lately but I can really improve, I really can! Just give me another chance!" said Dexter.

"Dexter, I've given you many, many chances. More chances than most managers, and especially store owners, would give. I hate to say this...but..." Dexter cringed. "I'm not going to fire you today. Do you want to know why?" he said. Dexter only managed a nod.

"Because the woman who got you this job, my wife's mother, who you will recall is also your grandmother, is coming to dinner tonight. And the only thing that could possibly ruin my dinner more than having her visit is having her visit and find out that I fired you that same day. You are here because it helps my blood pressure to stay low. It's not low now, but I suspect when I leave this room I will feel better. I just wanted you to understand..." and here he leaned forward in the chair, and yet somehow still loomed over Dexter, "...that your job hangs in a very fine balance right now. If you are late again, and I mean late as to be after eleven-thirty, you will be fired. Mother-in-law or no, I will just have to accept my aneurysm and untimely death as the price of running a store properly." McGuinness sat back in the chair, adjusted his tie, and then stood to leave.

"Mr. McGuinness..." began Dexter.

"If the next words out of your mouth are not 'Yes sir.' and 'I will not be late again, sir.' We'll both regret my outburst."

"Yes sir. I will not be late again, sir," said Dexter, in a small voice.

"Good." McGuinness pushed past him and opened the door to the hallway. He stood outside the door, and looked down the hall at the Mirror. He smiled and smoothed his hair. Dexter was just about to close the door when McGuinness said:

"Dexter, I noticed you hugged the wall coming into the store again today," he said.

"Um...sir...it's just that...." Dexter tried to think of anything other than the real reason.

"Is there something you want to tell me, or should I just assume you have another strange and endearing personality quirk your grandmother will bore me with tonight?" said McGuinness. Dexter swallowed anger and embarrassment.

"I'm just strange sir. You've said so yourself," he said. McGuinness smiled at him again.

"I thought so. Just don't do it when there are women browsing the intimates, you'll make someone call the police on you," said McGuinness. "Now, get to work." McGuinness paused and looked down the corridor at his reflection in the Mirror again. He gave himself a thumbs up and walked into the store. Dexter looked out into the empty hall for a moment, thought about slamming the door shut, and closed it without causing a scene at all. He set his backpack down next to the security console and fell into the chair with a heavy sigh. He looked at the TV monitors showing the interior of the store, and then glanced at the one from the outside loading bay. Nothing, yet. The crowd still hovered outside, which boggled Dexter's mind.

"Don't any of you have better things to do than sit outside a store before it opens?" he said. Thinking of the hooded teens he ran into on his way in, he scanned the crowd for them but couldn't find them. Frowning, he pulled the tape out of the overnight recorder and put it in the VCR. He put it on fast forward. Nothing of interest in the night, like normal. Yes, Dexter was certain today was as normal as any other. It was, in fact, the third most exciting day of his life, but he didn't know that. He looked at all the monitors again, spotted McGuinness standing uncomfortably close to one of the cashiers, and pulled out the book he was reading. The book was nice and old, and sometimes Dexter would catch himself smelling the pages.

Man. If I opened a bookstore I could just sit at the counter and smell books all day, he thought to himself as he flipped to where he left off. Absorbed in his book, he did not notice when a young woman came in with the rest of the crowd. The monitors, in a show of extravagance on McGuinness's part, were color. The woman Dexter did not see had shoulder-length dark hair, a medium complexion, and an attractively curvy figure. She was wearing a dark-blue button-up shirt, jeans, and pink tennis shoes. She was, on the whole, far too well-dressed to be shopping in a place like McGuinness's Fine Clothing. Dexter might have recognized her from the night before, but as we said, he wasn't paying attention. She carried a shopping bag from McGuinness's in one hand, as though she needed to return something...

*****

Rosemary Carter stared into the store she visited the night before with some friends. They were all a bit tipsy from celebrating a (not Rosemary's) bachelorette party, and one of them, Rosemary could not remember now who it was, had mentioned this terrible store...

"You won't believe what they sell in this place!" she said. "I saw a sweater with three wolves embroidered on it, with more wolves on the sleeves, and a wolf on the back!" she giggled.

"How many wolves is that in total?" someone else laughed.

"However many wolves too many!" said the first girl as they all laughed together and sipped their drinks. The festivities were tame but fun: dirty word games, novelties like edible underwear and sex toys, naughty straws for their drinks, and things like that. They were all twenty-something women with jobs that required them to maintain some decorum even outside of work, so going to a male-strip club or bar-hopping was out of the question for most of them. Rosemary, intrigued, said:

"What store? Is it open this late?" she said. Someone looked at her watch.

"You mean eight is late now?" said her friend.

"It's eight?" several exclaimed.

"We got started at six!"

"It feels much later!"

"Well, whatever, this place is open late anyhow. It's like...Guiness's Clothes or something like that," said her friend, taking a sip from her drink.

"Let's go!" said Rosemary.

"Noooo! More partying!" came many replies.

"We can get some ugly wolf sweaters to wear around!" said Rosemary "and we can party like we're in the woods! Awoooo!" she said, howling.

"Awooooo!" echoed many of the girls, before everyone got the giggles. It was a long moment before anyone could speak.

"All right, let's do it!" said the first girl.

"I'll call us a cab, since all you bitches are drunk!" said Rosemary, who got showered with straws and wrappers and other things as the girls laughed. The cab was arranged, and shortly a van showed up out front to take them to the famous McGuinness's Fine Clothing. The ride over involved lots more giggling and the telling of inappropriate jokes. The cabby, who loved parties, joined in on the fun. When they got to the store he promised to wait for them. They swarmed through the doors, and spent the next hour making nuisances of themselves for the cashiers and McGuinness. Dexter was too busy laughing at their antics in the security room to be of any help whatsoever.

Rosemary got away from the group and started browsing the sweaters, giggling to herself and holding some up for her friends to see when she found one especially noteworthy. The last of these was an embroidered wolf fighting a bear, with an eagle on the back across the shoulders.

"You have to try that on!" said one of her friends when she brought it back to the group to show off.

"Yes! Yes, try it on!" they all agreed.

"Oh, all right!" giggled Rosemary. They rushed to the Mirror in the back, and Rosemary was laughing to herself in the dressing room as she pulled the sweater on over her bra. She stepped out of the room and nearly had a heart attack laughing with her friends, many of whom fell to the floor. Rosemary managed to pull herself together long enough to catch a look of herself in the mirror, and started to have another laughing fit...but it died in her throat. She looked at the sweater, and at her friends. They all suddenly seemed distant, and as though they were caught in an old film that moved too slowly, their actions paused and jerky. She looked back in the mirror and saw herself standing there, somehow different. Her reflection was suddenly a version of herself that was better. The woman looking back at her in the mirror never had petty grudges, and went to cool parties, and was the center of attention in a good way rather than in a way that made her look foolish. She was at a loss. She looked at the sweater, and at the mirror, and then checked in her wallet to make sure she had money. Her friends were all agape when she bought the sweater a few moments later, and insisted on wearing it the rest of the night.

    The next morning, slightly hung over, she was still wearing the sweater but had taken off the rest of her clothes in an effort to sleep comfortably. It turned out all the embroidery was extremely uncomfortable, so sleeping in it was a mistake. She took off the sweater, and her chest was covered with a bright red indention of the wolf fighting a bear. She fell back in the bed and stared at the ceiling, and immediately regretted the movement as it made her head ache. She stood up slowly, put on a neutral t-shirt that went past her thighs, and walked into her kitchen. Her stomach did some flips when she looked in her fridge, so she poured herself a big glass of orange juice and drank it sitting at the table. She brought the sweater into her kitchen, and now laid it on the table to get a better look at it.

    Chaucer, her yellow tabby, strolled in and meowed at her. She reached down and scratched behind his ears while she drank her juice and looked at the sweater. The cat twined around her legs and purred like a little motor. The sweater sat there, looking stupid. *How did I look so different last night in this shirt? It can't have been the drinking. We were tipsy, but...* She spent a long while staring at the shirt, drinking her juice, and petting Chaucer. When she was finished with her juice she felt better, so she rinsed her glass and checked on Chaucer's food and water, for which he was quite grateful. She went into her bathroom to brush her teeth, but her attention was suddenly caught in the mirror. Her reflection, pale, splotchy, and very much a bad morning look, held her rapt. She felt like she was a double exposure, looking in the mirror. As though she was superimposed over something, or something was superimposed over her. She saw two faces...

...and woke up on the floor of the bathroom, with the faucet running. Chaucer stood over her, mewling and looking worried. As worried as cats ever look, anyway. She sat up. *What happened?* She felt the back of her head, but it wasn't tender or bruised. Her headache was still there, but lessened. *Did I pass out?* She stood with caution, holding onto the vanity, and tried to look back in the mirror, but was afraid to. She brushed her teeth in a hurry and all but sprinted out when she finished her morning routine. While she put on her make up, she kept glancing at the bathroom door. Half-way done, she stood and closed the door altogether. She finished and stared at the sweater. *Something weird is going on here. The sweater, passing out...the mirror.* She gathered up the sweater, stuffed it in the paper bag from the store, and decided to head back to find out more and to return the sweater. *I wasn't* that *drunk,* she thought.

So, there she was the next morning, staring through the windows with a group of people who were talking excitedly amongst themselves about the various treasures they would find. Rosemary put a little distance between herself and the others, clutching the bag to her chest. She bumped into a pair of young men with hoodies. They didn't look at her, but she apologized quietly and moved farther down. The store opened right on time when the owner came to the front, all sharkey smiles, and unlocked the doors.

"Welcome to McGuinness's Fine Clothing! Enjoy your shopping experience, and if you have any questions please do not hesitate to ask me!" he said. Excited shoppers, a dozen or so, rushed past him and began browsing. Rosemary just stepped in when she felt his gaze lock on her. She sensed it was not her face he was staring at. She looked at him smartly and said:

"I have a question."

"Yes ma'am, I'll be happy to help," he said.

"Where may I return an item?" she asked.

"Oh, I'm sorry that you want to return an item. Did you find some sort of defect?" he said.

"No. It's just a horrible sweater and I bought it in an altered state of mind," she said.

"May I see the sweater, please?" said McGuinness.

"Uh...sure," said Rosemary, who took it out of the bag and handed it to him. McGuinness shook it out and looked at it. He was frowning and his face was growing red, but then he looked inside the sweater and smiled.

"I'm sorry, but we can't accept this return," he said.

"I've got my receipt, though!" said Rosemary. She showed it to him, but he didn't even look at it. His eyes were still traveling.

"I understand that ma'am, but you've removed the tags from the sweater, so we can't take a return for it. I'm terribly sorry," he said. Disgusted with his ogling, Rosemary just stuffed the sweater back into the bag and walked away to her car. She could feel the man watching her leave. She threw the bag into the back seat and climbed in the front. She stared intently at the store. She felt certain she needed to get in there and check out the Mirror again. There was something about it...

While she was otherwise occupied, she did not notice the two men in hooded sweatshirts watching her from inside the store.

"What if she drives away, what then, Jig? I'm not goin' back to Mother empty-handed, I'm not!" said one.

"Shhh, patience, Cutter! She been glamoured by deh Mirr'r, she'll be back!" said the other. They hid amongst the clothes and watched Rosemary sit in her car. Rosemary gathered her composure, and decided to go back inside to look around. She got out of her car, and noticed the two young men from earlier looking at her, who turned and wandered into the store. She didn't like that, but...that Mirror...She felt in her purse and grasped the reassuring cylinder of her pepper spray. It was still early in the day, with plenty of light, and there were people inside the store, so she wasn't too worried. And she could always give them a taste of chemical deterrent.

She stepped back in and looked around for McGuinness and the two hoody guys. The guys she couldn't see, but she could see McGuinness off pestering someone towards a dark area in the back. She kept an eye out that way and for the two men, and started walking towards the Mirror. She caught sight of it, but there was a small group of people all trying to see themselves in the Mirror at the same time, so she went and browsed around. She started looking through the button-up shirts to find something to actually try on. If she had to look in the Mirror, she could at least be convincing about it. She shopped for about ten minutes while the people around the Mirror thinned out. Rosemary picked out a black button-up with an embroidered dragon that only looked somewhat terrible and began walking towards the mirror. The last woman standing in front of it seemed satisfied and walked off with her clothes.

Just as Rosemary was about to step in front of the Mirror, a short little man with a face reminiscent of a Chinese lion statue pushed in front of her. Rosemary decided not to make an issue of it, so she just walked back into the dressing room area. When she stepped in front of one of the dressing rooms, the door sprang open silently and one of the men in hoodies rushed out and grabbed her around the waist and mouth while she was turned away. Her hands got tangled in the shirt she was holding and she could not get to her pepper spray. The man pulled her quickly and silently into the room and his partner closed the door.

Rosemary started to struggle and get a scream out, but the one who closed the door punched her in the stomach, and all the air in her rushed out. Through squinted eyes filled with tears, she could just see the assailant in front of her. He stood a little taller than her, which seemed to mark him a juvenile, and the hood of his sweatshirt hung low over his face. She couldn't see any of his features at all, and in fact there seemed to be a sinister darkness in the shadows of the hood. Rosemary's knees got even weaker and her heart grew icy like a sudden blast of northern wind when she saw one pull out a knife. She was sweating and panic clenched her throat. She tried to scream again but couldn't get her wind back.

"Take a looksee Cutter and see if the Bob is in front of the Mirror, yeah?" said Jig. Cutter nodded and cracked the door to the dressing room. While he was looking out Jig held Rosemary tight against him. His body was hard and wiry against her back.

"Nice lookin', you is," he said.

"Alls clear, Jig. Time to go home to Mother," said Cutter. When Cutter turned to say this, Rosemary got a good view of his face. It was swirling darkness, like black smoke that stayed confined as though under a clear mask of a face, with only a pair of green cat's eyes shining through. Rosemary tried to scream again, which earned her a painful pull on her hair and Jig's sinister whisper in her ear:

"Try again, missy, and you won't be so nice lookin' anymore cause we'll let Cutter have a go 'atcha, and...well, his name's Cutter, innit?" Rosemary just sagged, tears flowing down her face now. Cutter put his knife against her ribs and Rosemary gasped as the sharp point pressed cold against her skin. Cutter then stuck his head back out the door and looked around. He nodded and they proceeded to both carry/drag Rosemary towards the end of the hall...

...which is just when Dexter happened to glance up from his novel, to see two young men dragging a woman towards the Mirror. He saw a door in the Mirror, one he could have sworn he'd seen hundreds of times before but wasn't there. And one of the hoods reached into the mirror, and pulled the door open. Dexter's stomach dropped. The two men proceeded to throw the woman bodily through the door, and then step through themselves. Just as the second one was about to step through, he seemed to feel Dexter watching him. He looked up into the security monitor, caught Dexter's eye with his own green cat eyes, and winked. The door slammed shut, and Dexter fainted as all the lights and TVs in the room suddenly went out.

About the Author

Jeff Hewitt is currently an independent author working hard on his third book, Men of Gods. When he is not reading or writing, he enjoys brewing beer, playing wargames, and challenging his friends in myriad boardgames. He is married to the beautiful Megan, who is currently working towards her dream of becoming a nurse. They have three dogs in place of carpet critters (for now,) and they are: Sophie, a Pembroke Welsh Corgi, Beasley, an American Jerk-Faced Terrier, and Penny, a handful. They live in Northwest Georgia.

You can find links to purchase books directly from the author on his website, www.jeffhewitt.net

All e-books available in most formats.